SHATTERED CURSE

SHADOW CITY: DEMON WOLF

JEN L. GREY

CHAPTER ONE

DESPERATION STRANGLED me as I linked, *Cyrus!*

My only salvation from insanity was that I could still feel our mate link, meaning he wasn't dead.

That didn't mean he wasn't hurt.

He didn't respond. His last words echoed through my mind— black wolves were attacking his group and for Sterlyn to protect me. He'd gotten cut off before he could finish his sentence.

Despite our suspicions that this meeting was a trap, we couldn't allow the men who'd captured Cyrus and Sterlyn's former packmates to injure them. The dark wolves had captured Mila, Theo, Theo's mate—Rudie, and Chad, and they'd offered an exchange—them for me. If we refused, they'd begin cutting off body parts. I knew they would follow through on that promise. The malevolence wafting off the dark wolves that had attacked us made my skin crawl, leaving me with no doubt they meant what they said.

If it weren't for my excellent wolf vision, the dark wolves would have blended in with the night. Plus, the musky, overly sweet scent of these enemy wolves overpowered the smell of the surrounding cypresses and redbuds. All the usual sounds and scents present in the forests of southeast Tennessee, several miles outside of the elusive Shadow City and its bordering towns, Shadow Terrace and Shadow Ridge, were obscured.

Even the raccoons and squirrels were silent as if all could feel the evilness—or like they sensed a looming natural disaster.

Natural disaster.

I'd have laughed at the irony if terror hadn't been crushing my chest. My entire focus was narrowed on my mate. He was in danger and needed me.

I connected to the pack, wanting to hear from someone else, and asked, *Is everyone okay? I lost touch with Cyrus.*

We've been swarmed, someone answered. *There are at least two against each of us, including the regular wolves.*

The regular wolves. My chest knotted. As the protectors of Shadow Ridge, each wolf in Killian's pack was strong and well trained, but they didn't have the silver wolves' extra advantage of drawing power from the moon.

Quinn, hold your ground the best you can, Darrell linked. *We're on our way to help you.*

I didn't know Quinn well since I'd stayed away from most of the silver wolf pack until recently, but he was one

of the pack members who hadn't caused problems for Cyrus. That meant a hell of a lot in this time of war.

My wolf surged forward, her magic fueling my body with greater speed.

We're on our way too, Sterlyn linked. *Griffin and I are shifting now.*

Oh, should I shift too? I hadn't wanted to spend the time to do it, but maybe it would help me get to Cyrus faster.

Sterlyn replied, *Don't. It'll be confusing with you looking the same as our enemy. I'd hate for someone to attack you by mistake.*

My throat closed. I hated it but staying in human form was safer for all of us.

"Annie!" Ronnie yelled from a few steps behind me. Vampires ran faster than wolves, so she caught up to me easily. Her copper hair whipped beside me as her sugar cookie scent tickled my nose and her emerald eyes gleamed. "We need to strategize before walking into yet another trap."

We didn't have time to talk, only react. "The strategy is simple—kick ass and find Cyrus." I loved my foster sister—she was one of the most important people in my world—but my mate and my pack were in danger.

I couldn't live without Cyrus.

Hell, I refused to be without him.

She'd feel the same way if she were in my shoes, but I wouldn't waste energy arguing with her. I'd stay on course, and I wasn't being stupid. Sterlyn, Griffin, Sierra,

Alex, and Ronnie were right here with me. I wasn't running into harm's way alone.

We do need to be smart, Sterlyn linked. Through our pack link, I could feel her concern. She was petrified of losing her twin. Cyrus was the only immediate family she had left, and she'd only recently found out he existed. *But I think we're okay. Darrell and Killian's groups weren't attacked. They're running south to ensure they aren't flanked. Once they've checked out the area, they'll make their way back to help us fight.*

I repeated the information to Ronnie, and my sister relaxed a little.

In this part of the forest, the cypress, oak, and redbud trees grew several feet apart, providing enough space for a car to drive through, unlike near the silver wolf pack neighborhood. As we ran toward Cyrus, sounds of rumbling engines alerted me to a nearby road. I was still new to my wolf, having shifted only a handful of times since the day Cyrus and I had mated, so I wasn't great at judging distance, but I'd bet it was no more than a couple of miles away.

Snarls and whimpers became deafening. We'd be upon Cyrus and his captors in seconds, and I pushed my legs to move faster.

I don't know what happened, but over half the attackers vanished, Quinn replied.

That changed nothing—Cyrus was still missing and not responding to us.

Silver and dark black-blue fur flashed between trees. Adrenaline pumped through my body.

We were finally here.

Something blurred past me and Ronnie, and the scent of syrup assaulted my nose, informing me it was Alex, Ronnie's mate. The form rammed into a dark wolf that had pounced on the back of a silver wolf, digging its claws into my packmate's fur.

Alex slowed and came back into focus. His angular features seemed sharper than normal with his golden-brown hair disheveled. His sun-kissed skin was slightly darker than Ronnie's, but paleness shimmered underneath, which I could see more clearly now that my supernatural side had been released. I assumed it came from him being a vampire.

Ronnie blurred forward, her dagger magically appearing in her hand. She attacked an enemy wolf standing on its hind legs. The demon blade slid through its neck like a knife through butter. The dark wolf's eyes bulged as it crumpled.

My stomach rolled. The spilled blood reminded me of horrible things from my past: my best friend running into a road after a ball and getting hit by a car, a crazed vampire messing with my mind and draining my blood, and all the death and destruction I'd experienced since then.

I went numb.

I hoped I'd never get acclimated to this kind of brutality. I averted my eyes, searching for one person in particular.

The most important person in my life.

Cyrus.

But everywhere my gaze landed, he was missing.

As if he'd vanished.

Killian's pack had paired up to fight the dark wolves, and I realized how much bigger the dark wolves were than the regular wolves. These dark wolves were similar in size to the silver wolves, who were larger and stronger because of their angel blood and ties to the moon.

Something to dissect with the others after the fight. I ran forward, bracing to defend myself or attack any dark wolf that got in my way.

Maybe if I'd been a demon like the witch coven that had hidden me as a baby had thought, it would have made fighting this enemy easier. We didn't know what we were up against, despite my animal fur matching the fur of these strange wolves.

Something slammed into my side and smashed me into a sturdy oak tree. The bark scraped my skin, and blood dribbled down my arm, the metallic scent hanging in the air. The dark wolf sniffed like it enjoyed the smell, and I stared into its cold, ice-blue irises.

The look was more malicious than I'd imagined. This wolf thrived on causing pain and injury.

My blood ran cold. There was no telling what they had planned for Cyrus, and I wouldn't let anyone, especially these assholes, hold my mate captive.

Silver fur flashed behind the wolf's head, and Sterlyn's lavender-silver eyes glowed as she steamrolled it into another tree. The wolf's head hit the trunk with a *whack*, and its ebony eyes rolled back as it fell with a thud.

Are you okay? she asked, scanning the fight around

us. Even in animal form, her body was tense. She spun around, ready to fight another wolf.

I was far from okay. *When we find Cyrus, I'll be better.*

Howls from a mile away alerted us that more wolves were coming. I rushed past Sterlyn, ready to wreak havoc. They must have taken Cyrus closer to the road.

Babe? I squeaked through our mate bond, hoping he'd finally respond.

Silence greeted me and yanked on my chest.

Something's off, Darrell linked. *Their numbers are smaller than the scents in the area—like they want us to think there's more of them. Only a couple of wolves sneaked up behind us. Nothing makes sense, but we're almost to you.*

At least, they were coming to our aid. *Yeah, same here. Quinn and the others had twice that number of attackers, and half of them disappeared without a trace.*

They're up to something. Sterlyn sounded annoyed. *Please get here as safely and quickly as possible. There's no telling what they have planned, but we can't leave. They might expect us to retreat, and they could bring the fight to wherever we go. We need to end this here.*

She was right. Running wouldn't make a difference. If we hadn't shown up here, they would've attacked us back at the pack housing. At least here, our homes weren't under attack.

A dark wolf snarled and charged at me. I inhaled deeply, channeling all the training Cyrus had given me since I'd arrived at the silver wolf pack for protection.

He'd told me to watch where the person looked—that was usually where they planned to attack.

Strangely enough, the wolf was aiming for my leg. A non-fatal wound. The alpha didn't want me dead. He'd said he wanted to bring me *home*.

My hands clenched. Cyrus was my *home*, and he wouldn't be taken away.

I spread my feet shoulder width apart and braced for the attack. I had to time this right; otherwise, the attacking wolf could counter my move.

This entire meeting had been a distraction and a setup, Sterlyn grumbled through the link. *This ends now.*

That was a plan I could get behind.

The wolf opened its mouth, ready to clamp down on my leg. I kicked it right in the snout. The wolf whimpered loudly as its head jerked back and its body dropped.

I rushed over and kicked it in the head again, knocking it out.

Glancing over my shoulder, I watched as Ronnie and Alex fought a wolf together, and Sterlyn lunged at a dark wolf attacking her mate.

Only a few dark wolves were left, and the other silver wolves were handling them.

I'm going to look for Cyrus. I jogged toward the road, following the tug of the mate bond. The connection was strange—I could feel him as if our link was an invisible rope.

Darrell trotted beside me in his wolf form. *I'm coming with you.*

It hadn't taken long for Killian and the others to reach us.

Thank God.

I turned. The rest of the silver wolves and Killian's pack had joined the fight. Our numbers were now triple our enemies', and despite the slaughtering that they were receiving, they continued to put up a fight.

It bothered me that they weren't retreating. They were willing to die for a cause but for what?

I didn't have time to figure it out. I focused forward again and hurried to find my mate.

Darrell sprinted ahead, taking the lead. I wanted to shift, but if I ran into the alpha prick who'd pretended he would trade our packmates for me, I needed to be able to speak with him. I had to tell him everything I was going to do to him so I could watch the terror in his eyes.

That was a vile thought, but I didn't care. These assholes had come here to hurt my friends and family. Their plan to kidnap me just made the whole situation worse. We hadn't done anything to these wolves, and this was the second time they'd sought us out to harm us.

Various sweet floral scents were thick in the area. I couldn't tell how many distinct scents there were, but it was definitely a large number.

Darrell lifted his head and sniffed. *That's what we smelled on our way to join you all here. There are at least thirty scents, and they're strong, meaning the wolves must be the ones that left the fight not long ago.*

Tensing, I tapped into my wolf so I could use her amazing vision, but I saw nothing out of the ordinary.

The half moon was high in the sky. We'd been out here longer than I'd realized, and it was approaching midnight. Cyrus was the only one missing from our pack.

Snarls sounded in front of us, and I froze. Five wolves trotted out of the trees, blocking us.

That told me everything I'd feared—they were preventing us from reaching Cyrus.

My wolf eased forward, brushing against my mind.

Darrell linked with the pack, *We could use some backup here.*

We're on our way too, Sterlyn replied. *Griffin and I are shifting now.*

Good. We needed to get past these wolves, and the dark wolves were an even match for the silver wolves.

Three dark wolves charged Darrell as two made their way to me. I lifted my hands, making it clear I planned to fight them. I wouldn't lie down without a fight.

My breathing turned rapid as the two circled me. Determined to keep them in my line of sight, I tracked their movements.

Darrell whimpered, and my heart sank. I couldn't help him. Every time I glanced at him, the wolves took advantage and circled closer.

Paw steps ran toward us, and Sterlyn and six others appeared.

The incoming threat was enough for the two circling me to strike. The one on my right launched forward, and I punched it in the snout. He jerked back just as the other wolf slammed into me.

I fell forward, not able to stop, and the wolf's jaws clamped onto my arm.

I screamed, unable to swallow it as the sharp pain jolted up my arm. It was worse than the claws that had gouged me just days ago, during our first fight with this enemy. Blood poured down my arm and into my mousy hair. The corners of my vision darkened, and the world shifted as the dark wolf dragged me toward the place where Cyrus might be. With each step, its teeth shredded my skin, but I wasn't sure that was its intent.

My breathing turned erratic. If I didn't hold myself together, I would pass out. Forcing my lungs to fill slowly added to my misery. The air sawed through my throat, and tears streamed down my face. Remembering the exercises Cyrus had forced me to do, I pushed through.

If panic took hold, I might as well just hand myself over to the enemy.

And I couldn't do that. The point was to save Cyrus and the other captives, not get myself in the same situation.

My heart pounded, pushing adrenaline through my body. Breathing still hurt, but my head cleared a little. I had to act.

With my free hand, I punched the wolf in the jaw. It flinched but didn't loosen its grip on my arm.

"Let go!" I screamed, not sure what else to do.

A wolf with sandy fur dove under my arm and attacked the wolf holding me. Griffin. He sank his teeth into the wolf's throat and ripped it out.

Blood gushed to the ground and spattered my arm as my captor's mouth went slack and released.

Bile inched up my throat, but car doors slammed close by. My wolf grew alert. I pushed the dead wolf away, ignoring the moisture on my arm.

I would deal with the blood later. *I'm going,* I linked with the others, not wanting to say it out loud.

Sterlyn appeared beside Griffin and pawed at the ground. *Let me go with you.*

The three of us ran toward the road as the sound of tires squealed against the asphalt only feet away.

No! We had to get Cyrus before they got away.

CHAPTER TWO

MY HEART POUNDED SO HARD that I wouldn't have been surprised if it exploded from my chest. Our mate bond was present but dimmed, as if Cyrus wasn't accessible. The warmth was still there and stronger than the other links, but it was like he was asleep.

Cyrus! I linked louder, trying to get a reaction from him. I needed him to fight back, but the silence was deafening.

Sterlyn, Griffin, and I ran through the last line of trees and onto the asphalt road. The only light came from the stars and the moon, but with my wolf sharing her magic with me, it seemed nearly as bright as day. A white van sped away with a half-mile head start.

The three of us raced after it. Sterlyn was the fastest because she was silver and in animal form. My wolf howled heartbreakingly in my head, and I wanted to cover my ears, though it wouldn't do any good, seeing as the noise was internal. At least, with the amount of adrenaline pumping through me, I didn't feel the pain in my arm.

Even with Sterlyn's speed, the van outpaced us dramatically, and it soon hit a curve and vanished from view.

We need to regroup. Sterlyn stopped, breathing raggedly. *We're wasting time and energy trying to catch up to it.*

Jaw clenched, I ran harder. Her words infuriated me, despite being extremely logical. She was right. There was no way we could catch up with them, but I couldn't do nothing. "I'm not giving up."

Griffin ran in front of me, preventing me from moving forward. He shook his head, and I didn't have to link with him to understand what he was telling me: Don't be stupid.

Yeah, he wasn't my alpha.

Sterlyn was.

I pivoted on my heel, desperate to get around him, but he countered my move. My hands fisted, and though he was my family, I would kick his ass if he didn't get out of my way.

"Move," I said slowly, deliberately, wanting him to realize how serious I was. I didn't need his permission to continue.

He growled and crouched, making sure I didn't pass him.

I get that you're upset, Sterlyn linked and approached me. She glanced at Griffin for a second, using their mate link to communicate.

It didn't matter. I was going after my mate. I wouldn't sit around with my thumb up my ass, waiting for something bad to happen to him.

She stepped in front of Griffin, approaching me cautiously. *Going after him angry like this will only get you captured, which will tell them that you're irrational and all they need to do is hurt him to make you do whatever they want.*

Crap. That snapped me back to reality. Damn Sterlyn and her reasoning skills. *I need to do* something. *I can't stay here knowing they have him.* Tears fell down my cheeks, and I didn't bother brushing them away.

We will do something. We're going to get my brother— your mate—back. Sterlyn's purple-tinged silver eyes reflected the moon, making them look magical. *But we must be smart about it, or things will only get worse. Look where we are now.*

My heart tugged, wanting to go after him. I inhaled deeply to clear my head. We were in the middle of an isolated road shrouded in darkness. Luckily, there wasn't any traffic, or a human surrounded by two wolves would've raised a lot of questions.

I was being reckless, but I didn't have it in me to leave yet. *We don't have a plan.*

Then we make one. Sterlyn trotted to the side of the road and stepped between two redbuds, knowing I would listen. If I continued my crazy course and Cyrus got hurt worse because of it, I wouldn't be able to live with myself. If I didn't do anything and something happened to him, I wasn't sure I could survive that either.

Griffin herded me after his mate. Unlike Sterlyn, he didn't trust me to make the right decision.

Smart man.

I sighed. One thing was clear: if I chased after the van, I wouldn't catch up with them now. My only solace was that they wanted me and would surely be in touch. I would willingly give myself to them if they released Cyrus, but I'd keep that thought to myself. No one needed to know what I was open to doing. If they did, they wouldn't let me be involved in saving him.

My chest tightened, and a scream lodged in my throat as I forced one foot in front of the other, following Sterlyn. My wolf howled in protest, making the feat damn near impossible. All this time, I'd thought I'd been through the worst experiences I'd ever go through, but *nothing* compared to this. It hurt to breathe, and it hurt not to at the same time, but my oxygen had been taken from me. Walking in the opposite direction from Cyrus was the hardest thing I'd ever had to do, which was saying something.

Everything inside begged me to go after my mate.

A long exhale from Griffin confirmed he didn't think I'd give up either. He remained behind me, expecting me to turn and run.

For some reason, that helped. I had no choice but to follow Sterlyn. Besides, from what I understood, she could alpha-will me and make me listen. I didn't like the idea of anyone taking my freedom away, and though I knew her well enough to know she wouldn't want to control me, she wouldn't hesitate if she believed it would keep me and Cyrus safe.

What's everyone's status? Sterlyn linked to the pack.

We're all accounted for, except Cyrus, Darrell responded. *We have some injuries, but nothing fatal.*

Why did they only take him? That was the piece of the puzzle that didn't fit. *Was he the closest to them?*

One of the closest, but multiple dark wolves attacked, and half of them went after him right away, Quinn interjected. *That's how they got him so easily. We were racing toward all of you, wanting to make sure Annie wasn't in danger.*

Of course, Cyrus's main focus had been on getting to me, just as mine was to get to him now. *How would they know to target him?*

We didn't kill all the dark wolves the other night when they attacked. Sterlyn trotted in front, her silver fur standing out in the darkness. *Cyrus was distraught when you were injured, and everyone could tell the two of you cared for each other. Also, we did tell the dark wolves you had a mate. So, between those two things, they probably had an inkling it was him. The smell of your scent mixed with his would've confirmed their suspicions.*

Darrell's displeasure crashed over me like a wave. *Just like during the previous attack, they ran in circles, combining their scents to make it hard for us to get a count.*

Who the hell are these people? Tonight, the silver wolves had held a slight advantage, but maybe that was because we hadn't underestimated them.

I noticed that during the first attack, Sterlyn linked. *But tonight, they seemed a tad smaller, despite us being larger with the moon waxing.*

I hated puzzles, and my life turning into one didn't sit well with me. I liked organization and control. *How many different wolf shifters look identical in wolf form?*

A flying squirrel leaped from one branch to another, causing my lungs to move easier and my arm to throb. The animals were returning, indicating that any looming threat was gone. They feared the dark wolves and probably sensed the same ickiness I did around them.

Blood trickled from my injury and mixed with the blood of the wolf Griffin had rescued me from. I needed to clean the wound when I got back to the house before an infection set in ... if I could even get an infection.

I thought silver wolves were the only ones. Sterlyn slowed. *Maybe Rosemary will know something about the dark wolves. Besides, we'll need her help to retrieve Cyrus.*

Thank God. Sterlyn was already forming a plan.

We stepped into the clearing where the silver wolves and Killian's pack were waiting.

"Annie," Ronnie gasped as she ran to me and pulled me into a hug. "I was about to go looking for you, but Alex told me if you were in trouble, the silver wolves wouldn't be staying put." She sniffed, and her arms tensed around me. "You're hurt."

Being in her arms allowed the tears to flow again. When she tried to release me, I held on tight and cried. "It's nothing serious." I pulled away and stared into my sister's eyes. "They..."—my voice cracked as a sob racked my body—"took Cyrus."

"They *what*?" Alex rasped, anger lacing each word. "How did that happen?"

I told them about our connection, the doors slamming, and the van taking off. "The only reason I'm not falling apart is I still feel him."

"Mila, Theo, and the others aren't here either. They had no intention of releasing them." Alex exhaled. "Let's go back to the neighborhood to strategize."

Having Alex on board with finding Cyrus eased some of my turmoil. With Rosemary, the vampires, and the wolves, surely we could rescue him. I had to believe I would make it through this. "How are we going to find him?"

Your mate connection, Sterlyn answered through the pack link. *Though that's what the dark wolves are banking on.*

"Maybe Eliza can help." Ronnie pulled out her phone. "I'm sure she has a witchy spell we could use. She told me to call if anything happened, and this qualifies."

Since Ronnie wasn't a wolf, I had to fill her in on what the wolves were saying through the pack link. "Sterlyn said I can find him through our mate connection. We don't have to drag Eliza into this." I wanted to protect our foster mom as much as possible. She was a witch but trying to stay out of the supernatural world. We didn't know why, but then, we all had our secrets, even though I was sick and tired of them.

Let her call Eliza, Sterlyn linked. *We can use your*

mate bond, but it'll take some time. The farther away he is from you, the harder it'll be for you to track him. I'm sure they're taking him to their pack. They'll want to have all their wolves on hand when we come to save our own. Griffin says a location spell will work faster, even with the drive to Lexington. He doesn't trust the witches in Shadow City, or we'd ask for their help. If we find them quicker than the dark wolves figure we will, it will give us an edge.

If a location spell would help us find Cyrus faster, then I was all for it. "They said it'll be faster if Eliza can do a location spell."

Ronnie nodded.

"Do you have service out here?" My chest expanded. I'd figured we'd have to call her when we got back to the neighborhood.

"I do." Ronnie pushed the contact.

Let's head back, Sterlyn instructed, and everyone moved.

I heard the line ring as if I were the one with the phone to my ear, which still struck me as odd. I was still acclimating to my supernatural abilities because my wolf had been repressed for eighteen years, and I'd first shifted only a few days ago.

Eliza answered, "Ronnie, what's wrong? Is Annie okay?"

"She's f—" Ronnie's nose wrinkled. "She's in one piece."

"What the hell does that mean, girl?" Eliza asked with annoyance.

Ronnie huffed. "Those wolves tried to take her again,

but she's still in one piece. However, they took her"—she paused and glared at me—"Cyrus and other pack members."

I'd been putting off telling Eliza that Cyrus and I were mated. She'd looked at him with such unease that I didn't want to deal with any more drama.

"The silver wolf who saved her from the vampire?" Eliza said.

"Yes, and we need your help." A family of raccoons scurried away at the sound of Ronnie's voice.

Eliza cleared her throat. "With what?"

"Locating him," Ronnie said simply.

There was a long pause. She was going to say no. I didn't know what her issue was with Cyrus, but she could at least point us to where the enemy was taking him. My birth mom had taken me to Eliza's coven to hide me from a demon that was hunting me, which just added to my confusion about everything. "Tell her—"

"I hate this," Eliza said, cutting me off, "but if what you said is true, I guess it's time to face the music. Head to Lebanon and call me when you're thirty minutes out. It's time to get answers. Don't bring a large group. It'll draw attention." The line cut off.

"Did she just tell us the city her coven lives in?" I hadn't expected that. She'd been bound and determined to protect them.

My blood turned cold.

Ronnie placed her phone back in her pocket. "Apparently so, but that's a good thing. We'll get there quicker, wasting less time."

That was true, but I couldn't shake the chill.

As we continued our trek through the woods, I focused on my connection to Cyrus, needing to feel him. I'd do everything in my power to make sure he got back here where he belonged.

Even the scent of the hydrangeas no longer comforted me. Instead, it caused a deep ache inside me, worse than any physical pain I'd been in. Those flowers had always been my favorite, so it made sense that Cyrus smelled like them mixed with his musk.

The silver wolf pack neighborhood came into view. There were fifty houses, though half of them weren't finished. The construction had been rushed a month before the slaughter of Sterlyn's pack. They still planned to finish the houses, but the pack had taken on the responsibility since enough houses had been completed to accommodate the remaining members. Each home had the same one-story floor plan, which made building the houses efficient.

The completed houses were closest to this entrance to the neighborhood, while the unfinished ones sat in various states of construction, nearer to the clearing where the silver wolves trained. Solar panels had been installed on each roof for power and to keep the town off the grid.

Everything looked the same, normal, down to the cars parked in the driveways, which made Cyrus's absence feel even more wrong. All that kept me moving forward was our need to hurry to meet Eliza. To save him, I'd have to stay patient.

Stomach tightening, I picked up my pace as the wolves took off at a run.

"Come on," Ronnie said, and she took my hand, pulling me toward the dirt road that went through the center of the neighborhood. I barely noticed the rows of three houses set on each side of the street.

My connection to Cyrus grew colder and fainter, and I crumpled to the ground. "No!"

CHAPTER THREE

MY ENTIRE WORLD dimmed as the connection between Cyrus and me grew lukewarm. I rubbed my chest, hoping the friction would reignite the bond.

"Annie!" Ronnie exclaimed and squatted beside me. "What's wrong?"

All I could do was let the tears fall down my face. I hadn't cried this much since Suzy's death, and not even that compared to now.

Ronnie placed her hands on my shoulders to make me look at her. Frustration leaked into her voice as she said, "Alex, I don't know what's wrong. I don't see any shadows, but it's like she's been injured again."

There was no doubt about that. I was more than hurt —my heart had been obliterated. I'd thought I understood what broken felt like, but I hadn't.

I'd only been cracked.

This was a whole new level of pain. The only thing

that scared me more was what would happen if I stopped feeling Cyrus entirely.

Exhaling, Alex crouched beside me. "All I see is the same arm injury."

The way he said that grated on me, and I pulled myself somewhat together. "What does that mean? Could they be doing something to Cyrus? Is that what I'm feeling?" My voice rose with fear.

The past couple of weeks, I'd been so determined to be seen as strong and capable, and that facade had crumbled in seconds. I couldn't get myself to care. All I could focus on was Cyrus.

Something tall with long silver hair ran toward me. Even though my vision was blurred by tears, Sterlyn's musky freesia scent filled my nose, and her trepidation fueled mine even more. She linked, *You felt it too?*

With the pack link, I could communicate more easily. *My connection with Cyrus grew colder.*

Mine did too, Sterlyn replied earnestly.

I wasn't sure if that was good or bad. It wasn't just our mate bond that had been affected, but I wasn't sure I liked it being pack wide, either. *What does it mean?*

He's far enough away that we can't link with him like normal, which isn't surprising since they're wolves and know how these things work. I figured they would take him far—if we rely solely on your mate-bond connection, it will take longer to track Cyrus, Sterlyn answered while pushing calm toward me.

I embraced the sensation as the terror receded from my chest. Even though I didn't like not feeling him, the situation wasn't unusual. Now that she'd put it into perspective, it did mirror my faint links with the two silver wolf shifters who were away visiting Mila's parents' pack. Mila's daughter, Jewel, had gone there, needing time to mourn her father, Bart. She hadn't split off from Cyrus as alpha of the silver wolves—at least, not yet—the way Mila and her allies had. Darrell and Martha's daughter, Emmy, had gone with Jewel, and though I hadn't met them, our connection as packmates still pinged in my chest.

"Are you okay?" Ronnie asked.

Again, I was worrying my poor sister. Good thing she was immortal, or I'd be putting her in an early grave. I sniffled, needing to get my shit together before the rest of the pack got out there. I was Cyrus's mate, for goodness' sake.

"The wolves moved Cyrus outside the link distance, so his connection to us is weaker," Sterlyn said with unease. "It's impacting Annie more than any of us."

Wiping the tears from my eyes, I blinked the world back into focus. Sterlyn stood behind Ronnie, her silver hair cascading down her shoulders and her light olive skin glowing faintly in the moonlight. So much goodness radiated from her; she was someone I'd follow anywhere.

Alex's eyebrows shot upward. "That can happen to mates?"

Griffin stepped from the tree line, a twig sticking out of his honey-brown hair. His shirt hugged his six-and-a-half foot muscular frame as he marched toward us, his hazel eyes darkening as he looked at his mate. "That's one reason I hate it when Sterlyn and I split up. I don't ever want to be in a situation where we can't talk."

Pressure settled on my chest as my throat dried. If I couldn't talk to Cyrus, how would we know if he was in trouble?

"Will you shut up?" Ronnie growled. "You aren't helping matters."

Determined to keep it together, I inhaled. "He was just being honest. No reason to get upset with him." I couldn't fall apart. That wouldn't accomplish anything. I had to be strong, not only for the pack but for Cyrus too.

Killian jogged over to us, his cappuccino hair blowing in the wind. His dark chocolate eyes scanned our growing group. He stopped next to Griffin. He was only an inch shorter than his best friend. "I called Rosemary—she's on her way."

My heart lifted. Rosemary was one of the strongest members of our bunch. "Who's going? Eliza said to keep the group small." One thing was clear: my furry self was going. No question.

"Our core group." Alex motioned to everyone standing around me.

Sierra dashed toward us, her dirty blond hair, pulled into its usual ponytail, flying back behind her. Her gray eyes slitted as she stared Alex down. "I *better* be part of that equation."

"Well—" Alex started.

Ronnie lifted a hand, cutting him off. "Of course, you are. No road trip and rescue mission would be complete without the mouthy friend."

"Right." Sierra nodded her head so hard it would have been comical if I'd been in a laughing frame of mind.

Finally finding the strength to climb to my feet, I stood. My arm screamed in protest, but I pushed the pain away.

"Here." Ronnie bit into her wrist and held it out to me. "Sip, so you can heal faster."

My stomach roiled. "I'm good."

"You need to be at full strength to go after Cyrus," Ronnie said, her irises sparkling. "A little sip is all you need."

I winced as I attempted to settle my stomach. If this got us out of here quicker, I'd do it. I licked the blood from her wrist, not wanting to take more than I had to. The sweetness was delicious, but knowing the source ruined the pleasant taste. The pain in my arm eased immediately as the wound scabbed over.

"We need to get moving so when Rosemary arrives, we'll be ready to go." I almost couldn't ignore the urge to get in the car and speed to Lebanon. If we hadn't been an hour closer than Eliza, I probably wouldn't have had the patience to wait for Rosemary. But there was no point in rushing to get there, only to wait.

"I'll get my things and head over to Cy—" Killian cringed. "Annie's house."

His refusal to say Cyrus's name brought a lump to my throat.

"Oh, my God." Sierra scoffed. "You all act like I say things without thinking, but he's so much worse."

Killian's mouth dropped. "What? What did I do?"

"He's kidnapped, not dead." She placed her hands on her hips. "You can say his name."

Not able to stand here and listen to more of the conversation, I took off toward my home—if I could even call it that without Cyrus there.

"Smooth," Alex deadpanned behind me. "Way to get on him and make it worse."

"How about we just stop talking," Ronnie scolded everyone, "and focus on getting ready to leave?"

A warm arm looped through mine, and Sterlyn fell into step with me. She whispered, "He'll be okay. He's a survivor."

"I know, but at some point, he shouldn't have to simply survive anymore." I hated that, for his entire life, he hadn't felt loved or wanted. He hadn't felt whole. I knew what it felt like because something had always been off with me as well. We'd both grown up feeling abandoned, unworthy, and not able to connect with our wolves the way we should, but he'd also grown up feeling unloved.

Just when we'd finally found each other and a feeling of peace within ourselves, something this horrible had to be thrown our way, like fate needed a laugh. "He deserves so much more than battling one thing after another."

Sterlyn stepped closer to me, our shoulders brushing. "It's not fair. Each one of us here has suffered more than our share. You and Ronnie not knowing who you are, your time at Shadow Terrace ..." She glossed over that, knowing she'd said enough. We didn't need to talk about my time as a blood bag. "Cyrus being taken from my family and raised in an unloving home, Griffin losing his father, Killian's entire family being killed, Alex's brother losing his humanity and trying to take his soulmate from him, and me watching the slaughter of my entire pack and having nowhere to turn. Let's not forget that when Cyrus and I found our uncle, he was taken too soon from us.

"We all have baggage, but that's what makes us stronger and more empathetic. These circumstances not only build our character and fuel our motivations but force us to rely on the people around us. Because of these trials, we found a new family, one not forged of blood. Not that we don't mourn the family we lost, but in our greatest times of despair, we found the will to move forward and love once more. In tragedy, there can be beauty. It might just take a minute for us to see what opportunities unfold."

Her words settled over me, speaking to the part of me I hadn't expected to access without Cyrus, and giving me the courage to ask the question, though I feared the answer. "Do you think we will find him?"

"Yes," she answered.

The temptation to hold my breath was strong, but I forced myself to breathe. I hadn't wanted to ask, because if Sterlyn didn't think we could, I'd give up hope. But the air remained clear; only the smells of the redbuds and cypresses surrounded us.

She hadn't lied. She truly believed we'd find him, and that was enough for me.

"Annie," Darrell called.

I stopped and found him and Martha hurrying toward us. They'd just come out of the woods, back in their human forms.

His midnight-brown hair fell to the side like long bangs, and his blood-orange eyes scanned the area for a threat. "What do we need to do about Cyrus?"

For him to address the question to me startled me. I wasn't sure why he wasn't looking to Sterlyn for guidance. "We're meeting Eliza. She has an idea of where they took Cyrus."

Martha's aqua eyes widened. "Already? How is that possible?" She ran a hand through her dark auburn hair, which cut off at her ears.

"When I was a baby, my birth mom gave me to Eliza's coven, and they brought me to her, meaning these wolves probably live close to the coven." Even though the coven had thought I was a demon, which still didn't make much sense to me. Eliza had seemed almost as upset as I'd been at the fact that I wasn't a demon.

"When are we leaving?" Darrell rubbed his hands together.

Sterlyn frowned. "We need you to stay here."

"What?" Darrell's face fell. "But Cyrus—"

"You're the most respected wolf here, and everyone trusts you." She gestured to the houses. "They need stability, after the past few days."

He chewed on his lip. "But I would be more helpful if I came with you."

"Honey." Martha took her mate's hand. "I know you want to go save one of your alphas, but she's right. Four of our own left the pack and were captured within a week, not to mention, we've been attacked twice when we're supposed to be hidden. Now Cyrus has been taken. We need you here, and not just to be everyone's rock. What if the dark wolves attack us again while they're gone?"

Could they? I linked with Sterlyn. The thought of leaving the rest of the pack vulnerable didn't feel right, either.

It's unlikely. They're preparing for us to come for Cyrus.

Griffin strolled to Sterlyn's other side and placed his hands in his jean pockets. "Good point. We'll get some of Killian's most trusted packmates to stay here while we're gone. Better to have more wolves on hand if things go sideways."

Even if the enemy wolves didn't attack, having more allies on hand couldn't be a bad thing. Yes, this place was supposed to be off the grid, but we'd seen how well that had turned out. We couldn't hide any longer.

Wings flapped overhead, and I looked skyward in time to see Rosemary lower herself to the ground. Her large charcoal wings flapped majestically, and her long mahogany hair blew over a backpack she somehow wore without hindering her wings. Her fair skin glistened. "If you hadn't told me where to come, I wouldn't have found this place. Your father did well in picking the spot. Close by, but far enough off the main road that no one is likely to fly by accidentally." Her dark purple stardust eyes surveyed the area.

Sterlyn gave a small smile. "I'm sure he would've loved to hear you say that."

The angel folded her wings inside her back and headed toward the Navigator. "Are we ready?"

"Not yet." But now that we were all here, we were wasting time. I turned to Darrell. "Can we count on you?"

Something shifted in his eyes, but I wasn't sure what it meant. He rasped, "You can always count on me."

That was all I needed. I turned and hurried to the house to get ready to leave, the rest of my friends and family following close behind.

WE'D BEEN in the car for an hour and a half. Alex had insisted on driving his Mercedes SUV, so he, Ronnie, Sierra, and I were riding with him, while everyone else rode with Griffin and Sterlyn.

The fancy car, with all its gadgets and leather, made me uncomfortable. The last thing I wanted to do was mess it up and upset Alex.

Sierra sang "Living on a Prayer" at the top of her lungs, flinging her head from side to side. Alex had turned the music off once, but Sierra had been unde-terred, singing her own mashup of songs. After a while, the old vampire gave up and turned the radio back on, grumbling that at least the instruments drowned out some of her annoying singing.

At first, I'd been worried about Alex and Sierra being stuck in the car together, but she was great comic relief and tempted me to smile from time to time. Also, the dynamic between the two was fun to watch. They liked each other but pestered the hell out of each other as well.

"Why don't you call Eliza?" Ronnie asked as she glanced in the rearview mirror.

Under normal circumstances, I'd have laughed or told her to do it, but it was something to do and would keep my mind busy.

Within a ring, Eliza answered, "What's taking you so long?" There was an edge to her voice like she was under duress.

CHAPTER FOUR

MY STOMACH DROPPED as fresh turmoil charged through me. "What's wrong? Are you okay?"

Eliza huffed. "No, I'm not okay. This whole situation is a horrible mess."

"Is someone with her?" Ronnie turned to me, which made her hair spill over the back of her seat.

If there was, I wasn't sure what we could do about it. "Is someone hurting you?"

"Tell her to blink twice if she needs help," Sierra said, all traces of mirth vanishing from her face.

A disgruntled groan escaped Alex. "We can't see her. How would that help anything?"

"No one is hurting me. Why would you ask such a thing?" Eliza sounded more like her normal grumpy self.

Ronnie relaxed, but annoyance filled me instead.

I wasn't in the frame of mind to deal with her attitude. "Oh, I don't know. You bit my head off because we weren't there yet. We were worried someone had found you, but nope. You're back to your curt ways."

"You're not the only one going through a hard time." Eliza cut to the chase, treating me like a child again. "I haven't seen my coven in nineteen years. This is difficult for me."

Yeah, this shit ended now. "Right. We're *all* struggling, so maybe you can lose the attitude. We're in this together."

Ronnie snorted then covered it up with a cough.

Both of us were surprised by what I'd said, but I wasn't sorry. Eliza had a way of belittling us, even though she didn't mean to. She was a great, loving parental figure, but she was rough around the edges. Hell, we all were.

After a few seconds, Eliza exhaled. "I'll text you where to meet me. I've notified the coven, and they're preparing a place for us to stay."

"Stay? We're supposed to get Cyrus!" There was no way in hell I would be close to him and not do anything.

"We're driving in the middle of the night, and we still need to determine his location," Eliza said slowly, attempting to speak normally. "If you rush in there, you'll get us all captured, if not worse."

Ugh, I hated that she was right. The sun hadn't even risen since it was four in the morning. "We can meet you at the coven."

"No," she said sternly. "I need to arrive with you."

Whatever. I wasn't going to argue. It'd just take longer. "Send the address my way. See you soon. Bye." I hung up as my leg bounced with nervous energy. I'd assumed we'd go rescue Cyrus as soon as we got to Lebanon. But no. Things couldn't be that simple.

They never were.

Ronnie settled back into her seat now that we knew Eliza wasn't in trouble. "Do you think we'll learn why Eliza stayed away from her coven all these years?"

I laughed. "I seem to find out what's really going on at the most dramatic times, so possibly. I think things are building to where it might slip out, even if she doesn't want it to."

"Same with me." Sierra laid her head on my shoulder. "I'm always the last one to know anything. No wonder we're besties."

Ronnie growled, "Bish, back off."

"Don't worry. You're my bestie, too." Sierra placed her hands over her heart and closed her eyes. "Even though you are one of the worst offenders when it comes to leaving me out."

"What!" Ronnie jerked her head back around. "I am not."

"Uh." Sierra wagged a finger. "Yes, you are. Let's see everything I found out last: you turning into a vampire, getting engaged—"

I couldn't listen anymore. "You weren't the last to know all that. *I* was."

That effectively shut her up, and she cringed. "Yeah, that's true. I'm being an ass."

That hadn't been my intention. "I get it. You were last to know out of the group that was in the know."

Alex shook his head. "Annie, Veronica didn't hide anything from you to hurt you. She was trying to protect you."

"Oh, I know." That was always the excuse. "But no more of that. I'm a wolf shifter and part of this world. No leaving me on the sidelines anymore. No matter what."

Apparently, losing Cyrus had pushed me to my limit. I had a wolf telling me I belonged to him and kidnapping my mate and four other pack members to force my hand. Maybe if I'd known about my supernatural nature from the beginning, no one would be in harm's way. Maybe I would've been better prepared to face these wolves. So many maybes I'd never know the answer to.

"I promise." Ronnie's eyes glistened with unshed tears.

The point hadn't been to hurt her, but I had to draw my boundaries, and it might as well be now—when we were about to go up against another enemy. My stress and sleep deprivation probably weren't helping matters.

Warmth spread through my chest, thawing the coldness. I gasped and rubbed my breastbone, reveling in the presence of my link to Cyrus as it flared back to life.

Sierra lifted her head and looked at me. "That was a stark change in your demeanor. Why are you smiling?"

I laughed, suddenly completely joyful. I'd been worried that Eliza might have unknowingly sent us somewhere the wolves wouldn't be, but all that concern washed away. "I feel him again."

"Oh, thank God." She leaned back in the seat. "We're getting close."

Cyrus? I linked, desperate to communicate with him. Even though it hadn't even been twelve hours since his abduction, time had crept by, feeling like years.

When I was about to give up, he responded groggily, *Annie? Please tell me that's really you.* His concern flowed into me.

Of course it's me. My heart pounded. I had no clue why he would ask that.

Discomfort wafted from him. *I didn't know if I was imagining things. The connection went so cold. Wait, why is it warm?*

We're getting close to you. Eliza knows where they took you. I hated that I couldn't hold or smell him. I'd give anything to be in his embrace. *Did they hurt you?*

I felt Sterlyn join the connection.

I want to tell you both the story at the same time, he explained. *The dark wolves descended on us when you were talking to their alpha. We all took off, trying to get back to you so we could fight together, but while we were searching for Mila and the silver wolf captives, a few dark wolves attacked. Their entire focus was on me. One had been waiting for us in human form in a tree, and he jumped down and whacked me over the head with a club. I was knocked out before I even hit the ground. Did anyone get hurt?*

That was a tricky question since we were all emotionally distraught. I looked out the window, watching the trees flash by.

Sterlyn answered, *Everyone made it out, but not Mila and the others. Have you seen them?*

They were in the back of the van. The dark wolves never planned on swapping, even if they had gotten Annie. I woke up before we reached their home base. Cyrus's remorse slammed through the link. *I'm so sorry I let you two down. You need to turn around and go back home. I got myself into this mess. I'll find a way out of it.*

I didn't have to be a psychologist to know why he was acting that way. *That's not happening. Stop with the whole I-need-to-prove-myself act. You don't have a damn thing to prove. You were right beside us, going into a situation we all knew would be volatile. Any of us could be in your place, and they sought you out because of me. If anyone should feel responsible, it's me. Don't you know by now that I love you and will always have your back, no matter what?*

Something unreadable flowed off him, pissing me off even more. It was as if he was debating whether to believe me.

Everything she said is true. Sterlyn's steadfast emotions charged through the link. *You're my brother. No, we didn't grow up together, but you are an important part of my life.*

But I've let you down most of all. He sounded broken. *I trained the people who slaughtered our pack and killed our parents. I was so awful to you, even after you took me with you instead of leaving me behind for Dick and the others to punish. I—*

Stop it, Sterlyn replied sternly. *You didn't know what was going on. They lied to you and manipulated you since you were an infant. They manipulated us all. Of course you resented me—I would've felt the same way if I were you. Is that why you didn't tell me the pack was struggling?*

This conversation was long overdue, and I wished they could have it in person, but if Sterlyn didn't confront him with a few home truths, he might act rashly to prove himself before we got into a position to help him. At least it was happening, and I hoped that reason would speak to him.

You trusted me with them, and I didn't want to ruin that.

Alex took an exit off the interstate and crossed a bridge. We had to be getting closer to where we were supposed to meet Eliza.

We're a team. Sterlyn opened herself up more to us, and her feelings of acceptance and love enveloped us. *All of us. I know you're a strong and good man. That's why I trusted the pack to you, but I need to know I can count on you to be honest with me about what's going on. We're supposed to support one another and know that, even when we get ourselves into horrible situations, we can rely on one another. We're only as strong as our weakest link, and if you believe you aren't worthy of acceptance and love, we will all pay for those insecurities.*

I loved Sterlyn's loving directness. She was an enigma at times. One moment, she was the kindest person I'd ever known, but other times, when needed, she was a warrior. She was the perfect type of leader who knew when to be soft and when to have a stern hand. No one, not even Eliza, channeled those two qualities in tandem.

In other words, don't do anything rash since you two are refusing to leave? His constant inner turmoil eased.

My chest felt lighter and fuller with the hope that he might have found a little peace. Baggage like ours was hard to lose, but if we grew a bit each day, we could accomplish more than we ever had before.

If you do anything to jeopardize yourself, I will hurt you, I teased, but there was truth behind my words.

He must have picked up on the sentiment because he replied, *I don't doubt it.*

Now that we have that settled, what do you know about where you are? Sterlyn asked, moving straight to business. *Any landmarks or pack numbers?*

I didn't see much. The back of the van had no windows—we were in complete darkness. Discomfort penetrated the bond. *When we got here, they pulled the van right up to the building they're keeping us in. It's made of all wood and looks as if it's seen better days. Twenty wolves were waiting for us, but they injected us with something. I woke up when Annie linked with me.*

Knocking him out hadn't been enough; they'd had to drug him unconscious, too. There was no telling what these assholes were willing to do. The idea that I was from that pack upset me. If I'd been raised there, would I have ended up just as cruel? A scary part of me considered it a real possibility.

I would hurt that alpha and make him pay for everything he'd put Cyrus through.

"We're here," Ronnie said as Alex pulled up to a dirty, empty gas station.

Eliza's older Camry was parked at the edge of the lot.

I linked with Cyrus, *Hey, we reached Eliza. Give me a second.*

She's with you? He replied with surprise. *I thought she hated me.*

Hate is a strong word. I'll link with you once we've talked but let me know if anything happens. I love you. In fairness, I didn't think Eliza was a fan of his. She looked at him as if he caused her pain. But I'd never tell him that.

Okay, you two be safe. Cyrus paused. *I love you both.*

We blew past the pump and pulled up next to Eliza's car.

My foster mom's light caramel hair was twisted into a messy bun, and the corners of her sea-green eyes were tense. She looked at Ronnie, but a smile didn't cross her face. Usually, she didn't look her age, but today, she looked every one of her sixty years. I imagined part of that was due to the strain of seeing her coven again soon.

As Griffin pulled in behind us, Ronnie and I rolled down our windows.

"Is this everyone?" Eliza rasped, her fingers tapping the steering wheel.

Ronnie smiled. "This is the crew."

"You could have driven less conspicuous vehicles." Eliza frowned, her jaw tense. "We're supposed to stay under the radar."

"These are the safest cars we have." Alex pursed his lips. "I thought they'd be fine."

She waved a hand. "It doesn't matter. I just thought you'd bring Ronnie's Mazda."

"We got rid of it before the wedding, remember?" Ronnie interjected.

Sterlyn rolled down her window and asked, "What's the plan?"

"Follow me," Eliza said, put her car in drive, then pulled onto the road.

"I admire and respect Eliza, but—" Alex started.

Sierra snorted. "You do realize whenever you speak the truth, even when it's negative, you don't have to start with a qualifying statement. You're still saying she's an odd bird, which I love. Why waste time with pleasantries? You're done with a conversation, you hang up. Someone is getting on your nerves, you tell them to quiet down. Why do people gotta get all butt hurt if someone doesn't follow normal social etiquette?"

"You two act alike. That's why you love her so much." Alex followed Eliza.

"That's the nicest thing you've ever said to me." Sierra beamed and patted herself on the back. "I knew you'd compliment me sooner or later."

Throwing a hand up, Alex sighed. "I give up."

"You probably should," Ronnie chuckled.

After ten miles, Eliza turned onto a gravel road. A dust cloud blew around us as the car jerked and bumped over ruts.

Alex grumbled something about his car getting dirty, but we all pretended not to hear him. That was the last thing we were worried about.

Soon, we were approaching a group of eight women and two men standing in the road with nothing behind them. They were hanging out in the middle of nowhere. A woman in the center with warm beige skin lifted a hand, a light forming in her palm. She thrust it forward, her straight, midnight-black hair blowing back as the light barreled toward us.

CHAPTER FIVE

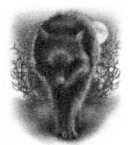

MY WOLF WHINED inside my head and tried to surge forward. Friction from whatever the witch had thrown at us made my skin crawl.

Eliza jumped out of her car and held her hands skyward until the air calmed. "What the hell, Circe!"

"Mom!" The woman dropped her hands, and her rich brown eyes widened. The man beside her touched her arm as Circe said, "I'm sorry. I didn't recognize you."

Uh ... *Mom?* Surely, I'd misunderstood her.

The man's forehead lined, and his long jet-black hair made his ivory skin appear paler in the darkness. He frowned, his icy green eyes filled with uncertainty.

"It's been nineteen years. Of course, I don't look the same." Eliza approached the group slowly, unsure of her welcome. She glanced at the man beside Circe. "Aspen, it's good to see you again."

He lifted his chin.

Her daughter shook her head. "It's more than that. Your hair is different."

"Trying to blend in while not looking exactly like I used to." Eliza scanned the group, and when her eyes landed on the younger woman next to Circe, she touched her chest.

The girl was around my age, maybe a couple of years older. Her eyes were chestnut brown, and her long, bronze-brown hair stood out against her sky-blue T-shirt. "Grandma?"

Holy *shit*, I hadn't known Eliza had a daughter, let alone a granddaughter. What had happened to make her leave these people she so clearly loved?

"Oh, sweet goddess. Aurora." Eliza's voice cracked. "You're a woman."

"I hate to interrupt this *tender* moment," a witch with long, ruby-red hair said from beside Eliza's granddaughter, "but when you said you were coming, we didn't realize you were bringing company. We were protecting our home."

Sierra fidgeted next to me and hissed, "Why didn't she tell them about us?"

Good question. "Your guess is as good as mine." My chest was so tight I thought my lungs might collapse. I wondered if Ronnie was feeling the same, but I couldn't turn my head to look at my foster sister.

"Probably because they wouldn't be a fan of this many people coming. Plus, we're a mixed bag of supernaturals," Alex whispered as if he, too, was afraid they'd hear us.

"Dude, the windows are rolled up." Sierra leaned forward and pointed at his window. "They can't hear us. They're witches."

Alex rolled his eyes. "If someone spelled us, they could. We have to be careful."

"Wouldn't they be able to hear your whispers, then?" Sierra arched her brow, calling the vampire out.

He glared at her. "Depends on the spell, but we don't have to make it easy on them."

"You two," Ronnie groaned. "Stop. You bicker like an old married couple, and I'm not a fan. He's mine, hussy."

Sierra plopped back in her seat and crossed her arms. "Oh, he is, all right. I can't handle his grumpy old ass. He needs to loosen up."

"I'm loose enough." Alex lifted his nose. "But thank you for your concern."

Now they were getting on my nerves. "Will you two shush? I'm trying to listen to their conversation."

Alex's irises turned navy. He probably didn't like being scolded. Tough.

A middle-aged lady on the right edge of the group stepped forward, her golden-brown complexion adding to her beauty. "You stayed away all these years to protect us, and now you roll up with two vehicles full of strangers. That sure comes across as shady." She crossed her arms over her white tank top and nibbled on her plump bottom lip. Her very curly midnight hair ended just past her shoulders. Her charcoal eyes searched for something in Eliza.

"It wasn't an easy decision, but I couldn't ignore their

plea for help." Eliza straightened her shoulders and met the woman's gaze. "Cordelia, you were right all those years ago. It took people I love facing another tragedy for me to see the truth."

One of the girls who looked close to my tender age of eighteen tossed her wavy, milk-chocolate colored hair over her shoulder. She stood between the ruby-haired witch and a third girl, who also looked close to my age. The milk-chocolate haired girl said, "Maybe a phone call or a visit without your new coven would have sufficed. Did you think about that?" She propped a hand on her hip, wrinkling her black top, and narrowed her coffee-colored eyes.

"Selene, that's enough," the ruby-haired woman snapped, her onyx eyes focusing on the girl. "This is our former priestess, even if you don't remember her, and we will treat her with respect. Do you understand?"

Selene's head jerked back, but she nodded, her jaw twitching.

Most of the witches were not thrilled with Eliza's return. I felt horrible for her. She'd stayed away to protect them, but I understood where they were coming from. It was easy to feel abandoned instead of protected, kind of like I did with my biological mother.

Finding out that Eliza must have done the same thing to her own daughter and granddaughter had my stomach squirming. I wasn't sure how I felt about it.

"You're a good parental figure, Herne," Eliza said with deep respect.

"Even if we don't agree with your decision, we must

respect it," Herne said, but there wasn't any warmth in her words. "Please forgive Selene for speaking out of turn." She turned her head to the girl and gestured to Eliza.

Selene exhaled and muttered, "Yes, I'm sorry."

"Why are you here?" the woman at the far left demanded, staring Eliza down with her ocean-blue eyes. Her hair was obsidian and matched her black crop top and dark jeans. The only color she wore was crimson lipstick. With her porcelain skin, it gave her a vampiric appearance. "Not only did you bring two vehicles full of people, but they're flashy and draw attention."

"Sybil, I know that." Eliza tensed, not liking being questioned. "They're from Shadow City—"

A tall, brown man rasped, "Are you *serious*?" He stepped toward Eliza, but Cordelia grabbed his arm and said, "Eliphas, calm down."

"She brought people from *Shadow City*. The very city our rival clan inhabited when it was supposed to be us!" Eliphas fisted his hands, his slate-gray eyes filling with hatred. "Why should we welcome these witches into our home?"

A twenty-something woman tilted her head, causing her curly, dark brown hair to fall to the side. Her brown complexion glowed, and curiosity appeared in her ink-colored eyes. "Shadow City? I thought that was a legend."

"Me too, Kamila," said the last girl, who hadn't yet spoken. She stood between Sybil and Selene. She leaned forward, and her artic-blue gaze landed on Circe. "I know you told us the story, but it was so long ago. I thought maybe the city had vanished or something since we've never been near it." Cheeks turning pink, she pulled some of her wine-colored hair forward to cover part of her face.

"It's real, Lux. Before we relocated here twenty-one years ago, we lived thirty minutes away from it, though we made sure to never get too close." Circe inhaled sharply. "Let's cut to the chase. Why are you and these people here?"

Eliza rubbed her hands together. "You know I wouldn't have come here, let alone brought anyone else with me, if I'd seen another way."

The steadfast woman I'd grown up with clearly felt uncomfortable. No longer able to watch her face these people alone, I opened my car door and climbed out.

She spun around and pointed to the door. "Get back in that car."

That was the problem—she always wanted to do things on her own without any help. From what I'd gathered, that was one reason she'd left her coven. Instead of relying on them to get her through whatever she was running from, she'd left them behind.

There was a chance I would piss her off more by not listening, but I wasn't a child. I was a mated woman and desperate to rescue the man who meant everything to me, along with some former pack members who'd gotten caught in the crossfire. "She came here because of me. If you're going to be mad at anyone, it should be me."

"She isn't a witch." The man next to Circe scowled. "What the hell is going on, Eliza?"

"Aspen, you know her." Eliza turned her back to me, facing the group again. "She's the child you sent to me."

"That's Annabel?" Circe's face paled. "Why did you bring her here?"

Annabel? My stomach dropped as my head tilted back. I'd never been called that name before, but Annie made sense as a nickname.

"Remember when I asked you if any wolf shifters lived around here?" Eliza said carefully, glancing at each witch. "Apparently, that's what she is, even though you told me she was a demon. Now those shifters have taken members of her pack."

The witches didn't seem shocked, and a lump formed in the back of my throat. They'd hidden what I was from Eliza.

"Who else is with you?" Herne asked, standing tall. "You brought the girl we purposely sent away to our doorstep—what other trouble have you brought to us?"

That pissed me off. They just assumed we were trouble when they were the ones who'd sent me away. I marched over to Eliza and stood beside her, refusing to cower to these witches, even if they could hurt me with a flick of their hand. "My friends are *not* trouble. They're here to help me."

Two car doors opened, and I didn't have to turn around to know Ronnie and Sterlyn were getting out of the car, too. Their distinct scents of sugar cookies and musky freesia surged through the air.

Eliza huffed, not happy that more people were getting out of the cars, but the damage was done.

"Like Eliza said, we aren't here to alert anyone to your presence or tell anyone back home where you live." Sterlyn lifted her hands as if in surrender. "We're here to get our pack members back from the dark wolves who took them, including my twin brother."

Circe's mouth dropped. "You're a ..."—she glanced at Eliza, who nodded, then back at Sterlyn—"silver wolf. An alpha."

"Yes, and my twin brother is my beta. He's acting as alpha while I work with my mate, Griffin, the Shadow City alpha, to turn things around there." She pointed to Griffin, who'd stayed in the driver's seat of the Navigator, his hands on the steering wheel like he was ready to get the hell out of there quickly, if necessary.

"Is this a joke?" Circe gasped and looked at her mother. "Because it isn't funny."

"No, it's not." Eliza shook her head. "Now you understand why I'm here."

"If she doesn't want to help us, we can figure things out for ourselves," Ronnie said, unimpressed with the coven.

I loved my sister, but sometimes, she was rough around the edges and didn't trust new people all that much. That was one reason I'd been so shocked she'd stayed in Shadow Terrace after knowing these people for only a short time. Now I understood—she'd found the world she belonged in, just like me.

Play along, Sterlyn linked with me, realizing I wasn't willing to go. *Your sister is trying to end this standoff.*

Everything inside me said not to leave, but I couldn't force someone to help us if they didn't want to. Using every ounce of willpower I had, I turned and headed to the car. When I reached the door, my heart dropped. They were calling Ronnie's bluff.

"Wait," Circe said. "I'm not saying we'll help you, but let's go to our meeting room to discuss the situation further. Aspen and Eliphas, please reset the perimeter spells once the others have come inside."

Eliphas bowed his head slightly. "Yes, my priestess."

Aspen scanned the vehicles, examining everyone inside before his attention landed back on the four of us. He said to Circe, "If you need me—"

"Aspen, you're my son-in-law. Do you really think I would've brought these people here if they were a threat to my family?" Eliza's usual gruffness had returned. "I left to protect all of you, and I wouldn't put you at risk. Yes, there are vampires, shifters, and an angel, but they've protected these two girls that I love as much as all of you."

"An angel?" Aurora beamed. "A real live angel?"

He nodded reluctantly. "We'll meet up with the rest of you once we're done recasting the spells."

"Park your vehicles in the gravel lot next to the community house," Circe commanded and headed down the gravel road.

Should we offer to give them a ri— Before I could finish the word, the air vibrated and rippled like a piece of plastic wrap in the wind. I stumbled back, not sure what the hell was going on, but this definitely wasn't normal.

None of the witches seemed concerned. Like a mirage, a picture of a neighborhood flickered into view as the eight women walked through the warped air.

There wasn't any uncomfortable friction. Instead, the neighborhood appeared right in front of our eyes. The houses were all designed in a gothic style with the same gray stone. Each one was three stories high, with an attic at the top and a window in its center. Herbs and flowers grew in planter boxers out on the front porches.

Eliza climbed back into the Camry and drove past the witches, who were walking to our destination. Alex followed Eliza, followed by the Navigator.

"Is this a good idea?" Alex asked, on edge.

I had to admit something odd was going on. The witches weren't thrilled with Eliza returning here or with my presence, and they'd acted strangely when they'd seen Sterlyn.

So many secrets swirled around us, and I had a feeling, if we didn't learn them, we would never truly know what we were up against.

Eliza drove to a building made of the same stone, but that was where the similarities ended. It was three times larger than the others and only one story.

We pulled in beside her, and as I climbed out, I watched Eliza rush to her daughter. She lifted a hand, and then the noises that surrounded them vanished.

Oh, hell no. She was keeping something from us. I marched over, determined to learn what she was hiding.

CHAPTER SIX

SYBIL SPLIT from the group and blocked me from approaching Eliza and Circe. Her ferocious scowl and pale skin clashed against her dark hair and clothes, giving her an intimidating air. She snarled, "What do you think you're doing?"

Six months ago, if someone had talked to me like that, I would've laughed and avoided confrontation. I'd been a people pleaser to a fault, but the past few months had changed me, and all she did was piss me off for thinking she could treat me that way. "Nothing that concerns you."

My wolf brushed against my mind, lending me strength. She didn't like the way Sybil was treating me, either.

My sister appeared beside me, her irises darkening to hunter green. As usual, she had my back. "That woman is our mother, even if we aren't related by blood. We have every right to talk to her."

"She may have raised you, but not well," Sybil sneered. "This is coven business, and you are not witches."

Alex appeared beside Ronnie and said simply, "They only recently learned about the supernatural world. You can't blame any missteps on them."

Sybil said as she glanced over her shoulder at Eliza, "I don't. I know *exactly* where the blame goes."

This woman radiated so much animosity. If the coven all felt the same way, there was no way they would help us. I couldn't even fathom why they'd helped my birth mother in the first place.

The rest of our group stood on my other side, presenting a united front.

Sterlyn stepped close to me, her shoulder brushing mine, and linked, *Witches aren't known for liking outsiders, especially in their living areas. They let us inside, showing they'll likely help, but we don't want to antagonize them.* She cleared her throat and smiled gently at the witch. "We don't mean to make any of you uncomfortable. I know what it's like to think you're hidden, only to have people show up suddenly. It's not the best feeling in the world, but Annie only wants to save her packmates, and the whispers make her feel like there are secrets."

"If you want our help, she'll have to get used to it." Sybil looked down her nose at us. "Because we do have secrets, and there are things we will *not* share with outsiders, no matter who you are to the former priestess."

Rosemary positioned herself at the end of our

lineup on the left-hand side. Her wings expanded and fluttered slowly like she was stretching them after the long car ride. "Then expect the same treatment from our group."

Sierra wrapped her arm around Rosemary's neck, careful to avoid her dark wings, and snapped, "What she said."

Cordelia strolled over and stood by Sybil. She pursed her lips and crossed her arms. "You came here for our help. Not the other way around. A lack of transparency will get you nowhere, and most of us are looking for an excuse not to help you."

Griffin puffed out his chest next to Sterlyn. "If Circe decides to help us, you won't have much of a choice."

"She won't make us help you if we don't want to." Sybil smirked and rocked back on her heels. "Unlike alpha shifters, priestesses don't force their people on most matters unless the coven is at risk. Your packmates being taken isn't a witch problem."

Brows furrowing, Killian scratched the back of his neck. "Our packs handle things the same way. We don't force anyone against their will, and when it matters, we rally to the same side anyway."

"Sure." Cordelia rolled her eyes. "We totally believe you."

"Shouldn't you?" Sterlyn tilted her head, her eyes turning more silver despite the lightening sky. "You could tell if we were lying, unless something is inhibiting you from sensing it."

Sybil flinched before she could stop herself. "Let's

just say, I don't trust Eliza all that much, and I wouldn't put it past her to spell you so we couldn't smell your lies."

I didn't know witches could hide the smell of a lie. "Wouldn't you feel the magic if she had?"

"Not with a strong, experienced witch." Cordelia tensed. "And Eliza is one of the strongest witches I've ever met."

"That's one of the nicest things I've ever heard you say about me." Eliza had taken down the sound barrier. She chuckled.

It rubbed me the wrong way that we didn't know what Eliza had spoken to Circe about, but they were done. Circe's solemn expression revealed nothing.

"That's all I got." Sybil dropped her hands. "You did abandon us, after all."

"Enough," Circe said sternly. "You know things weren't that simple."

Something truly bad must have happened to cause Eliza to leave. But if I pushed the issue now, it would alienate the witches further. In order to get Cyrus back, we would need whatever help they were willing to give.

"Before we make any hasty decisions, we owe Eliza the respect of hearing her request." Herne motioned to the door. "She did lead us for over twenty years."

When none of the witches argued, Circe clutched Aurora's arm, and the two of them made their way to the door.

"After you," Sybil said and rubbed her fingers like she wanted to cast a spell on us.

She'd totally light our asses on fire if she could get

away with it. Everything inside me screamed not to turn my back on her. "I—"

"Thank you," Sterlyn interrupted and linked to me, *They won't do anything until they hear Eliza out. They would get in trouble with Circe, even if they don't want to admit it. Even though you're uneasy, use your wolf to amplify your senses as we walk inside. They don't trust us, so they won't let us follow them. Someone has to give in, and we're the visitors.*

"Go on," Eliza said, validating everything Sterlyn had told me. My foster mother hung back with the others, which appeased me enough to follow her daughter.

Griffin hesitated, feeling the same way as I, but Sterlyn took his hand and led our group behind the others.

Her confidence and leading by example were what I needed to force myself to head into the house.

As I passed Ronnie, she looped her arm through Alex's, and the three of us moved as a unit. They didn't say anything, but Ronnie's face scrunched like it did when she was arguing. She and Alex were talking, using their mate bond.

I wished there was a way I could link with Ronnie as I could with Sterlyn. It would come in handy right now, with Eliza acting so strangely. We were the two people who knew her best out of our group.

Killian, Sierra, and Rosemary followed us. I heard another flutter and glanced over my shoulder to see that Rosemary had her wings extended, shielding our group from the witches.

"I don't like that angel," Selene whispered. "She makes me uncomfortable."

A grin teased the corners of Rosemary's mouth.

When we entered the house, I paused. The space was a surprise.

This wasn't a house at all. The entire building was one gigantic room. Thick, stained-wood support columns had been given double duty as bookshelves. Each column held several shelves filled with old leather books. The floor was rough, unfinished wood, and there were herbs placed around each windowpane and above each doorway. They looked like a mixture of brown and red roots. A hint of poppy and a spicy musk wafted from the bouquets.

"What's that?" I asked and sniffed, as if the scent alone would give me answers.

The others entered the building behind us, and Eliza answered, "The yellowish root is Angelica root, which wards off evil, and the reddish-tinged root is bloodroot, which prevents curses and evil spirits from entering the dwelling." She looked at her daughter. "I'm glad you continue to use the mixture."

Circe frowned, lines marring her face. "We learned our lesson when we didn't."

Eliza stiffened. "What do you mean?"

Silence was her answer, and Eliza's nostrils flared.

She hated being ignored.

Always dependable, Sterlyn spoke, preventing the tension from getting worse. "Like I said, we're very sorry for troubling you, but we're hoping you can tell us the location of the dark wolves that attacked our pack. We aren't here to cause problems or ask you to do anything you aren't comfortable with."

"Your presence makes us uncomfortable enough," Sybil said lowly. "So I'd say you haven't managed to achieve that."

"Sybil, I said that was *enough*." Circe pivoted to stand in front of the troubled witch. "One more outburst, and you won't be allowed to stay in attendance. Do you understand?"

The witch's cheeks turned almost the same shade of red as her lips. When she didn't argue, Circe turned back to our group.

"Besides—" Eliza started.

Circe lifted her hand, cutting her mother off. "I want to hear it from them, not you." Power rolled off Circe as she put her mother in her place. "By bringing them here, you've shown you think they're worthy of our help. Let them speak for themselves so we can decide."

Eliza frowned, and her nose wrinkled begrudgingly, but she said nothing else.

"The dark wolves—the ones you hid me from—found me. I—I don't understand how or why, other than whatever spell you put on me weakened until it broke. They attacked my pack and took the beta—our acting alpha—and four other members after failing to get me." My heart clenched as I held back from speaking Cyrus's name.

"Why would they do that?" Aurora asked with concern, her brown eyes filled with terror.

I wasn't sure what she meant—why did they want

me, or why had they taken those five people. Either way, the answer came back to one word.

Me.

Sterlyn placed a hand on my shoulder and sighed. "They want Annie because they think she's part of their pack. She's the same type of wolf as them. They captured four of our wolves after their first attack and tried to make a trade for her, but they never intended to give us our pack members back. I don't know why, but when we realized the meeting was a trap, we tried to retreat. That was when they captured our fifth pack member, my twin brother and beta of the pack—"

Eliza doesn't know he's my mate yet, I interjected, not wanting her to let it slip. I'd planned on telling her, but things had happened so fast, and she was so determined to hide my magic again that I hadn't had the chance. "They're doing whatever it will take for me to give myself up to them." They'd upped the stakes by taking my mate, and they would continue until I turned myself over. That thought upset me even more.

"It doesn't matter—we won't let them have her." Ronnie nodded and straightened her back. "We'll figure out a way to take these assholes down."

Eliza jumped in. "Why did you tell me that a demon wanted her? Why didn't you tell me she was a wolf?"

"When her mother came to us, she didn't tell us much, other than her child had been promised to a high-ranking demon." Circe turned to the large window that took up over half of the wall, where faint pinks across the horizon hinted at sunrise. "She wouldn't tell me anything more, except that if we wanted the balance of good and evil to remain stable in the world, we needed to hide the girl and that giving her up was the most loving thing she could do."

Griffin squinted. "And you just ... did it? No more questions asked?"

"Oh, we asked questions, but she refused to answer, saying the more we knew, the greater the risk to us. She didn't want the baby to stay here because it would be too close. We needed to send her child farther away, and we couldn't tell her where." Circe rubbed her forehead and closed her eyes as if a headache was coming on.

"We could tell she wasn't lying." Herne's eyes softened as she glanced at me. "And if what this woman said was true, then not only was the baby at risk but our entire world too. We took a vote, and we called Eliza."

Cordelia paced in front of us. "Only four of us talked to the woman. Goddess, we didn't even know her name, but her words held an eerie truth that left us all unsettled. When she allowed us to cast a truth spell on her, there was no question. We had to hide the baby."

"A truth spell?" Alex's face twisted. "I'm three hundred years old and never heard of one."

"Of course, you haven't." Eliza snorted. "You've surrounded yourself with the Shadow City coven. They never seek the truth, and they're rather corrupt."

"I've never heard of a truth spell either, and I live outside the city." Killian shoved his hands into his pockets. "Griff, have you heard of a truth spell?"

"No, I'm with Alex on this one, but I don't trust

Erin," Griffin growled, naming the leader of the Shadow City coven. "I wouldn't be surprised if she has kept its existence a secret. We could use the spell to nail Azbogah for all his half-truths and lies of omission, and she wouldn't want anything bad to happen to him."

"I still want to meet that angel," Sierra said longingly. "I've heard so much about him, yet I've never seen the douchebag."

Lux laughed, then tried covering it up with a cough. Aurora smiled.

"You don't." Rosemary shivered. "He's horrible. One day, I might actually punch him."

"Not if I get to him first," Alex growled. "He tried to *force* Veronica to turn."

"We're digressing." Sterlyn lifted a hand and looked at Circe. "What *do* you know about Annie's mother?"

"Not much." Circe's shoulders slumped. "All we wanted to do was keep the balance. That's our coven's primary responsibility."

"If you had all these spells in place, how did she find you?" Eliza exhaled noisily. "She shouldn't have been able to stumble upon this coven with the mirage."

Circe grimaced, reminding me of a child. "We didn't have it in place."

"You *what?*" Eliza shouted.

CHAPTER SEVEN

ELIZA WAS furious that her coven hadn't had spells in place to conceal themselves all those years ago, but I had no clue why. "You didn't have *our* house hidden."

"Why the double standard?" Ronnie asked, bouncing on the balls of her feet.

"We were living in a neighborhood with people constantly coming and going. The spell would've been broken as soon as I set it up." Eliza motioned to the witches. "But they're all witches, so it would've been possible."

"The spell breaks anytime someone breaches the perimeter." Alex rubbed his chin. "That's why the two men are setting it back up."

Eliza walked to a column and leaned against it. "The three of us had different schedules, so it would've been too complicated to reset the spell continually. I did have spells around the backyard to alert me if someone tried to sneak up on us."

"Ah!" Ronnie snapped her fingers. "That's how you found out Annie and I were sneaking out that night."

"As soon as you stepped into the wooded lot, the magic woke me." Eliza laughed, her eyes twinkling with mirth. "You two were so shocked when I raced out there."

We'd made sure to be extra quiet, and until today, I'd never known how she'd heard us. I guessed that was what happened when you had no clue you were living with a supernatural being. "Ronnie was so mad at me. She didn't speak to me for days."

"You talked me into it, and we got caught after you swore nothing bad would happen." Ronnie crossed her arms. "I didn't like Eliza being mad at us."

Sierra patted her chest. "If I'd been there, we would've gotten out of there even with Eliza's magic fingers."

"Magic fingers?" Killian grimaced. "Bad choice of words."

Rosemary scoffed. "And you wouldn't have been able to see what she spelled. You would've just caused more trouble, trying to talk them into running before Eliza caught up."

Something unreadable crossed Circe's face as she listened to the banter.

Brushing off the conversation, Eliza stared her daughter down and pressed, "After what we'd gone through, you didn't think to hide yourselves?"

"We moved, and we were hoping for a fresh start." Circe rubbed her temples. "For several months, we lived here without anything strange happening. Aurora, Lux, and Kamila were able to toddle around the woods without us worrying about taking down the spell."

Eliza clicked her tongue in disapproval. "I wondered how someone found you. I thought it might have been when you ran into town, but I guess they didn't have to wait for you to show up."

I'd been on the receiving end of that look one too many times. This wouldn't end well.

"Well, excuse me for not taking criticism from the woman who not only left her family but her coven as well." Circe held her head high, reminding me of Eliza.

Jaw tense, Eliza pushed herself off the column and said lowly, "I did what was in the best interest of the coven."

Herne marched over to Eliza, and the younger witch placed her hands on her hips. "You did what was best for you. You left your daughter, who'd just gone through the same trauma as you. She not only had to console a baby that had been kidnapped but had to step into a coven in a leadership role."

She stuck her finger in Herne's face. "I'd been training Circe to take over. Don't act like I abandoned her."

"You did, Mom, but it's not relevant now." Circe turned to our group. "We aren't here to argue about the past. There's no reason to fight over what was or wasn't done. We need to share facts and decide what to do next."

When Eliza opened her mouth, Sterlyn interjected, "You're right. I take it Annie's mom found you here?"

Exhaling slowly, Circe closed her eyes before speaking. "Yes. We didn't share what coven we were, just like she didn't share what pack she was from or why a demon wanted her child. Neither of us was interested in the other's secrets. To protect the balance of our world, we snuck the baby away, and Aspen met Mom to give her Annabel."

"Did she ever come back to check on me?" I asked before I could think through whether I truly wanted the answer. Did it even matter? The answer would only hurt.

Selene's face lost its scowl as if she understood what I was going through.

"We can't be sure." Cordelia smiled sadly. "Either way."

"Why not?" That seemed like it would be easy to figure out. Either she had come back, or she hadn't.

Rosemary rubbed her hands together. "Because they put up the spell to hide the neighborhood, right after they handed you to Eliza."

"Yeah." Circe inhaled deeply. "We'd gotten involved enough. We bound Annabel's magic and sent her to Eliza."

The way she was acting made me think she wasn't telling me everything, but I didn't want to push things...yet.

"Does that mean you won't help us?" Griffin rolled his shoulders. He tried to come off as relaxed, but I'd been around him long enough to know he was anything but.

Sybil snarled, "She just made it clear that—"

"That's fine. We'll leave. We don't want people to help who don't want to." All of this was my fault, and I didn't want to cause the coven more pain. Something traumatic had happened before my mother ever showed up, asking for help. They didn't need it stirred up again.

The gothic witch paused, her face smoothing as some of the anger disappeared from her expression.

"I agree." Sterlyn placed a hand on her neck. "We don't want to cause problems. We thought maybe you'd know more about the pack than you do."

"You won't force us to help?" Herne's brows lifted high enough that they disappeared behind her long bangs. "Not even the vampire and angel?"

Alex shrugged. "Once upon a time, I might have tried to force your hand or find a way to make you owe me, but since I met Ronnie"—he looked lovingly at my sister —"I've realized there is a better way of doing things."

"And you think the same?" Circe asked Rosemary.

Pulling her wings into her back, Rosemary tugged at her shirt. "We're strong, and we got this far. We'll be fine on our own."

"Before we leave, there's one thing I need from you." Eliza glared at our group, not thrilled that we were letting the coven off the hook. She seemed determined, not only to help us but to get her coven to help as well. We needed to figure out what was going on here. "The pack link bond will take us to their location, but if you could help me with a location spell, we could get there quicker."

The door to the building opened, and Aspen and

Eliphas entered. The two men walked to their spouses and surveyed the room.

"What's the decision?" Aspen asked, standing between his wife and daughter.

Circe crossed her arms and stared at Eliza. "Mom asked if we'll help them with a location spell so they can find the dark wolf pack quicker."

Aspen's forehead lined. "You won't help them beyond that? From what the wolf who brought Annie told me, the pack is huge."

"We gathered the same thing." Killian strolled to the window, focusing on the brightening sky. "They've sent at least fifty different wolf shifters to attack us, and no women or children, meaning their pack is even bigger."

My stomach sank. I was probably the only one who hadn't thought about that. I was the least experienced among us, but I didn't give a damn. I would be right there with everyone when we went in to save my mate and the others.

The link between Cyrus and me was back to its normal, warm temperature, and I sensed a peacefulness on his end. He had to be resting, and I needed to keep my emotions level, so I didn't bother him. "Cyrus mentioned that, when they arrived, there were ten more shifters he hadn't seen before they were drugged and moved into their holding area."

"Drugged?" Alex grimaced. "I was hoping he'd have some insight on the layout."

"That's not a huge deal." Rosemary gestured out the

window. "If they give me a location, I can fly over it and see what I can glean before we make a move."

The witches glanced at one another, somehow speaking without words.

Can they link like we can? I'd thought only mates and wolf shifters could do that.

Sterlyn glanced at me. *They can't, but they are attuned with nature and thus themselves. They can't communicate as clearly as we can but enough to get a consensus.*

"Fine, we will help you with the location spell," Circe said and looked at her daughter. "Go grab a map, a goblet, and jasmine incense." Her eyes shifted to the rest of us. "And we need from you something that belonged to one of the shifters."

"I thought you might." Sterlyn removed a ripped piece of cloth from her pocket. "This is part of the shirt my brother was wearing not even half a day ago."

"Perfect," Herne said and took the cloth. "This will work."

The witches formed a circle, and Eliza joined the lineup, standing next to her daughter.

Circe frowned but didn't say anything as Aurora brought the materials over. She placed the map on the ground and set a dark goblet on top of it filled three-quarters of the way with water. Once that was positioned, she sprinkled the jasmine incense on the map and placed the four candles in the positions of North, South, East, and West. Then she stood between Eliza and Circe.

Once Aurora was settled, Herne placed the cloth on

the map. She dipped her fingers into the water and splashed a few drops onto the cloth, then went to stand between Selene and Lux. The eleven witches began to chant, and the temperature dropped by several degrees.

Ronnie took Alex's hand and stepped closer to me, her body tense.

We'd never been around anything like this, and I didn't feel comfortable either.

"*Dea, adiuva nos invenire personam,*" the witches chanted together over and over.

Suddenly, the candles lit, and the incense swirled in the circle.

"This is so cool," Sierra whispered and stepped closer.

Killian grabbed her arm, holding her in place, his eyes glowing. He must have commanded her to stand still.

The witches continued to chant as the jasmine swirled and the candle flames grew larger. I'd expected the flame to be large instantaneously.

Moments passed, and just when I was certain they couldn't locate Cyrus, the flames shrank until they extinguished, and the jasmine dissipated. The witches all opened their eyes at once.

Eliza snatched the map from the floor and held it out to Rosemary. "We're here, and that's where they're keeping him."

"Got it." Rosemary grabbed the map and placed it into her pocket. "You all go get some rest while I scope out the area. Just text me where you'll be."

"Mom," Aurora said. "Can't they stay here? We have

plenty of room, and I'd like to spend time with Grandma, especially since she's the only grandparent I have." The young girl flinched. "If she wants to."

Hugging the girl, Eliza buried her face in the young girl's hair. "I'd love nothing more than that, but we have to respect your mother's wishes."

Sadness coursed through me. I'd never known what Eliza had left behind until today. Something had always haunted her, but she'd never talked about her past. Ronnie and I understood feeling out of place all too well, as if something was missing, and maybe that was what had forged the strong bonds that kept the three of us together and gave us the strength to keep going.

Circe glanced at Aspen. He squeezed her shoulder, and she exhaled. She looked at her daughter and said, "Fine. They can stay here."

"Are you sure that's a good idea?" Sybil asked.

If that witch could, she'd have removed us from their land immediately. At least, Circe seemed compassionate, though she wasn't thrilled with the situation either.

Hell, none of us were.

"I'll be back shortly." Rosemary walked out the door, and her wings exploded from her back as she took flight.

"Kamila, please take them to the guest house while I stay here with Aurora and Mom," Circe said, not willing to leave the two women alone.

"Yes, Priestess," Kamila said and opened the door. "Follow me."

As we exited the building, I could feel witches watching our every move from the surrounding houses. I suspected only the strongest had met with us, keeping most of the coven protected. I'd never felt so under the microscope before, not even when I'd learned about supernaturals and everyone was watching for my reaction. Had that been just a few weeks ago? It felt like forever now.

The neighborhood was quiet, with most of the others still asleep or at least in their houses. My eyes wanted to shut so badly that I wasn't sure I was up to meeting anyone else.

We walked two houses down, putting us right in the middle of the neighborhood. Kamila led us onto the white porch of a dark stone house and opened the door. "Here you go."

Inside, a brown leather couch and loveseat framed a red brick fireplace. Just beyond the living room was a kitchen with gray cabinets, a firewood stove, and a refrigerator. Stairs stood directly in front of the door leading up to the second story.

"Upstairs, there are three bedrooms and two full bathrooms," the young witch said. "And the attic on the third floor includes a full-size bed. You should have most everything you need. We'll come check on you when your angel friend returns." She pivoted on her heel and marched out the door.

"That was short and sweet," Sierra grumbled and yawned.

Sterlyn nodded. "I agree, but we're all tired and irritable, which means we need to rest while we can."

Though I was exhausted, the last thing I wanted was

rest. Everything inside me said I should be searching for Cyrus, but I couldn't do anything until Rosemary got back.

"You all take the bedrooms upstairs, and I'll sleep on the couch." Killian sat down and kicked back.

"Sounds like a plan to me," Alex said, taking Ronnie's hand and leading her up the stairs.

Sierra and I fell in behind them, with Griffin and Sterlyn following us.

When we reached the landing, the stairway cut around to the left, heading up another flight to the attic, and a long white hallway led to the right.

"I'm taking the attic, so I don't have to hear any hanky-panky down here." Sierra stuck out her tongue and continued up the stairway.

The five of us split into different bedrooms. I took the first one on the right, with Ronnie and Alex taking the room right next to mine. Sterlyn and Griffin took the larger bedroom on the left. None of us bothered to argue over who got which room.

Sunlight spilled into the room, so I didn't need to turn on the light. The white walls matched the hallway, and a full-size bed was set in the center of one wall. There was no additional furniture, which was fine. All I needed was the bed.

I crawled onto the mattress and laid my head on a rather flat pillow covered in a worn, yellow-stained pillowcase. There wasn't a comforter, just a light yellow sheet that I covered myself with. I closed my eyes and focused on the warmth of my bond with Cyrus. I wanted to talk to him, but after being drugged and injured, he needed all the rest he could get. I had a feeling we'd be fighting our way out of the pack.

Eventually, as I clutched the bond between us, I fell asleep.

———

PAIN RADIATED IN MY CHEST, and my eyes flew open. I glanced around the room, forgetting where I was, and reached for Cyrus. His side of the bed was cold ... and memories of last night swirled through my head.

Cyrus wasn't here.

Hurt flowed along our connection as another bout of agony ripped through me.

Then terror charged through me.

I wasn't in pain; Cyrus was. He wasn't okay.

CHAPTER EIGHT

CYRUS! What's going on? I couldn't breathe, and my fingers went numb. If Rosemary didn't get back here fast, I'd march to the witches and demand the location. Now that I thought about how they'd handled the map, it was like they'd prevented me from seeing it. At the time, I'd been so damn tired that I hadn't put the clues together. Further proof I needed rest before charging in for my mate.

Another flash of anguish wafted through the bond, closing my throat. *Cyrus!* I cried and pleaded. I needed to hear him, afraid of what his silence meant.

I'm fine, he linked, and his discomfort faded slightly.

My gut said he was hiding it from me. *You are not. Please, tell me what's going on.* I wasn't above begging.

They came in here to rough us up to get you to react. Concern flowed through our bond. *But you can't do that. We must think everything through before we act.*

Look, I slept. If that's not proof I'm being rational,

I'm not sure what else I can do. I'd fought the urge to leave and find him, trusting Rosemary to get the job done. I did trust her, but it felt wrong lying in bed while my mate and former pack members were being held captive.

Unfortunately, I needed the rest, and despite hating that he'd been injured, my brain was working better.

Somewhat.

I'm so sorry. The guilt was suffocating. The five of them were in this situation because of me. There was no way anyone could argue that point. Even though I hadn't meant for this to happen, good intentions didn't change our circumstances.

Love poured through our bond to me. It felt like he was trying to hug me through our link.

The connection heated as he channeled his emotions. *I'm not. When I met you, something shifted in my soul. For the first time, I've felt some sort of peace. The more time I spent with you, the more content I became, and it scared the living hell out of me. I knew you were making me into a better version of myself, and the thought of losing you petrified me. I hate that I wasted all that time being afraid. We could've been happy, but instead, I made us miserable.*

I was scared, too. I'd struggled with the same feelings at first. *You weren't alone, but—*

No buts, Annie. I've never been happy or at peace with myself until you. You've given me something no one else could ever provide. Hell, you literally complete me. Taking a few beatings is more than worth the sacrifice.

This entire situation sucked, and I didn't want him beaten, but what I feared was something worse than that.

Death.

Neither one of us could undo that. His death might not kill me, but I would want it to.

The front door opened downstairs, and I rolled off the bed to my feet.

I heard Killian grumble, "You took longer than I expected."

It had to be Rosemary. I ran out of the bedroom. The others must have heard Killian too, because the other two doors opened as well. Focused on hearing what Rosemary had learned, I ran down the hall and stairs without looking to see who followed me.

I had to remember I wasn't alone in wanting to rescue Cyrus and the others.

Rosemary stood by the front window, looking outside. The sun was lowering, and with it being the end of August, it had to be close to four in the afternoon. We'd slept most of the day.

The angel's lips pressed into a line as she pulled her wings into her back.

A warning shot through my body. Whatever she had to tell us wasn't good news. She was normally expression-less, not distressed.

Restlessness plagued me, and there was no way I could sit. I wanted to sprint into action. I stood next to the fireplace, bouncing on the balls of my feet.

"Here." Killian moved his feet off the couch and sat up so two people could sit next to him.

Sterlyn headed toward him with her hair slightly messy, adding to her beauty. Griffin followed close behind, his longish hair hanging in his eyes.

Alex and Ronnie sat on the love seat. My sister didn't try to talk me into sitting next to her. She knew me well enough to know I couldn't. In high school, she'd seen me so many times when I'd come home from volunteering at the children's group home after a rough night. I'd pace and vent, feeling like I needed to be *doing* something. This was like that feeling but more personal because I couldn't help the man I loved.

"Where's Sierra?" Rosemary glanced around the room. "I don't want to tell this story more than once, and you know how she can get."

With a grunt, Killian's chocolate eyes glowed as he linked with Sierra.

A door slammed from the third floor, followed by footsteps racing down the stairs.

Her dark blond hair stuck up in the back as she wiped the sleep from her eyes. Her lime-green shirt was wrinkled and so bright it was almost blinding. She yawned and shook her head. "What'd I miss?"

Rosemary arched her brow. "Nothing. We were waiting for you."

My patience was already stretched thin, and I wanted to snap at her to start talking. I didn't think that would go over well with the angel, so I bit my tongue.

What's wrong? Cyrus linked, discomfort pouring off him, but his pain seemed to be lessening.

For now.

I opened up the link to include Sterlyn and answered, *Rosemary just returned from flying over the dark wolf pack.*

Wait. You found us? Shock floated through the connection. *You can't—*

Only Rosemary went, Sterlyn interrupted. *Everyone else stayed behind. A few woke and ate some of the food that we packed after getting some rest so we can get a solid plan together with clear heads.*

That appeased Cyrus slightly. *You should all head back. I can figure out a way—*

Hell no. I couldn't handle hearing him dismiss us again. *Do we really need to have the same conversation?*

Sterlyn grinned.

No, he replied.

"What did you learn?" Alex asked as he wrapped his arm around Ronnie's shoulders.

Rosemary faced us. "Not much."

"Really?" Sierra asked with surprise as she made her way over to the couch and plopped down between Killian and Sterlyn. "Then why were you gone for so long?"

"I was trying to get a feel for the area." Rosemary twisted her hair into a bun. "The place has so many damn evergreens—as if they grew the trees around their houses and neighborhood to remain hidden. They trimmed the bottom in places for vehicles to drive through. The trees are huge, though, and I could only get a glimpse of the houses." Rosemary leaned her head on the wall. "I counted ninety-five log cabins, all one story tall."

"Were any people out and about?" Griffin chewed on his bottom lip.

"A few. Mostly women and children." She inhaled. "There were a few men, but it was hard to get an accurate count without being seen."

"Do you have a guess, though?" Sterlyn asked. "Like anything that could give us some sort of lead."

"They have at least fifty pack members there, but I think there are more." She rubbed her arms as she looked outside. "I've never seen anything like it. How well the place was hidden makes me think the community's lived there for a while. I could also feel a strange energy everywhere."

Strange energy.

I struggled to swallow. "What kind of energy?"

"I'm not sure." Rosemary threw her hands up. "It was so damn confusing, but there's something not right going on there, and I've never felt this before. It was sadistic, like the essence of the entire place is evil."

"Essence?" That didn't make sense.

"Angels can sense if something or someone is good, bad, or neutral." Rosemary yawned. "This place reeks of corruption."

Ronnie groaned. "What do we do?"

There was only one answer, but none of them would like it. "I have to go there."

"What?" Ronnie's head snapped in my direction. "Not happening."

Her thinking she had any sway in my decision was comical, though I couldn't fault her. If I'd been in her position, I'd be reacting the same way. "Think about it. We need to know what's going on there so we can get Cyrus and the others out. If Rosemary couldn't get that information from the sky, how else are we going to figure this out? Cyrus has already been hurt, and they'll keep hurting him until I can't bear being apart from him."

"They want *you!*" Ronnie exclaimed with determination. "If you go there, you'll be giving them exactly what they're after! That can't happen."

Taking a deep breath, I forced myself to calm down. Ronnie was only protecting me. Thankfully, Eliza wasn't here, or they'd be feeding off each other. This was how they always treated me when they didn't like what I had to say. "I'm not reacting. I'm saying we have no good alternatives."

"The witches can do something." Ronnie leaned forward in her seat and turned to Alex. "Tell her."

Alex grimaced, and Ronnie's mouth dropped.

I wasn't sure why my mouth wasn't open in shock either, seeing as he usually sided with Ronnie on all matters.

"No!" She pointed her finger at his face. "Don't tell me you think it's a good idea."

"I don't think it's a *good* idea," he started.

Ronnie dropped her hand and uttered, "Ha!"

"But ..." he continued.

Her body tensed as she glared at him. "But? You can't be serious."

"Love, I know she's your sister, and I don't want her in danger either, but it might be the best way to get the lay of the land so we can get everyone out of there," Alex spoke slowly as if to calm a beast sitting beside him.

I was glad at least one person didn't think I was insane. I didn't have a death wish, but we had to rescue them. I couldn't sit here and do nothing, hoping they released them.

Ronnie turned to her best friend. "Sterlyn, tell Alex and Annie it's too risky. The two of them have lost all reason."

When Sterlyn didn't reply right away, hope grew inside me. For once, people were listening to me and taking my ideas seriously instead of treating me like a child.

"This has to be a joke." Ronnie stood and raised a hand. "It doesn't matter. She's not going."

My sense of calm vanished, and my breathing turned rapid. "I wasn't asking for permission, Ronnie. You aren't my mother."

"Everyone needs to take a moment and calm down." Sterlyn motioned around the room. "We're in a horrible situation, and unfortunately, there are no right answers. When it comes to threats and supernaturals working against each other, good calls are rare."

"But putting my *sister* at *risk* is a solid option?" Ronnie scoffed and threw herself back onto the love seat. "I don't think so."

"These shifters are smart and have been together for a long time," Sterlyn said and got up to stand beside me.

The gesture spoke volumes, and her support moved

me. No one had ever stood beside me like this against Eliza and Ronnie.

Determined, Sterlyn stood tall, her commanding presence on full display. "If we rush in there together, we could all be captured. They have much larger numbers, and they would smell us as soon as we arrived. Let's say the witches spell us so they can't smell or see us—we'd still be walking around the place with no idea where to go. However, I don't know what else to do. She's the only person they'll take in, and she can link with me."

Griffin climbed to his feet and stood beside me in front of the fireplace. "Though not ideal, she is our *best* plan."

Ronnie's nostrils flared, and her face reddened.

"We won't let them keep her," Killian rasped from the couch. "I swear to you. I've already lost a sister, and I refuse to lose anyone else we consider family."

Family.

He and I weren't close, but that didn't matter. I was Ronnie's sister, which meant I was his, too. That was how this group worked, and I was ecstatic that I was becoming one of them.

Sierra rolled her eyes. "Even though I love giving this guy a hard time, there is one thing I know about him, Griffin, and Sterlyn. When those three put their minds to something, nothing gets in their way. If they say they won't allow Annie to stay there, they'll do everything in their power to get her out. And I do mean everything."

"And I vow to help them every step of the way, like I've done since the beginning," Rosemary promised, placing a hand over her heart. "I will always fight on the side of those who honor truth and justice."

Ronnie laughed, the sound devoid of humor. It was more proof she'd given up. "I've been outnumbered."

Thank you, I linked to Sterlyn. *I know that wasn't easy.*

Watching you walk up to that pack and let them take you in won't be easy. That, and Cyrus never forgiving me. But that pack will only get more brutal with him until you rush in without thinking, and we won't be able to stop you. This truly is the safest option for everyone involved. Sterlyn patted my shoulder, her eyes shining. *And I believe you're more capable than even you know.* She turned back to the group. "Let's go find Eliza and Circe to tell them what we've decided and see if they can help."

I hadn't thought about telling Eliza. She wouldn't let this one go. But it didn't matter. I'd made my decision and stood up to Ronnie; I could stand up to her, too.

"Let's go," Rosemary said. She opened the front door and walked outside.

The rest of us followed, my heart pounding with dread.

As if they'd been anticipating us, Circe, Eliza, and Herne were waiting. Eliza's face was set in a deep frown.

Circe gave her mom a look of warning then spoke directly to me. "We'll find a place close to the dark wolf pack for your group to stay when Annie turns herself over to them, but with one condition."

Holy shit, they'd been listening. I bet they had been the entire time, and they wanted something out of it.

CHAPTER NINE

CIRCE LOOKED at each of us, gauging our reactions.

I didn't have time for this. I needed to get to my mate *now*. "What is it?"

"That you allow Aurora and Lux to go with you," she answered simply.

"No," Eliza rasped, her hands clenched with rage. "Not happening. It's bad enough that you kept me away from them all day and that Annie will be heading into danger. Now you want to risk Aurora too? Unacceptable. I'll go with them."

Herne's dark eyes cut to the older woman. "I get that you walked away for a reason and couldn't lead—I don't blame you for that—but you're no longer the one making decisions. You passed that right to your daughter. So, if Circe says Lux and Aurora are going, that will be what happens. Besides, you're too emotionally involved, and you hate not being in charge. It would be a disaster if you went."

Herne had Eliza pegged perfectly. Her presence would cause more problems. "No one needs to go but me. There's no reason to put anyone else at risk."

Loud laughter escaped Ronnie, and she clutched her chest. "You really think I'm going to stay here while you hand yourself over to an insane, hidden pack? *Hell* no."

"The coven has agreed to help?" Sterlyn asked, moving to my other side.

Raising a hand, Circe answered, "Within reason. We agreed, albeit begrudgingly, that since we started this mess by hiding Annie in the first place, we need to help fix it."

At least there was that.

Griffin's shoulders relaxed. "Does that mean you can use a spell to hide us so we can save Cyrus and the other pack members?"

They could hide us? It made sense, but the thought didn't sit well with me. "But if we go rescue them, the dark wolves will attack again, and we won't be any closer to figuring out why."

"We'll move the pack to Shadow Ridge," Ronnie said eagerly. "Simple solution."

"First off, we're keeping the silver wolves hidden until they get settled before reintroducing them into society." Sterlyn sighed. "We'd have to deal with the council before moving them to Shadow Ridge, and we don't have another location large enough nearby. Our hands are tied."

Killian walked to the edge of the group and put his hands into his pockets. "Besides, Annie's right. Even if we get them back, the dark wolves will attack again within a day. I'm sure of it. The whole point is to get you. Even if we moved everyone, we wouldn't get situated in time."

True. The dark wolves had already shown their hand, and they would hunt us down. If we moved to Shadow Ridge, they'd come for us there. It wouldn't eliminate the problem.

"We're sending our daughters with you for two reasons." Circe lifted a finger. "One is to cloak you when the time comes, but you'll still need Annie to go inside and get an idea of where everything and everyone is. Cloaking all ten of you will take a lot of power, and they won't be able to do it for long." She raised a second finger. "And second, while Annie is infiltrating them and learning what these wolves want from her, Lux and Aurora can hide your scent, so they won't be alerted to your presence. That doesn't require as much magic, as it is relatively easy to do."

"Actually, that will work out perfectly." Rosemary yawned. "There's a remote motel a few miles away. We can stay there while we scout out the area."

"Ew." Sierra's nose wrinkled. "A remote motel doesn't sound like a place I want to be."

Alex rubbed the back of his neck. "I hate to admit it, but I'm on the same page as Sierra. When I thought about traveling outside of Shadow Terrace, I didn't expect to be visiting a coven of witches and sitting around a hotel room while Annie put herself in danger."

"It didn't look that awful." Rosemary shrugged. "But

we'll be harder to find than if we stay in the woods and one of the wolves stumbles across us."

The mood darkened again as the direness of the situation sank in. "It's getting dark—we need to head out now."

Herne nodded. "I'll get the girls, while you gather the things you need."

"We never unloaded the car, so we're ready when they are." Sterlyn ran her fingers through her hair and looked at the twilight sky.

"While she does that, it would be best if I shielded some of your magic," Circe said and stepped toward me. "The weaker you seem, the less interested they'll be in you. They tracked you down when your power began to unleash. I'm surprised Mom allowed it to happen."

The words hit Eliza as intended, and she sucked in a breath. "I told her I needed to perform the spell again. She was supposed to come home to Lexington to let me do it. I was trying to stay away from Shadow City—"

Their bickering wouldn't get things done any faster. "Are you sure that's smart?" If hiding my magic helped, I was open to it. I'd do anything to save Cyrus, but I wasn't sure this was a smart move. "If it's necessary, then okay."

"We'll hide it enough to make you seem unthreatening. We still want you to be able to protect yourself." Circe held her hands in front of her and chanted, "*Magia celare eam.*"

A breeze rustled the leaves of the cypress trees. The gust of wind grew stronger and stronger until a small tornado swirled around me.

"Annie!" Ronnie shouted, but Eliza hurried over and placed a finger to her lips.

If anyone else spoke, I couldn't hear it over the fierce rush of the wind swirling around me. After a few seconds, I grew worried because the spell felt never-ending.

I blinked at Circe, her face lined with determination. Her arms shook as she held them out, mouthing the words once more.

Something wasn't right. I attempted to lift my arms, but I couldn't. The wind held them at my sides as it swirled against my body. Though I could see everything, breathing became increasingly difficult. I felt like I was suffocating.

I was trapped.

Eliza rushed to Circe, her face pinched as she stood beside her daughter, mirroring her stance.

Now two sets of hands pointed at me, and the wind increased. Something raked over my skin, feeling like rug burns.

Sweat beaded on their foreheads as they continued casting the spell, their breathing labored.

Several witches walked out of their houses to watch the spectacle. One of them shouted something, but Circe quickly lifted a hand toward them, signaling for them to stop before focusing back on me.

Icy panic slid up my spine into my throat. Even the witches had varying degrees of surprise on their faces.

Annie, did they find you? Cyrus linked in my mind, his concern racing inside me.

I tried to breathe deeply through my fear. He had enough to contend with. I hadn't meant for him to feel my turmoil, but I was trapped, and hysteria was immobilizing me. *No, we aren't under attack. Wait, do they know we're close by?* Ugh, the only thing that could make this situation worse was for the wolves to find us here. Hopefully, they couldn't while we were inside the illusion spell the witches had in place, but I was afraid that even a close call might anger the witches into no longer helping us.

We needed their help.

I don't think so, Cyrus assured me, but he was on edge too. *But with what you're feeling—*

Of course. Between the pain and terror wafting from me, an attack was the most logical explanation. *The witches are trying to lock some of my magic away, so the dark wolves won't sense me as much.*

Why would they sense— He paused. Then anger ripped through me. *You better not be coming here. Annie, what are you planning?*

Yeah, I wasn't answering that. I didn't want to lie to him, but I also didn't want to tell him and have him react recklessly.

When I didn't respond fast enough, he linked Sterlyn in, *What are you two planning?*

I whimpered as the magic grated across my skin. If this kept up, I'd have a pile of it at my feet before the spell was over.

Cyrus's panic slammed through the bond. *Sterlyn, what's going on?*

I tried to lower myself to the ground, but the air kept me upright.

They're trying to bind her magic, and something isn't right. Sterlyn ran around me and yelled frantically, "Stop! She's in pain! You're hurting her."

The wind dissipated, and I fell to my knees with a groan, tears trickling down my face.

Copper hair blurred, and Ronnie materialized next to me. She hugged me, and I sagged against her, tense with pain.

"What the hell was that?" Sierra crouched beside me, glaring at Eliza and Circe.

"I ... I don't know." Circe's brows furrowed. "I couldn't weaken her wolf. At all."

Eliza stood in front of me and crossed her arms. "Annie, is there something you need to tell me?"

That was a loaded question, and whenever she put me on the spot like that, I tended to make the situation worse. I had to be smarter than normal, so I took a moment and cleared my throat. "Uh ... like what?"

"Only a handful of things are stronger than magic, and one is when you meet your other half and seal the bond." Eliza spoke the next words slowly. "Like I said, is there anything you need to tell me?"

Yeah, she knew. That was great. "Well, Cyrus, he's kind of my ... mate?" My voice rose like it was a question, though I hadn't asked a damn thing. I wasn't ashamed of Cyrus, but I was petrified of Eliza's reaction.

"Why wouldn't you tell me that?" Eliza scowled at me, then Ronnie. "And you should've had the sense to."

Eliza ran a hand down her face. "Now I understand why the magic dwindled so damn fast."

"Look, I didn't learn about it until recently." Ronnie lifted her chin and stood. "So don't give me an attitude."

"Neither one of you should be talking." I was so damn tired of fighting. "I didn't tell you because you kept looking at him like he disgusted you or something. I didn't want to deal with any drama until he was safe."

Circe turned to her mother. "Her mate is a silver wolf?"

"Apparently so," Eliza grumbled.

"Why does it matter?" I glanced back and forth between them. Something was going on, and someone needed to say something.

Hey, are you better now? Cyrus linked, pulling my attention away.

Yeah, I'm fine. I'm sorry I scared you.

Aurora and Lux walked out of a nearby house and hurried toward us with Herne on their heels. Both young girls were dressed in all black and had their hair pulled into low ponytails, and they each carried a duffel bag.

Thank God, they were ready to go.

Why are you apologizing? Cyrus asked. *Your well-being means everything to me. That's why you can't come here.*

I'm coming to save you and the rest of the pack. I was done with him trying to talk me out of the very thing he'd do if he were in my shoes. *I love you, and I could never live with myself if I didn't try.*

He paused, the words settling hard inside him. *Fine. I*

can't stop you. But, Annie, I will protect what's mine. I don't care what it takes—I won't let them hurt you.

My heart warmed, and I pushed my love toward him. *I feel the same way. I'll let you know when I'm close.*

Please, be careful, he pleaded. *I can't live without you.*

Aurora's irises were almost as dark as Herne's as she surveyed our group. "What happened here?"

"A spell gone wrong." Circe sighed. "But it doesn't matter. Are you two okay with going with them?"

"Of course." Lux beamed. "Those spells are easy—we won't have any problems."

Grimacing, Alex put his hands behind his back. "Are you sure two of your youngest members should accompany us?" He gritted his teeth and looked at the young women. "No offense."

"How many times have I said it? If you feel the need to say no offense, someone is going to be offended." Sierra blew a raspberry. "You'd think with him being three centuries old, I wouldn't have to tell him that."

"I'm older than him, and you have to tell me things like that, too." Rosemary shrugged. "Our age means we have no problem being truthful."

"Or rude." Sierra rolled her eyes. "With you two, those terms are interchangeable."

"Is she really lecturing me?" Alex puffed out his chest. "Her? The one who watches stupid movies and sings her lungs out in the car?"

"Just because I know how to have fun and you don't doesn't mean you get to criticize me." She smacked her chest for emphasis. "I can't help it if you have a stick shoved up your ass."

Alex inhaled sharply. "I do not have anything of the sort."

"We do *not* have time for this!" My frustration snuck through, but I didn't give a damn. "We need to go."

"I agree with Alex." Eliza stood straight. "I don't think Aurora and Lux should go."

"Mother, I'm trying to work with you here, but you can't go. You're too emotionally invested, and after you and me, Aurora is the strongest in the coven. I'm needed here, so she needs to go. Lux is her training partner, so it makes sense for them to go together. That is the last time you get to question my judgment."

Eliza opened her mouth to rebut her then closed it.

Before she could start another argument, I looked at the group. "Should we go?"

"The sooner we get there, the less prepared they'll be," Sterlyn said. "Hopefully, we can get everyone out in the next day or two."

Pulling the map from her pocket, Rosemary handed it to Griffin. "Here's the location. I'll fly to the hotel and meet you there. That way, you'll have room for both Lux and Aurora."

Not wanting to leave Eliza like this, I spun around and hugged the woman who'd raised me. Thankfully, my skin no longer hurt. The abrasive sensation had disappeared once the magic had stopped. "I'm sorry I didn't tell you. I just—"

"I get it." She hugged me back. "Please be careful.

You three girls are some of the people I love most in the world. I can't have any of you hurt, including the one who's stubborn enough to hand herself over to the pack who wants her. Do you understand me?"

I pulled back and smiled sadly. "I love you too, and I'll do everything in my power to make sure we all come back home. Every single one of us."

Ronnie hugged her next while Aurora stood awkwardly a few feet away.

I waited to see if she would hug Eliza, but she stayed put.

I couldn't blame her. From what I could tell, Aurora didn't remember much about her grandmother. Eliza was essentially a stranger to her.

"What about the spell?" Sterlyn asked as she headed toward our cars.

Lifting a small bag, Herne nodded toward it. "We'll handle it as soon as you get through the perimeter. The girls can let you back in when everyone comes back."

We all got into our car and drove away in silence.

WE CLIMBED out of the car at the Sleep Inn, the hotel Rosemary had mentioned earlier. The place didn't seem as sketchy as the angel had described. It looked like a decent place to stay, given the location and circumstances.

Rosemary landed in the nearby redbuds and stepped out of the tree line, her wings already hidden. She hurried to the trunk of the Navigator and grabbed her bag. "Let's go get a couple of rooms."

Yeah, I wasn't staying. The tug of the mate connection between Cyrus and me was almost too strong to handle. My wolf knew he was nearby and in danger. "I'm heading out. I've got to get to Cyrus and the others."

As expected, Ronnie slammed the trunk of her and Alex's SUV, frustrated that I was determined to go on my own. She didn't say anything, knowing there was no talking me out of it.

"You promise to link with me the entire time?" Sterlyn placed her hands on my shoulders, staring into my eyes. "I want you to check in once you get there, once you get settled, and every hour. If I don't hear from you besides when you're sleeping, we will come to get you, whether you've found Cyrus or not. Do you understand?"

"I do." Even though Cyrus was her brother, I could feel her struggling to let me go alone. It went against her alpha instinct, but she also knew I was our best chance of getting him and the others out, too.

"If you die, I'll bring you back to life to kill you again." Ronnie hugged me tight, almost cutting off my air.

I chuckled. "I wouldn't expect any less."

"The same goes for me." Sierra wrapped her arms around me and my sister, holding us both. "Because you're family, too."

Tears burned my eyes, but I blinked them dry before anyone could see. "I love you too, Sierra." Pulling myself out of their embrace before I could break down, I saluted the guys, Rosemary, and the witches. "I'll see you soon."

"Uh, I'm going with you." Rosemary handed her bag to Killian. "I'm going to fly over and make sure nothing goes wrong before coming back here."

"You don't—" I started.

"I'm not asking for permission," she said. "Guys, text me the room number I'm staying in."

"Will do," Killian answered.

I scanned the group again, then turned on my heel and hurried into the woods, ready to get to my mate.

When we reached the thickening trees, Rosemary whispered, "You better be safe and use your head. I'm taking to the sky." Her wings exploded from her back, and she patted my arm awkwardly before taking flight.

My wolf surged forward, eager to find Cyrus, and we took off at a run. I let her guide me, knowing she wouldn't lead me astray.

After a couple of miles, a branch broke not ten feet away.

I wasn't alone anymore.

CHAPTER TEN

MY BREATHING TURNED RAGGED, and the over-whelming urge to attack took hold.

They're here, I linked with Sterlyn.

I know it's hard but try to remain calm. Sterlyn pushed serenity toward me. *They'll think one of two things: that you're there to attack, or you're there to learn what we're up against and ultimately a rescue mission.*

Uh ... the last thing is exactly what we're doing. I wasn't sure how to get around that one. My heart hammered. Maybe this hadn't been the best idea. We didn't need me to be captured and add another person to the rescue list.

I doubt they'll ask you straight out. They'll try to outsmart you in your own game. Just play on the truth—you're there to learn more about your heritage. Remember to breathe, and if things get bad, let us know. We're prepared to leave the motel if it comes to that, but I don't think it will.

106 JEN L. GREY

Knowing they were ready eased some of the tightness in my chest. With Rosemary here, even if she had to carry my ass, we could get by until the others reached us. *Stick as close to the truth as possible?*

Exactly, she replied. *That's always the best way to do things. It prevents you from needing to lie, which I assume they can smell the same as we can.* She grew more serious. *They'll come out aggressively—be prepared. They may threaten you in case we're nearby to force us to attack. Stay levelheaded.*

Paws pounded my way as if they'd heard what she'd said. From what I could tell, twenty wolves were heading my way.

My wolf surged forward, and I had to hold her back. If I shifted, I wouldn't be able to communicate with them. Though they couldn't talk to me in wolf form, at least, they could hear what I had to say. If I was in wolf form, I would seem more aggressive.

The closer they got, the harder it became to breathe. I tried to keep my head steady, remembering all the advice I'd given the kids at the group home when I'd worked there: Listen to your heartbeat; relax your muscles; visualize a place that calms you. However, none of it worked. No matter what I did, the faint sound of paws running toward me seemed as loud as a train rushing down the railroad tracks.

Babe, what's going on? Cyrus asked, his concern wafting through me.

He'd been oddly silent since he'd found out I was coming. I could feel the conflicting emotions warring inside him, so I'd left him alone, not wanting to start an argument. He'd resigned himself to me coming, even though he wasn't happy about it. *I'm here. The dark wolves are heading toward me.*

Please, turn back while you can, he pleaded. *I can find a way out of here.*

I don't doubt that. Cyrus was one of the most capable people I'd ever known. He'd survived so much and without anyone to lean on. I didn't think I could've endured everything he had. *It's not that we don't think you're capable—it's that we're a pack, even the non-shifters. We don't leave anyone behind, which includes Mila, Chad, Theo, and Rudie.*

Just please be careful. I swear if they hurt you—

They won't. At least, I didn't think they would, not at first, but I was wise enough not to say it. *Besides, Rosemary is right above me, and Sterlyn and the others are only a few miles away in a motel.*

Wings fluttered overhead, and I glanced up to see Rosemary hovering just above the trees. Luckily, we were a few miles from anywhere, so a human seeing her wasn't likely. She probably shouldn't be flying that low, but it wouldn't do any good telling her to leave. She was there for me.

Some of Cyrus's concern eased, but it didn't vanish. *There are a ton of them here. Every once in a while, I pick up another scent. I'd say there are over fifty.*

Rosemary thinks there are more than double that, based on the number of houses she saw when she flew over earlier. We needed as much information as possible about them. Their numbers, their training, their...everything. *They're approaching now.*

Can you open your link so I can hear everything?

I wasn't sure that was the best idea, but he'd feel whatever I was going through, so if I didn't, he might get more worked up. *Uh, how?*

Just spread out your consciousness to your surroundings, like you want me to hear, he replied.

That wasn't super helpful. I tugged at our connection, trying to open it up more.

The wolves slowed as they drew closer and stopped just out of sight. I waited with bated breath for their next move as I continued to manipulate the bond.

My chest grew warmer, and the link felt as if it beat throughout my body. *Did it work?*

Yes, I can hear the wolves breathing, he replied with relief.

When the dark wolves didn't move, I took the first step. They were waiting me out, and I didn't have the patience to play games.

Maybe if I tried to communicate with them, it would ease the tension of the encounter. "Hello. I know you're out there. I'm not here to cause any harm." Luckily, that was true.

A wolf huffed and moved in my direction.

None of the others followed him, easing some of my worry. If they were going to attack, surely, they would've all come together.

Stepping between two redbuds, the wolf narrowed its

eyes and bared its teeth. Something icky washed over me, coming from inside the wolf itself.

They wouldn't be friendly after all. Sterlyn's advice to breathe repeated in my mind. I forced myself to inhale. I had to think clearly. "I've come in peace." The slight stink of a lie wafted from me.

The wolf pawed at the ground as he sniffed and scanned the surrounding area.

That's exactly what someone would say if they didn't come in peace, Cyrus linked.

Opening the bond with him had clearly been the wrong choice. Not only was I in a horrible situation, fighting off my panic, but I also had a critic. *Excuse me for not being savvier about the art of conflict.* I couldn't hide my exasperation, though I regretted biting his head off. I wasn't the only one going through a hard time.

Regret poured into me as he linked, *You're right. I'm sorry. Just tell them you're there to give yourself up because that's the truth, despite me asking you not to.*

He couldn't resist the dig.

Sterlyn had said something similar—stick to the truth. "I'm here to hand myself over to your pack."

The wolf cocked its head as its overly sweet, musky smell swirled around me.

What the hell was he doing? Staring me into submission? I needed to get to the pack and see Cyrus. Being away from him this long was taking its toll on me. My chest tightened as I fought back a growl. I would not submit to this asshole, so we needed to move this along.

"Should I follow you?" I took a step toward him, and the wolf snarled, stopping me in my tracks.

The other pack members ran past me and fanned out. Cyrus pulled Sterlyn into our connection and said, *They're spreading out to make sure it's not a trap.*

We made a point not to go into the woods, so as long as they don't follow her scent back to the car, we should be okay, Sterlyn replied. *Which they shouldn't because humans are swimming in the pool outside.*

That was a godsend. Knowing our luck, if that hadn't been the case, they would have double-checked.

The wolf inched toward me and lowered his head, ready to attack at any moment.

I lifted both hands, wanting him to see I was unarmed.

He circled me, and I remained still, not sure what to do. He growled, and I glanced over my shoulder. He nodded his head forward, indicating the direction he'd come from.

We're on the move, I linked to both Sterlyn and Cyrus. I took slow, steady steps and hid my shaking hands. I didn't want the prick to know he unnerved me. I needed to appear confident and calm.

Everything I wasn't in that moment.

Tapping into my wolf, I channeled her help in determining where to go. I sniffed the air and followed the trail of scents that were grouped together...or at least that was what they wanted me to think.

I glanced upward to find that Rosemary was no longer close to the treetops. I saw a very faint hint of black from her large wings high in the sky. She was close, which kept my hands from shaking uncontrollably.

No animals scurried through the woods, which resulted in a strange silence. The only sounds came from the wind blowing through the leaves and the wolves following me.

The scent of oakleaf hydrangea filled the air as I passed by the white-flowered shrubs that indicated water was close by. The smell reminded me of my mate and made my heart ache, but I was getting closer to Cyrus. I had to remember that. Soon, I'd be smelling him and back in his arms—my true home.

Voices alerted me that we were getting close to the pack housing. I paused, needing to prepare myself. Though I'd been eager to get here for Cyrus, the pressure of what I had to do was building. Everyone was counting on me, and I couldn't let them down.

The wolf headbutted me, and I almost fell to my knees. I caught my footing. If I hadn't been tapped into my wolf, I would've landed on my face.

Douchebag.

"What the hell?" I rasped, reining in my anger. Lashing out wouldn't be helpful, but damn it, I didn't want to be a doormat either.

A low growl was the response, and he headbutted me again.

This time, I'd expected it. Not wanting to be manhandled, I planted my feet firmly and stayed upright. I walked slower, not wanting to cause a huge scene, but I had to stand my ground somewhat.

The standard cypresses and redbuds we'd been walking through thinned as evergreens replaced them.

We were getting close.

Soon, the only trees we walked past were the evergreens that were these wolves' signature. In the distance, a log cabin came into view, and the noises of people grew louder.

My stomach churned. Each step put me in more danger but turning around wasn't an option. My mate was here.

The short house we approached was strategically positioned between evergreens. The bottom half of the trees were cut out where they jutted against the home. They obviously maintained the trees so that they grew close to the homes without damaging the structures. The house had two windows in the front and a small front porch that led to the door. Five men stood in front of it, facing me.

They had to be waiting for me.

I see five men and a house, I linked with Sterlyn and Cyrus.

Cyrus replied, *If they do anything to you, I'll find a way to get to you.*

If he had found a way out at this point, he would've already taken it, especially knowing I'd planned on coming here. *It'll be fine.*

They want her, Sterlyn interjected. *They won't hurt her yet.*

Yet.

That was not comforting.

If you knew they would— Cyrus started.

Sterlyn cut him off. *We'll get all of you out before it comes to that. I swear. She has two days, at most, before the rest of us come for you, whether we have the information we need or not.*

Sooner if they start hurting her, Cyrus demanded.

I swear on the moon, she linked. *Annie, nothing bad will happen to you. We'll get you all immediately if anything even hints at going wrong.*

I wasn't worried that the wolves would hurt me. I wanted to learn everything we needed to about them, so we had an idea of what they wanted.

The men in front of me had been there the night Cyrus was taken. Just like that night, the tallest man stood in the center, with two men flanking each side. Something sinister wafted off them, the strongest emanation coming from the man in front—the alpha.

He ran his fingers through his longish brown-black hair, moving it to the side. His face had aged in the last two days, looking slightly older than forty like it had the night before, and his electric blue eyes were haunting. Those eyes narrowed as he examined me again. "I thought it was a dream, two nights ago, but here you are, looking exactly like I remembered."

What an odd thing to say. "What do you mean?"

"It really is freaky." The alabaster man chuckled. He was taller than the other four by a few inches, but his complete lack of pigment made him appear intimidating.

Almost as if they'd put themselves beside each other because of the huge contrast, the man beside him had rich, smooth, espresso skin and dark eyes. He was two inches shorter than the alabaster man, but his smirk was crueler. "I think a certain someone knows about this."

The two other men beside the alpha had to be twins. Their chestnut hair was cut short, and their warm beige skin was the same shade. The only difference between them was the one on the end was about an inch taller. They remained quiet.

"Oh, I agree. And the time has come." The alpha flicked his wrist. "Thanks, Huey, for bringing her here, but go scout with the others to make sure no one followed her."

They're searching for you guys, I linked with Sterlyn and Cyrus. *They expected you to come with me.*

We're staying put and going as far as ordering pizza. They won't find us, Sterlyn reassured me.

I was so glad I could link with them all. It made this bearable.

"I think it's time we finally got some answers." The alpha motioned for the twins to move forward and asked, his eyes focused on me, "Don't you?"

That was one thing I didn't need to lie about. "I do."

"Then, please, after you." He waved me forward so that I followed the twins and walked in front of him.

I didn't want to turn my back on him, but I had to play nice. He needed to think I was here to surrender. I forced my feet to move one at a time and schooled my face.

We passed the house and headed down a worn path. Each log cabin reminded me of the silver wolf pack neighborhood, and I guessed these houses had also been designed for efficiency and not uniqueness. Maybe they'd had to build them quickly. Another mystery.

We didn't pass anyone, but I noticed a few people glancing at us through their windows.

I wondered if they'd been told to stay inside. *I haven't seen anyone else outside.*

They probably expect you to be linking with us, telling us everything. They'll try to limit what you see. Annoyance surged through Sterlyn. *But that's okay. We have the witches. Just figure out what you can.*

Yeah, that would be easier said than done. We walked into an open area that had several benches in a semicircle, like a theater. They were positioned around a large tree with a worn patch of grass in front of it.

A sour taste filled my mouth. This was where the alpha talked to his pack, and they all sat around him, hanging on his every word.

Was this a cult?

"Go get my mate," the alpha commanded the alabaster man. "And Ken, don't give her any warning."

His mate. Why would he bring her here?

"Yes, Alpha." Ken hurried off, leaving me alone with the four other men.

The alpha steepled his fingers, and his hateful eyes flicked to me. "You're full of surprises."

"Uh...thanks?" I didn't know how to respond, but that felt like the safest option.

He laughed, but his face turned indifferent. Cold. "You aren't going to ask why?"

Clearly, he didn't like my lack of interest. "Okay. Why?"

"Because you somehow got away from this pack for what...eighteen years? Then you blinked in and out, alerting us to your presence, until you completely disappeared, but not before we located you. Now you're here, days before I expected you to arrive." He stepped into my personal space. "And I will find out how and why."

I gulped down a breath, and the alpha grinned.

He wanted to frighten me, which pissed me off.

Footsteps hurried back, and I heard a woman ask, "What's this all about?"

Looking for any reason to gain distance from the alpha, I took a few steps back and looked at Ken and the woman who had joined us in the clearing.

My breath caught as I stared at an older version of myself.

The woman's mouth dropped open, and she ran her hand through the same brown-sugar-colored hair as mine. Her honey brown eyes bulged. "Annabel?"

CHAPTER ELEVEN

MY WORLD TILTED as I stared at my birth mother. It was like looking into a mirror, and unlike the men around me, warmth radiated off her. I'd been so focused on finding Cyrus that I hadn't considered that running into her was a possibility. But, of course, it was—this was her pack.

The alpha chuckled. "That's what I thought the other night when I saw her, but how is that possible? Our daughter died a few days after birth. I heard her heart stop beating."

His words upset my stomach, and I tore my gaze away from my mother to look at the alpha.

He was my *father*.

I tried to swallow the vomit inching up my throat. I couldn't believe that, out of every male here, the alpha prick was my father. I couldn't imagine him raising me. Maybe my mother giving me up had been a blessing.

"I heard it stop t-too." My mother's voice broke. "I thought I'd lost her forever."

But how had my heart stopped beating? It couldn't have happened because here I stood. The witches must have done a spell...

My body froze as realization washed over me.

Babe, it doesn't matter to me who your parents are, Cyrus reassured. He could hear everything because I still had our connection open.

It's not that. I'd only been certain of a handful of things in life, and the most solid one was that nothing could tear Cyrus and me apart. Though we might be newly mated, our relationship was strong...secure. Now I'd learned the only thing I feared *could* tear us apart, but the longer I held it close to my heart, the harder it would be to tell him. *Didn't the witch who kidnapped you make it seem as if your heart had stopped beating, too?*

Pain washed over him and bled into me. *Maybe it was the same coven.*

He didn't say anything else, but he didn't have to. *Then it's no wonder Eliza looks at you that way. But if she was so guilt ridden, why did they do it again?*

It doesn't matter. It's in the past, and we can deal with it later. You need to pay attention to what's going on around you. Cyrus pushed away his hurt.

He was right, but the revelation still tingled in my brain.

The taller twin scratched his ginger-brown scruff. "Tate, there's only one supernatural race that can do something like that."

"You're right, Echo." The alpha nodded. "Witches. But how did they find us, and why did they hide my daughter?"

At least, I had the name of the alpha now—Tate. I hated calling him the alpha because it sounded too respectful.

Tate narrowed his eyes at me, the irises darkening. "Would you know anything about the witches?"

Annie, run, Cyrus commanded. *This won't end well.*

I'm not leaving you. I lifted my head, refusing to submit. *Besides, even if I ran, they'd catch me within seconds. Then our whole plan of getting information would have been for nothing.*

Something banged a few buildings down from me as Cyrus linked again, *Damn it, Annie.* He looped Sterlyn back into the conversation. *Things are going south. We need to abort this plan.* The logs of the building shook slightly, identifying where the commotion was coming from.

"She must know something," the dark brown man growled. "Her mate is freaking out. She's talking to him."

Yeah, they'd figured out Cyrus was my mate. We'd assumed that, but he'd confirmed it.

"I agree, Nyko," Tate said and grabbed my face. His fingers dug into my cheeks, making my jaw ache.

He wanted me to whimper and be scared, and even though that was exactly what I wanted to do, I wouldn't give the bastard the satisfaction.

A vein between Tate's eyes bulged. "Do you know the witches who did this?"

Nothing I said would improve the situation, so I remained silent. Besides, speaking would only cause more pain.

"Stop!" my mother exclaimed, moving forward to reach me.

Expecting her reaction, Ken wrapped an arm around my mother's waist and pulled her back against his chest. He rasped, "Midnight, remember your place. Don't get involved."

"Like hell I won't." Midnight fought against his grasp. "That's my daughter he's hurting!"

"Shut up." Tate's eyes glowed as his wolf surged forward. His words were laced with alpha will, and he directed the command at my mother.

She opened her mouth but couldn't speak. All that sounded were squeaks.

Cyrus's desperation to reach me slammed into me as the banging inside the building grew louder.

Don't hurt yourself. I'm fine. I wasn't sure of that, but for my mother to give me up, Tate's intentions must have been terrible. I had to bank on the fact he wouldn't kill me. Worst case: Sterlyn and the others would have to come into the pack to rescue us.

Tate's emotionless eyes focused on my face, and he turned red with anger. "Who took you? Aren't you upset that someone stole you from your family and pack? They hid you from us."

So that was how he would play it. I was going through a similar experience as those poor kids in the group home. For the first time ever, I truly understood their struggles, but I wouldn't let this awful person have any control over me. "Fuck you," I muttered, ignoring how his fingers dug between the upper and lower halves of my jaw when I spoke.

He released me, and before I could stretch my jaw to relieve the pain, he punched me in the same place he'd been digging his fingers into. My head snapped back, and pain exploded through the entire right side of my face.

A howl rang through the night. Cyrus's wolf had taken control. *Sterlyn! Help her!*

We're leaving! she replied. *Annie, hold on.*

Tate smiled cruelly as he watched me.

I rubbed my jaw, thankful it wasn't broken as my mouth filled with a metallic taste. He'd injured me, that was for damn sure, but my anger eased some of the pain. I spat my blood-tinged saliva on his black tennis shoe.

Instead of the rage I'd been hoping for, pride reflected in his eyes. "Are you sure that's smart? I won't stop until you tell me who took you."

"Bring it on." That wasn't smart, but bullies loved when people showed fear. If I crumbled, he would demand more and more information. I had to be strong to protect the people I loved. "I won't tell you a damn thing."

"Yet you came here?" He tapped his finger against his bottom lip. "Why?"

"You know why!" Like Sterlyn had said, they already suspected I was here with ulterior motives. Lying would only make things worse. "Why else would you take my mate?"

He threw his head back and laughed. The other four creeps chuckled along with him. I was missing something, but I had no clue what. "Is that funny to you?"

"Oh, child. Yes." He wiped tears from his eyes. "But it's a moot point. You're here, and that's all that matters."

My blood ran cold. Maybe coming here hadn't been the right call.

His body quivered as a cold smirk flitted across his face. He was getting off on my fear. "I'll ask you again. Who hid you?"

Just tell him, Cyrus linked as he banged harder against the walls. *Don't let him keep hurting you.*

The hurt and scared part of me wanted to do exactly what Cyrus suggested, but I couldn't live with myself if I did. "Screw...you."

"That's not very ladylike." Tate *tsk*ed. He went to punch me in the stomach, but all the training Cyrus and I had done while in human form kicked in.

I dodged his punch and kicked *him* in the stomach. He leaned over, cradling his side, and his goons descended.

Echo grabbed one arm while his twin clutched my other side. Nyko punched me in the gut like Tate had tried to do. Pain radiated, and the vomit I'd been swallowing down expelled.

I couldn't let a good opportunity go to waste, so I stumbled forward and puked on Nyko's bare legs. He backed away, but the damage was done as vomit slid into his shoes.

The twin gagged. "Oh, gods."

"Troy, keep it together," Echo choked. "She didn't puke on you."

Nyko stared at his legs, his face twisting in pure disgust.

"Lock her up in the extra house," Tate snarled, his voice low with pain. "I'll deal with her later."

A strangled sob broke through, and I locked eyes with my mother, who had tears and snot running down her face. She mouthed the words *I'm sorry*, but she had absolutely nothing to be sorry for. I wanted to tell her that, but she would only wind up in a similar state to mine.

All this time, I'd wondered what kind of mother could give up her child. I thought she must not have loved me enough, but now I realized the truth.

She loved me so much that she'd ripped her heart out to save me from this man and whatever his plans were for me. She hadn't wanted me to grow up in this kind of life. Then why had she gotten pregnant in the first place? Why put herself in a situation where she had to sacrifice me?

As the twins pulled me away, I linked with Sterlyn and Cyrus, *They're taking me to a house. Go back to the motel and let me see if I can figure something out before we abort the plan.*

Hell, no! The walls of the building Cyrus was in shook once again as he tried to escape. He was trying to reach me before they locked me away like him. *They need to come get you* now.

Me? If they come, they're getting you, too. Now I was getting angry, which I welcomed. Anything to dull the agony coursing through me.

Cyrus growled and replied, *I don't give a damn about me. They need to get you away before they hurt you worse. I told you this was a horrible idea. Sterlyn, get her now.*

Maybe— Sterlyn started, but I didn't need her siding with her brother.

Stop. I tried to dull some of my discomfort so Cyrus wouldn't feel it as much. *Give me a chance. If this happens again, I'll willingly go along with whatever the two of you think is best.*

Absolutely not, Cyrus answered. *You need to go back to safety now.*

What safety? He was oblivious. *I get that you want me safe. I want the same thing for you. That's one reason I'm here. But this man now knows I'm alive. He may never stop hunting me. The best chance we have is to stick with the plan and give me another chance with Tate.*

She's right, Sterlyn replied. *But if he hurts you again, we're coming after you.*

Sterlyn! Cyrus's fury was palpable. *If anything happens to her, I'll never forgive you.*

I hadn't been this enraged with him since before we'd mated. *Don't you dare push that off on her. I'm an adult, and this is my decision.*

She's right, but Annie, if things don't get better— Sterlyn linked.

I know. She'd already said they'd come get me. *I understand.*

The noise from the building stopped as Cyrus unlinked from our connection. His dismissal hurt, but I wouldn't change my mind. This was about more than saving him, though getting him out was my priority. I also wanted to learn about my heritage and what Midnight had tried to save me from. It had something to do with demons, and we couldn't ignore that. Not after what happened with Ronnie.

The twins walked faster than me, and my feet hit a root, twisting my ankle. I bit my lip to keep the sounds of pain from escaping.

They dragged me past a building with no windows, and Cyrus's faint scent slammed into my chest. That was where he was located. I linked with Sterlyn and Cyrus, *The place where Cyrus and the others are being kept is at the edge of the neighborhood.* At least, something useful had come out of this.

At the edge? Cyrus sounded surprised too. *I figured it would be in the middle in case someone escaped. And Mila and the others aren't here with me. They separated us.*

They must have you locked down tight, Sterlyn replied. *They probably didn't want to chance their enemies getting a layout of their location in case they could link with their pack. If you were able to get out, Cyrus, you would have when Annie was being injured.*

Shit. She was right. At least I'd found him, and there

were two buildings similar to his nearby. Mila, Theo, Rudie, and Chad had to be in one of them.

"Here you go," Echo grunted as he and his brother dragged me to a building next door to Cyrus.

It would be ideal if Mila and the others were in the third building beside mine. *I think they're keeping all three of us in neighboring buildings.*

Echo opened the door, and Troy shoved me inside.

I tripped over my feet and landed on my ass. They slammed the door, leaving me alone in the room. Taking a moment to sit, now that I was alone, I scanned the space. It was one large room with nothing but a full-size bed against one wall and a door to a small bathroom to the right. The inside was made of logs, just like the outside, and there wasn't any air conditioning. It was hot and muggy, but at least I was alone.

I climbed to my feet and winced as my ankle twinged in pain. I headed to the bed, which appeared to be clean with white sheets, and laid down, trying not to focus on the fact that Cyrus was so close, but I couldn't see or touch him.

My eyes grew heavy, and though I tried to keep them open, I soon drifted off to sleep.

A CLICK CAUSED my eyes to spring open. I jolted up in bed and prepared to fight for my life. I climbed to my feet, relieved that my ankle and stomach no longer hurt. Shifter healing came in handy.

The door opened, and Midnight stepped inside.

I braced myself to lunge, but she placed a finger to her lips, telling me to be quiet, and whispered, "If you want to see your mate again, don't make a sound."

My heart sank. Did I misread her or was Tate forcing her to try to get information from me? Maybe she hadn't been helping me after all.

CHAPTER TWELVE

THE SCREAM CAUGHT in my throat, and I swallowed it. It would only get Cyrus worked up. He was already upset with me for putting myself in this situation, but I had to come here.

I was going to take these dark wolves down.

Midnight glanced over her shoulder and focused back on me. "Well, do you?"

That threw me. "Do I what?"

"Want to see your mate?" she whispered, stepping into the cabin.

This had to be a cruel joke. Refusing to let her torment me, I remained silent. I had never wanted anything like I wanted to see Cyrus. Only two days had passed since I'd seen him, but it felt like a lifetime.

I sat back on the bed. She must have thought I was a huge idiot.

She huffed and shut the door, seeming on edge.

There was no telling what Tate had threatened to do

to her if she didn't get the information on the witches he so desperately wanted. I hated it. She might be a true innocent, but her life, like mine, wasn't more important than anyone else's.

The closer she got, the farther I scooted away from her and toward the wall, but it wasn't like I could get away from her. I could try to escape, but that wouldn't be smart. I'd bet there were wolves stationed outside in case I made a run for it.

I had to play the game and pretend to be here for sincere reasons. All the times I'd encouraged the children to be excited at the prospect of a new couple possibly adopting them ran through my mind. If they'd experienced what I had with Tate, no wonder they hadn't been happy about the prospect of meeting a potential new parent. This experience had reinforced my life's mission —to help kids in desperate need.

She lifted a hand, and I flinched. It pissed me off that I'd let her have any power over me.

Her irises darkened to a milky brown. "I won't hurt you."

"Sure," I bit out, angrier at myself than her. "You're either going to laugh when I beg to see my mate or slap me. Either way, it's abuse."

"No." She placed a hand on her chest, clutching her black tank top. Perspiration lined her upper lip, and she wiped it off with the back of her hand. "I'm being sincere. I'll take you to him for a couple of hours. I know you two need to be with each other."

The air was surprisingly free of sulfur. There had to

be a catch, and I tried to calm my excited heart. "Why would you do that?" I wouldn't deny that I needed Cyrus. The stress, distance, and horrible situation were putting a strain on not just our link but me emotionally and physically. I almost felt as broken as I had before we'd completed our bond.

"Because your bond needs to be as strong as possible, and you need to have a clear mind." She lowered herself onto the edge of the bed. She reached her hand toward me but stopped. "Your father wants to keep you apart to make you desperate."

I didn't understand how the fated bond worked, but I was already getting edgy. It made sense that I would begin acting erratically. "Even if this isn't a trick, someone would see us. That wouldn't end well for either of us."

"Your father and half the pack left to look for the witches." Midnight placed her hands on her lap. "They're following your scent to see if they can figure out where you came from."

Shit. Sterlyn.

Please tell me you're okay, I linked with her. Her end of the link felt calm, but it could be because she was drugged or unconscious like Cyrus had been.

When awareness floated through the bond, my concern eased. She replied, *Yes, we're fine. What's happening?*

They're tracking my scent. I was worried they might have found you. My body relaxed marginally. For all we knew, they were scoping out the area or about to attack.

She linked, *We thought of that when we ran into the woods to come after you when they were...er...earlier.*

Smacking me around? There was no reason not to state the facts. Glossing over what had happened wouldn't erase it from my mind. Hell, even when Alex had tried to make me forget that Eilam had used me as a blood bag, I hadn't fully blocked the memory. Instead, nightmares had haunted me until I'd finally remembered everything.

Yeah, that. Regret sailed into me. *But when we went into the woods that the pack is monitoring, the witches hid our scents. We've stayed inside since then.*

At least, we had something on our side. Sterlyn had been trained for things like this, and she considered alternatives I would never think of. *They're hunting the witches.*

They're cloaked, Sterlyn assured me. *I'll wake Aurora so she can contact Circe and let them know. We can at least make sure their perimeter spell is at full force with no holes, so the wolves won't be able to find them.*

That was a relief. I didn't want anyone harmed because they'd helped me.

"Don't worry," Midnight sighed. "They won't find the witches."

Her words startled me enough to bring my attention back to her. "What do you mean?"

She rubbed her hands together and frowned. "I honestly thought you were dead."

"Why? You'd—" I stopped. I didn't know if there

were any listening ears, so I didn't want to confirm anything.

"When I brought you to them, they took you away to discuss the situation with the rest of the coven. They had me stay in a large one-room house similar to this." She gestured around the cabin, but this place was a quarter of the size of the meeting room we'd been in. "When they came back, they said they'd come to an agreement, and I needed to take you home. They'd done everything they could for you."

That didn't add up. Someone had spelled my heart to sound as if it had stopped beating.

Distraught, she wrapped her arms around herself. "I begged them to keep you, but the girl who spoke to me— she was close to my age, I think—said the decision was final. They spelled us so Tate wouldn't smell the witches on us, and I took you back home. That night, when I went to check on you in your crib, your heart had stopped."

I didn't doubt her sincerity, but that might be why Tate had sent her. Not wanting to incriminate the witches, I asked, "Then what happened?"

"Tate freaked out for—" She paused and fidgeted uncomfortably. "—reasons. He had things to handle after your death, so I took you away to bury you. I set you down on a soft grassy knoll." She stared at the floor, lost in a memory. "I left to dig a grave, but when I went to get you, you'd vanished. I searched for you for years but never found you. I even went to find the witches again, but they'd vanished too. I figured that instead of helping us, they'd performed a death spell on you. All this time, I blamed myself for your death. That because I took you to them, I'd caused you to die." A sob racked her body.

My mind was trying to catch up, but my chest felt heavy. I figured Midnight had known about the plan, but the witches had made her believe I was dead for a reason —to protect her from Tate. It was both cruel and kind, a mixture I wasn't comfortable experiencing. "I'm sorry."

"No." She sniffled. "You didn't do anything. I caused this, and all for nothing because despite everything, you came back."

I hadn't considered how she'd feel about my return. She'd sacrificed so much to protect me, yet I'd walked right into this of my own free will. "He found me and took my mate. I couldn't not come."

"Oh, my sweet baby girl." Her hands shook. "I know. Destiny has a way of forcing its hand."

"Why—" I started, but she lifted a hand.

She leaned toward me, her eyes turning the color of honey. "All that can come later, but if you want time with your mate, we need to go."

Against my better judgment, hope sprang free in my chest. "I'm sure at least one person is guarding him."

"Yes, but that wolf owes me a favor. I tried to get him to let you escape, but he wouldn't." She stood and inched toward the door. "But he said he could let you inside for a couple of hours. That's when the wolves should be back. The longer we talk here, the less time you'll have with him."

Even if this was a cruel joke, I had to at least try. Midnight seemed to truly care about me, and this might be my only chance to see Cyrus before we escaped. "Okay."

She opened the door and lifted a finger before disappearing.

Antsy with anticipation, I practically ran across the room, standing a few feet from the door until she opened it again.

Sticking her head back in, she waved me on, whispering so low that even my wolf ears almost didn't hear her, "Hurry."

I followed her to the next building. The scents of Mila and the others washed over me, calming me. I could hear their murmurs, easing my worry about whether they were alive.

A man over six feet tall stood in front of Cyrus's door. His face was set in a serious expression, eyebrows furrowed and jaw tense. His hair was the same length as his black scruff, and he had a sand-colored complexion. He was lean but muscular, reminding me of Killian. Lips mashed together, he unlocked and opened the door.

A low growl came from inside as anger and anxiety wafted through my link with Cyrus. *Calm down. It's me.*

I know. There's no good reason why they'd bring you to me. I want to see you, but not if they'll hurt you while I'm helpless.

It's not like that. Not able to stop myself, I rushed past Midnight and the man. When I saw Cyrus, my heart both broke and filled with so much joy.

He wore a pair of black running shorts that weren't his. His chest was bare and showed a few faint bruises. I barely had time to revel in his muscular chest and six-pack abs before I launched myself into his arms, and he wrapped them tight around me.

What are you doing here? he asked and glanced at the door.

The guy who'd let me in rasped, "You have two hours," then shut the door.

I was so overcome with joy that I couldn't speak to him through our link. I pulled away and stared into his warm silver eyes. He had a foot in height on me, but I fit perfectly against him. I ran my fingers through his dark silver hair, filling my lungs with his unique scent.

A smile filled his face as he stared at me, and our love flowed between us.

Are you complaining? I teased, wanting to feel normal during the time we had together. *I know you aren't happy with me.*

He caressed my cheek. *Of course, I wanted to see you, but I don't understand why or how you're here. You need to leave before they catch you with me.*

Tate is looking for the witches, so Midnight—my biological mother—snuck me in. They said we have a couple of hours while he's gone. I won't question it. Maybe she was on my side. Unable to wait any longer, I kissed him eagerly.

I hadn't been sure I'd ever see him again, and I didn't want to take a single minute for granted.

He responded at first. Then he tried to pull away. I wrapped my arms around his neck, clinging to him. I linked, *What's wrong?*

He hurt you. He removed my hands from his neck and scanned me. *Are you still injured?*

I've healed for the most part. My jaw is a little sore, that's it. I cleared my head enough to scan the room. His building was just like mine, with a full-size bed against the wall and a bathroom only a few feet away. *Sorry if I worried you.*

You didn't do anything. He moved toward the bed, and metal clinked along the floor.

I glanced down to see he had an ankle cuff on one leg with a chain that gave him enough slack to reach the bed and bathroom. *What the hell?*

They have to make sure I can't get out when they open the door. Cyrus lay on the bed and opened his arms to me. *But I don't want to talk about that. Right now, I want to hold you.*

I didn't need to argue with that. I slipped in beside him and ran my fingers over his bruises. *They hurt you, too. How bad is it?*

It's nothing I haven't handled before. He wrapped his arms around me, and I laid my head against his chest and listened to his heartbeat. It was the most beautiful sound in the world. For the first time in days, I felt at home.

Anywhere Cyrus was, even in a horrible place like this, he was my home. I'd rather be here with him than anywhere else in the world. This was where I was meant to be.

God, holding you feels better than I remember. He kissed the top of my head, burying his nose in my hair.

I closed my eyes, memorizing how it felt to be in his

arms. My eyes burned as I breathed in his scent. Most likely, we wouldn't get to see each other for another day or two. I pushed away the negative thoughts to focus on the here and now.

I'm sorry you got roped into this. Cyrus tensed. *If I hadn't suggested you come back with me—*

Stop. I pulled back and stared into his granite irises. *For the past several years, something tugged me down to Shadow Ridge. I didn't understand it, but southeast Tennessee always called to me, and when I searched for schools in that area and Shadow Ridge University popped up, I knew I was meant to go there.*

Still, you went back to Lexington. Cyrus frowned. *If I just—*

Will you let me finish? I glared at him.

A small smile peeked through. *I guess, or I might get into trouble.*

I stuck out my tongue at him but continued. He had to understand. *When I went back to Lexington, I still felt the tug, and it wasn't from the horrible dreams. It was you. The buzzing I feel when I touch you is what I yearned for when I sought out Shadow Ridge University. You were the reason I was drawn there because you were close by. Even if you hadn't come back to Lexington, I would have found a way back to you.*

His breath caught as he searched for something inside me. *I went back to Lexington to protect you because the thought of someone else doing it drove me insane.*

If it's anyone's fault, it's fate's, but damn it, Cyrus, I wouldn't want it any other way. He had to believe me. I desperately needed him to.

His pupils dilated as the scent of his arousal mixed with mine. We'd bared our hearts to each other, and our wolves were desperate to be close. I ran my hands down his chest and paused at his shorts. *I take it these were gifted.* I'd only ever seen him wear jeans.

He exhaled unhappily. *They gave them to me since I was naked when I got here. This is my second pair—I ripped the other ones off when I shifted, trying to get to you.* Regret poured off him, crashing over me as his arms tightened around me. *I'm so sorry I couldn't protect you.*

Remember when I told you I needed to train in case someone couldn't be there? I'd decided that before I'd realized I was a wolf and just after a random vampire outside the group home had attacked me. After getting settled into Darrell and Martha's house, I'd snuck out to figure out a way to train myself, and Cyrus had found me. I'd told him I needed to know basic skills to protect myself. *This is why. You won't always be there to protect me. It's inevitable. That's why I need to be able to protect myself.*

You shouldn't have to. His arms tightened. *I hate that this happened.*

We weren't going to waste our two hours together doing this. I refused. I lifted up and kissed him, desperate to taste him. *Please, let's focus on each other.*

He slipped his tongue into my mouth.

His cinnamon taste overloaded my senses, and my body heated.

Someone could walk in at any moment, he linked, despite our tongues dancing.

I didn't give a damn. *Then I guess we'll need to make it fast.* I kissed down his neck and slipped my hand inside his shorts.

Annie. He groaned as I stroked him. *They could be listening.*

You better claim me again to make sure they know. I bit his neck and moved my hands faster.

His hand cupped my breast as his fingers kneaded my nipple. His touch had my wolf howling inside me.

Damn it, I can't think straight. He removed my hand from his shorts and rolled on top of me. He positioned himself between my legs as the chain raked against the floor.

I started to remove my shirt, but he caught the hem. *Don't take it off. I won't be able to focus if I know there's a chance someone could come in and see you topless.*

Whatever it takes, as long as you don't stop, I vowed, desperate for us to connect.

A smirk crossed his face as he unfastened my shorts. He reached down for the sheet at the end of the bed and threw it over us then lowered my shorts and removed them from one leg. *We need to hurry and make sure you stay covered.*

His hand slid between my legs, but I shook my head. *I'm ready.* The longer we took to connect, the likelier we could be interrupted, which added a thrill to the moment.

Are you sure? he asked.

Instead of answering, I leaned forward, sliding his

shorts off his hips, and wrapped my legs around his waist, coaxing him inside me.

A moan left him as he moved his hips, slipping in and out of me. His wolf surged through his eyes, and my wolf responded. This wasn't about making love but about connecting in a primal way. We were in danger, and who knew when we'd get a moment like this again.

He thrust, increasing the friction inside me. His body covered mine as he captured my lips with his again. My body moved in sync with his, and we opened our connection, feeling each other's love and pleasure.

Within minutes, an orgasm ripped through us. The combination of his pleasure and mine caused my body to quiver. When we both came down from the high, he rolled off me and helped me back into my shorts. He then redressed and laid on the bed beside me.

For the first time in two days, I felt complete. He cuddled me against his chest, and I fell asleep, safe in his arms.

THE SOUND of the door opening woke me. I sat up, surprised to find Midnight there instead of the guard.

The area around her eyes was tense, and she glanced over her shoulder at the woods. "Come on, we've got to move. He's almost here."

CHAPTER THIRTEEN

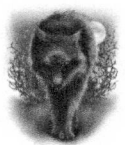

EVERYTHING inside me demanded I stay in Cyrus's arms. I breathed in his musky sweet hydrangea scent, trying to make sure I held it close in my memory. He held me close, as if he were having the same battle. Then he released his hold.

You better go, he linked. *I don't want him to find you here after what he did to you earlier.* His jaw twitched as anger coursed through him.

Unfortunately, he was right. If I wanted Tate to believe I was at his mercy and had no ulterior motives, I had to be careful. *Fine.* I kissed him again, needing another second with him.

I almost expected him to pull away, but he succumbed to both us and our wolves, desperate to remain together.

Midnight cleared her throat and warned, "Seriously, he'll be here soon. We need to make sure the room airs out before he gets back."

That was enough to force me out of bed. If Tate came here first, we needed time to let my scent dissipate. I rushed to her, glancing over my shoulder at my mate one more time. *I love you.*

A pained expression crossed his face as he swallowed hard. *I love you, too.* His eyes glistened with unshed tears.

Every ounce of me wanted to hurry back to him and ease his pain, but I couldn't, which made me hate Tate more. It was his fault we were in this damn situation.

The shifter who'd allowed our visit stood a few feet from the door. Tendons in his neck bulged, his pulse visible. His elbows were close to his body as he surveyed the woods.

If I hadn't been on edge before, I sure was now.

Midnight grabbed my arm and pulled me toward my building. My wolf surged forward as I listened for the shifters, but I didn't hear anything. I could, however, feel an evilness charging toward us. There was only one creature I viewed as that vile, and that was Tate.

Loud banging on the walls of Cyrus's room caused me to pause. He was going crazy like he had when Tate had been hitting me.

Midnight shoved me inside the room, her strength taking me by surprise, and I stumbled a few feet when she released me.

"What the hell?" I rasped in both anger and surprise. *Is he hurting you?* I linked to Cyrus, ready to declare war on Midnight. I didn't give a damn if she'd given us time together.

"Get in the shower and get into bed," Midnight said as she reached for the door. "Get his scent off you. *Now.*"

"There's something wrong with Cyrus. I need to go back." I couldn't stand by and let him get hurt. "That shifter must be—"

"Tanner isn't doing anything to him." She raised a finger, looking every bit like a mother. "Connect with your mate and check if you don't believe me. He's doing that to hide your scent."

I'm fine, he confirmed. *I'm just working up a sweat to overpower your scent with mine before jumping into the shower.*

The two of them were on the same page. *Thank God.*

I'm sorry. I didn't think about how it would sound. More pounding came from his direction. *But this is the only way I can protect you.*

"Go," Midnight said. "Take a shower and get into bed. He'll be here in ten minutes." She arched a brow, watching me.

The sun would be rising soon, and he'd expect me to be asleep. If he checked in with me, it would be strange if I was awake after taking a beating like that. I forced myself to move, though I didn't want to wash off Cyrus's scent. But they were right. No one could know we'd been together.

After turning on the shower, I rummaged through the small cabinet underneath the sink and found a thin white towel and a bar of soap. There was no shampoo or conditioner, but the soap would get me clean.

As I placed the bar of soap on the edge of the white

plastic tub, the front door opened and shut, indicating Midnight had left. I heard the *click,* confirming I was locked in. I hated having my freedoms stripped, but I had to remember why I'd come here—to save Cyrus and the others.

When the small bathroom grew steamy, I almost cried in relief. I'd expected to take a cold shower, thinking they'd strip me of all the niceties to break me. I hated taking cold showers, and Ronnie would make fun of me about how pink my skin got every time I bathed.

Holding on to that memory, I stripped down and placed my clothes next to the thin towel on the pedestal sink. Luckily, my clothes already smelled like him from our time back home.

I stepped into the shower, letting the warmth hit my back and loosen my stiff muscles. I wanted to take my time and enjoy the shower, but I was in a hurry. I forced myself to wash my hair and body quickly, and I was dried, dressed, and back in bed a few minutes later.

I fanned my hair out against the pillow to dry it and focused on my link with Cyrus. *Are you getting some rest?*

Getting out of the shower now. Then I'll try. If we're going to get out of here, we need to be ready. We might only get one chance, and even then, it might not be under the best circumstances.

The way our luck was going, we wouldn't get out of here without a fight. It was like something was working against us. But I wouldn't trade a thing. Cyrus was my other half, and as long as we were together, everything would be worth it.

———

I STARED at the ceiling as I lay in bed. I had gotten some sleep, but not nearly enough. Every few minutes, I'd wake up to the sounds of talking or someone walking by. I'd hold my breath and pray they weren't heading to see Cyrus or the others.

Something buzzed in the air. The energy felt similar to the magic flowing inside me, yet different. Darker, grittier, and slimy. I had to think about something else to distract myself from the weird sensations.

Sunlight shone through the bottom crack of the door, my only indication that it was daytime. Tate and the others had gotten back shortly after Cyrus and I had settled into bed. I'd expected him to come see one of us, but he hadn't.

Heavy footsteps headed my way, and I sat on the edge of the bed. I didn't want Tate or one of his idiot shifters to come in and find me lying in it. I didn't need to invite something horrible to happen.

A shiver ran down my spine at the possibilities.

The footsteps drew closer, and my heart pounded in my ears. This couldn't be a coincidence.

Tate's overly musky smell wafted through the crack of the door. He was coming here, which was bittersweet. I didn't want to see him, but I'd rather he come to me than Cyrus.

I stood and faced the door as it swung open.

Even though I'd only heard one pair of footsteps, I still was surprised to see Tate alone, without one of the four men who were always with him.

He stepped into the room and closed the door behind him. He examined me as he steepled his hands. Maybe that was his trademark gesture—he'd done the same thing when I arrived.

He wore a black shirt and jeans, the same outfit as before. It must be his signature look. He remained silent and leaned his back against the door.

If he thought I would break the silence, he'd soon realize that wasn't the case. I had no interest in talking to him. My goal for coming here was to save the five people who belonged back home. He wanted answers more than I did.

Time stood still as we stared at each other in challenge.

After a while, he exhaled and dropped his arms. "I think we got off on the wrong foot."

Ah. Since beating me hadn't worked, he was trying another angle. "You mean kidnapping four pack members and my mate? Or physically assaulting me?"

He winced, but his eyes remained cold. "Both?"

Yeah, he wasn't fooling me, but I'd play along. "Oh, well, there is a way to rectify that."

"How so?" He put his hands into his pockets.

"Easy." I shrugged. "You let Cyrus and the others go."

A loud laugh escaped him. "That would make everything all right?"

"Yup. That's the best way to show you're sorry." There was no way in hell he'd do it, but a girl had to try.

"Then you'd want to leave with them." He touched the section of his chest his heart lay under. "And I wouldn't get to know my daughter."

"That's why you took them and beat me?" I wouldn't drop it. "Because you wanted to get to know me? Was it a test to see how strong I am?"

"That was me acting out in anger." He tried to smile sadly, but it fell short. He was a horrible actor. "Which was wrong, but I can't change the past. I'd like to start over."

This conversation was already going in circles, but I had nothing else to do. "My answer still stands. If you want to prove you're sorry, let the five of them go."

"And you won't stay." He lifted his hands. "How about this? Give me a few days, and I promise to take care of them. In three days, we can have this conversation again and see if we can come to an understanding."

I wanted to ask what the catch was, but if he knew I was on to him, this helpful ruse would end. He'd promised to trade me for Mila and the others the night they'd taken Cyrus. He had no intention of following through.

Since he was attempting to appear like a nice guy, I could use the act to my advantage. "Do I get to come and go as I please and meet the pack? It's not very nice to lock your daughter in her room, right?"

"When you say come and go...?" He lifted a brow.

"I mean just around the pack. You do have my mate

and friends here as collateral if I leave." I wouldn't leave without Cyrus. He surely had to know that.

He tapped a finger against his lip as he considered my suggestion. His expression pinched in displeasure before it smoothed back into a mask of indifference. "No leaving the pack grounds, and you must have a chaperone with you at all times until our three-day agreement is up."

That wasn't necessarily what I'd meant, but I'd take it. "Deal." I smiled sweetly and batted my eyelashes.

"Are you ready for breakfast?" he asked and nodded toward the door.

I hadn't expected him to say that. "I get to leave here to eat?"

"That's what you want, right? To get to know the pack?" He opened the door and gestured outside. "You can't do that in here."

This was exactly what I needed, so I didn't want to hesitate and have him change his mind, but I also didn't want to seem too eager. I linked with Sterlyn and Cyrus, *He's letting me out to eat breakfast with the pack.*

What? Cyrus's surprise, relief, and suspicion intermingled in a confusing combination. *Are you sure it's not a trick?*

Sterlyn linked, *I'm not surprised. Between not getting any information out of you yesterday and not finding the witches, this is the only strategy he hasn't tried.*

The pretend caring father? The façade wasn't believable, but he seemed to think he was doing a good job. *Let's just say he shouldn't quit his day job.*

"Are you coming?" he asked warmly despite the corners of his mouth tipping downward.

Shit, I'd hesitated too long. "Yeah, sorry. It's just overwhelming." Between learning he was my father, meeting my mother, and everything in between, *overwhelming* didn't cover the extent of my feelings. I forced my legs to move, and when he didn't budge, the horrible realization that I would have to walk near him made me want to freeze. I didn't want to be close to him in any capacity, but I took a deep breath.

Is he doing something? Cyrus asked.

No. I just have to walk by him. I stepped outside and saw five women hurrying deeper into the neighborhood.

"Follow them," Tate instructed from behind me.

He wanted to keep an eye on everything I did. I hated that he was smart, but that didn't mean I couldn't glimpse at my surroundings. I kept my head forward, making a point to not come off like I was taking notes. As I followed leisurely behind the women, I informed Sterlyn and Cyrus of my conversation with Tate.

We'll get you out tomorrow night, Sterlyn linked. *He has a plan and wants you to think nothing's going on, but he chose that number of days for a reason.*

I'd thought the same thing. *That's my fear, too.*

That's why I didn't want you to come here, Cyrus replied, but he wasn't angry like when I'd first arrived. The time Midnight had given us together had soothed us enough to get back in sync. Mates were meant to be together, not ripped apart.

And that was why I'd had to come. *You know I had to.*

I know, he agreed. *But that doesn't mean I have to like it.*

That I couldn't argue with. I scanned the area, but it was more of the same: log cabins every fifty yards surrounded by trees. The neighborhood was large, but it felt like part of the woods.

A building five times the size of my cabin came into view. Shifters headed inside, and I was surprised by the numbers.

Inside the building, the rows of tables reminded me of a school cafeteria. The men laughed, having a good time, while the women sat next to them with lifeless expressions. No matter where I looked, I saw the same thing over and over. Even the female children sat expressionless while the male children played.

There was something terrifying about the entire scene. I stopped in my tracks, unable to comprehend what I was seeing.

"Hey, sweet thing," a guy cooed from the table closest to me. He reached out and clutched my hand, his khaki eyes perusing me as malice smacked me in the chest. He grinned, revealing yellow teeth. "I see Tate brought another woman for one of us to mate. I call dibs."

I jerked away, but he tightened his hold.

I wouldn't be manhandled like this. Not again.

CHAPTER FOURTEEN

HIS SWEATY HAND gripped harder as he tugged me closer. "You sure are pretty."

"I'm taken." I lifted my chin and wrenched away.

His hold was firm, and I moved only an inch. He laughed and waggled his brows, his face twisted in sadistic pleasure. "Oh, she's a feisty one. Those are the best to break."

He emitted something disgusting.

This asshole was almost as bad as Tate. Without considering the consequences, I punched him in the jaw, and his head snapped back. His hold loosened enough for me to twist my hand out of his. I spun and kicked him in the stomach, and he fell backward off the bench. He landed on his back with a *thump*.

The entire building went silent as everyone turned in our direction. A woman three seats down from me placed a shaky hand over her mouth, like she couldn't believe I'd protected myself—which pissed me off. These women expected to be treated like that. This was completely unacceptable.

I'd deal with that later. If I took my attention off this guy, he could attack me again, and I might not notice in time.

"You bitch," the man growled and slowly climbed to his feet. His oily face turned red, and his chest heaved. "You'll pay for that."

Cyrus linked with me as his trepidation took root, *Babe, what's going on?*

Before I could respond, the older man sitting on the other side stood and fisted his hand in my hair.

I couldn't believe they were treating me this way, and my father wasn't doing anything to stop them. Fine. I didn't want his help. As the older man yanked my head toward him, I didn't fight the motion. Instead, I surged back, letting the back of my head hit the man in the face. A *crack* told me I'd broken his nose.

"*Hody shid!*" he growled but didn't loosen his grasp as I'd hoped. He yanked me sideways, and I almost fell.

Annie! Cyrus linked.

I managed to stay on my feet, and he released me, ripping out some of my hair in the process. My scalp stung, and my eyes glistened with tears, but I blinked them back, refusing to cry. *I'm fine. Just putting some jerks in their place. I'm so damn glad you trained me.* I spun around, ready to protect myself. I wasn't a fighter like Sterlyn, but damn it, I'd do everything I could to defend myself.

I hate to admit it, but you were right. Cyrus's frustration bled through. *I'd hate to think about what would've happened if we hadn't trained.*

"That's enough," Tate growled and pointed at the older man and the younger one. "She isn't meant for anyone here."

I didn't like the way he'd worded that, and the fact he'd stepped in after they'd pushed me around hadn't gone unnoticed. He probably wanted me to be put in my place like the other women here, but fortunately, I'd been raised by a strong woman who was a coward to no man. I bared my teeth at both men and Tate as I repeated, "I already have a mate."

"Don't remind me," Tate scoffed and wrinkled his nose. "Anyway, no one touches her. This is my daughter."

"*What?*" the man with yellow teeth asked, his eyes bulging. "That's Annabel? I...I didn't know. I thought she died."

"So did I." Tate stood in front of the door, the center of attention. "Witches spelled her and stole her as a baby. Last night, a large group of us tried to find the coven that took my sweet, precious child from me."

Even the words didn't sound sincere. His whole act appalled me, but I had to play along. *It's over now. We're heading to get breakfast. Tate finally stepped in.*

I'm sure he did, Cyrus responded. *Be careful. I don't trust him.*

I don't either.

Someone is coming with food. Link with me soon?

Yeah, go eat. I wished he was beside me. *I love you.*

I love you more. Anxiety wafted between us. *Pay attention to everything, but don't get caught.*

That was the plan.

"Did you find them?" a bulky shifter in the far corner called out.

Tate shook his head as a vein bulged between his eyes. "We did not, but we will soon." He flicked his eyes to me before staring at the rest of his pack.

I wouldn't be sharing anything with him. There was no way I'd turn over the very people who had saved me all those years ago. My short time here had made me realize how different my upbringing would've been had I remained here. The thought of who I might have become terrified me.

The nagging question of how Eliza and her coven might have handed Cyrus to evil people lay heavy on me. They'd protected and saved me, but Cyrus had been stolen from a loving family and placed into enemy hands. The same sacrifice but with opposite results.

Another damn thing we needed to answer later.

"I'm here to introduce my daughter to the pack. She's finally back where she belongs." Tate attempted to smile lovingly at me, but his demeanor fell short. I wasn't sure the man could feel joy. The corners of his mouth tipped upward but reminded me of a baby working on a full diaper. Whenever a toddler got that look on their face, it was every leader for themselves. The last one in the room got to change the diaper, so if you weren't aware of what was going on, you'd think a bomb was about to go off.

In fairness, I guessed it could be considered it a stink bomb.

The men who'd been ogling me tore their gazes away, and I breathed a little easier.

Tate placed his palm at the small of my back, and the urge to flee took root. I stilled my body and didn't step away, despite my stomach protesting. This was a temporary issue that I had to endure to rescue the others, and I wondered how many times I would have to remind myself of that.

"You see, I protected you," Tate said as he led me down the center of the room.

No, he hadn't. I'd bet he'd hoped those two would manhandle me into submission before stepping in. I'd saved myself, but instead of being ornery, I remained quiet.

We reached the other side of the room, and he turned me toward the left corner. My gaze swept the area for threats. My head pounded from where my hair had been ripped out, but I refused to show my discomfort. I forced my hands to remain by my sides as I walked with my shoulders straight and proud.

Midnight sat with the four men who were always around Tate. Three of them had a woman beside them, but the men didn't seem interested in talking to them. Their attention was on their alpha and me.

No one sat beside Midnight. My eyes focused on the spot to her right, at the end of the table, where I wouldn't have to sit next to Ken. I had a feeling Tate intended to seat me by the man.

As I moved to take the seat, Tate wrapped his arm around my waist and pulled me to his side.

Something unsettling coursed through me where our bodies touched. Even if he was my biological father, I didn't want to be this close to him.

"Honey, why don't you sit at the end so our daughter can sit next to both of us?" Tate suggested, gesturing to her plate of eggs and bacon. "Since we lost so much time, it'd be nice if we could talk to her."

Midnight's lips mashed into a firm line, but she obeyed, sliding down a spot. She seemed unhappy about me spending more time with him than I was. Surely, she had to know I wouldn't betray her.

"Are you sure it's smart, having her here?" Nyko sat across from Tate and sneered at me. "She should be locked in that room until she informs us about the witches' location."

"Maybe she doesn't know," a woman with a warm beige complexion suggested from beside Nyko.

Nyko snapped his head in her direction and rasped, "You weren't spoken to, Uma."

She averted her peridot eyes to her plate of food and tucked a piece of her long, light caramel bangs behind her ear. "Right. Sorry."

I wanted to tell her she didn't need his permission to speak, but I bit my tongue. This was how their pack operated. Though it was terrible, I couldn't risk making more waves. Besides, if I said something, it could be turned back on me, forcing me into a situation where I might have to lie, which wouldn't be good for anyone here.

Ken leaned forward and looked around Tate at me. "Are the witches still nearby?"

The musky scent of a regular wolf swirled around me as a young woman around my age put plates of food in front of me and Tate. She didn't speak and kept her gaze fixed on the wall, making eye contact with no one.

"Thank you," I said as I grabbed the fork from the plate.

Her eyes widened, and Tate laughed heartily.

"You don't need to thank her," he chuckled and gestured for her to leave. "That's her job."

Just when I'd thought I couldn't think any worse of him, he proved me wrong. Needing something to do before I spouted off, I stabbed several pieces of egg and stuffed them into my mouth.

"Wow." Echo snorted and sipped his coffee. "If she keeps eating like that, nobody will want her."

Did he just fat shame me? I stared at the prick sitting in front of Nyko and next to his twin brother. He had to be the only one of the five unmated. I grabbed three pieces of bacon and took a large bite. As I chewed my food, I opened my mouth, making sure to enunciate every damn word. "Maybe you should be more worried about yourself since you're the only one here who can't snag a woman. Besides, I'm mated, so I don't give a damn if my looks and weight aren't up to your standards." Could this guy think that I was promised to him? Surely not.

Midnight coughed, covering her mouth with her hand. The corners of her eyes wrinkled, informing me she was trying to hide her laughter.

"I'm not the one you need to worry about," Echo grunted. "You need to learn your position in this pack."

"Oh? And what exactly is that?" I placed the fork down, my appetite gone. "To be passive and get beaten up by men twice my size?"

The young girl next to Troy froze and used her honey-pecan hair as a shield as she looked away from our group. Her reaction told me more than I wanted to know. Troy abused her regularly.

Troy slammed his hands on the table. "Listen here. You better not give Minx any ideas."

"Enough." Tate lifted a hand and gestured for him to sit. "Annabel will see how things operate soon enough, but we must teach her the ways of the pack. She wasn't raised with us, so she doesn't know any better. I'm sure we can all agree to be a little lenient with her for the moment."

The four men smirked like there was a joke I wasn't privy to.

Tate turned to me. "And you need to respect the men who protect you. There are things you will come to understand and learning to hold your tongue will benefit you."

"What do I need to understand?" I forced myself to pick up the fork again and eat. I had to keep my strength up even if the food sat like lead in my stomach.

"You'll learn soon enough." Tate pointed at my plate. "Now eat up. Then we'll assign you a job to help out the community."

Sitting quietly was good enough for me since having

to interact with these five men would make things worse between us. If I didn't talk, it would help with the perception that I was giving this a fair try. I focused on my plate and pretended to tune out the conversation the five of them were having. I wanted them to lower their guard and say something telling.

As the men finished up, I quickly ate the rest of my food. I'd purposely taken my time, not wanting to finish before we were ready to go. Midnight and the other women hadn't spoken a word the entire time, and I realized they stayed silent out of self-preservation. Every time one of the men asked a question, a panicked expression would cross her face, and she'd answer quickly.

"Why doesn't Annabel help me tend the garden?" Midnight asked as we all stood from the table.

Tate rubbed his chin, contemplating her suggestion, and nodded. "Fine, but Echo, I want you to go with them. I'll be there after my meeting to check on her."

The taller twin puffed out his chest like it was an honor to babysit me.

Tate didn't want me out of their sight for long in case I tried to escape. I'd take any reprieve I could get from the other four. I picked up my plate and cup and looked around for where to bus it.

Nyko laughed. "She really is clueless."

Before I could respond, Midnight caught my eye.

"There are people who clean up here." Midnight took the items from me and placed them back on the table. "Come on, let's go work off the food." She looped her arm through mine, guiding me toward the door. She didn't bother saying anything to Tate as we left.

It surprised me that they were mates. He seemed very indifferent to her and acted as if she were a bother. I hoped Cyrus and I never got like this, although there was one huge difference between their relationship and ours. Cyrus treated me with respect and cherished me. Tate didn't value anyone but himself.

I had so many questions, but I couldn't ask them with Echo following close behind.

The other three mates walked next to us as we moved across the pack houses, heading away from where I was staying. I took in every house we passed, realizing Rosemary's count had been damn accurate.

This pack was so much larger than the silver wolves, and I knew nothing about it. It was time I rectified the situation. "What is this pack?"

Midnight hesitated for a second before continuing our quick pace. "What do you mean?"

"Every pack member born into this pack has a dark blue-black coat." Maybe she didn't know anything else. "Most wolves are different colors. I only know of one pack where the members have the same shade of fur."

"This pack is similar to the pack you just described," Midnight said, but there was something unsettling in her tone. "All our descendants, like you, have the same color of fur for the same reason."

"Similar? Descendants?" The silver wolves were the descendants of angels, so I didn't understand how that was possible.

Troy's mate's pearl-blue eyes focused on me. "Haven't you heard of the balance? Of good versus evil?"

"That for every positive energy, there must be a negative?" Ken's mate asked. Her gorgeous golden complexion contrasted starkly against his alabaster tone. Her smokey-brown eyes stared at me steadily, and I swore there were flecks of glitter in them.

The visual gave me the answer, and I felt like I couldn't breathe. "Are you saying what I think you are?"

"Yes," Midnight answered. "If angels created silver wolves, what do you think created this pack?"

The word was simple, but I had to force it off my tongue. "Demons."

I closed my eyes, hoping she'd tell me I was wrong.

CHAPTER FIFTEEN

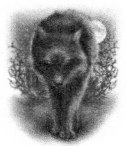

"TOOK YOU LONG ENOUGH." Echo chuckled condescendingly. "Did you really think your little plaything's race was all that special?"

I spun around and glared at him. I spoke slowly to ensure there was no room for confusion. "He is my *mate*. Don't you dare understate what our relationship is, and he *is* special. He's more of a man than any of you are, yet you insinuate that I'm the slow one."

"Annabel," Midnight warned, but I couldn't contain my rage.

Babe, is everything okay? Cyrus linked, concern swirling between us.

Argh, sometimes our link wasn't ideal. I didn't want to worry him every time I grew frustrated, but given our situation, of course, my heightened feelings would cause him anxiety. *Just Echo being a jackass, but it's fine. Midnight is taking me to the garden to work with her, and they're filling me in on the origins of the wolf pack.*

"Listen here, *girl.*" He might as well have said *bitch.* "You need to understand your place in this pack. You may be the alpha's kid, but you're a female, which means you're only good for one thing..." He paused and chuckled. "Okay, maybe two."

The sexual innuendo was clear, but I had no idea what he meant about the second thing. "What're the two things?"

"You'll figure it out soon enough." A cruelness hardened him.

Midnight tugged me back into motion. "We need to keep moving."

I opened my mouth, but something in her face stopped me. Even though she hadn't raised me, I understood the look. She was telling me to shut up and trust her. It was the same strained look she'd given me last night when she'd taken me to Cyrus. I needed to know what she was protecting me from.

Going with my gut, I forced myself to listen to her. She'd had my best interests at heart since I was born, so maybe I should cooperate until something gave me pause.

The closer we got to the garden, the more the air around me charged with that strange sensation. What could only be magic rubbed against my skin, but it felt different from when the witches had tried to hide my wolf.

Midnight said, "We four mates weren't initially from this pack. Those who don't have the same fur are mated to people who were born into this pack. I'm assuming it's similar to how the silver wolves operate since you were fated to one of them."

"Fated," Uma squeaked. "Wait, you found your fated mate?"

"You aren't all fated?" I'd heard that people could have chosen mates, but for these women to endure this kind of treatment, the men must have something over them.

Uma shook her head.

That answered a question that had been nagging me. No wonder these men treated the females like shit. They weren't fated mates; they were chosen. If they'd completed the mate bond, wouldn't the men still feel a connection to these women?

"We fought it initially since my wolf—" I stopped, barely in time. I didn't want to say too much about my past in case I unknowingly gave them information about the coven.

"Your wolf, what?" the golden-complected woman asked.

"Indra, give her a second to get her thoughts together," Midnight chastised while giving me a knowing glance.

That name made sense for the woman, and it meant that Troy's mate was Minx. That information was useful. "It's fine." I waved it off. "I just struggled to connect with my wolf until Cyrus and I completed our mate bond."

"Damn witches," Echo grumbled. "They make every damn thing more complicated. I can't wait until we find them and make them pay."

That wouldn't be happening. I'd do whatever it took to ensure these wolves hurt no one else.

"I can't believe you found your fated mate." Minx sighed longingly. "I was brought here as a pup, and this place is all I remember."

"Did something happen to your pack?" From everything I'd learned about wolf shifters, even if her parents had died, her pack would've taken care of her.

She shrugged. "All I know is Tate found me when I was little and brought me here to safety. I owe him my life."

My stomach revolted. I'd been around him only a few times, but I already knew Tate wouldn't save anyone. He did things to make himself feel more important and gain control over others.

"What about the rest of you?" I was curious how these women had gotten here, knowing they hadn't been raised in this pack.

Indra attempted to smile, but it turned into a grimace. "My parents and I were traveling the United States several years ago. We visited Nashville and came through here. My parents met Tate in the city, and some things happened, resulting in me joining this pack."

Her wording didn't go unnoticed, but with Echo on our tail, now wasn't the time to ask more questions. I needed to choose my battles wisely. "What about you, Uma?"

"Me?" She nibbled on her bottom lip, staring forward.

I almost regretted asking her. Her body language

spoke volumes—she didn't want to talk about it. "If you don't want to tell me—"

"Nyko is my second mate." Uma's voice was devoid of emotion. "My first one died, and Nyko claimed me." Her bottom lip quivered, at odds with her emotionless statement.

There was a lot more to the story, and I had a feeling I wouldn't like it.

"How are Mila and the others?" That question had been hounding me since I'd arrived here. Tate had learned they'd left the pack when he'd used them against us, so they knew I couldn't pack-link with them.

"That's enough questions," Echo growled. "Now hurry up and get your asses to work."

We picked up our pace as we passed a few more houses surrounded by evergreens. A few men were on the rooftops, sawing branches that were growing down onto the roofs. A wooden privacy fence the length of a football field appeared ahead. Trees grew along the edges, providing some coverage to the area.

A cluster of log cabins was grouped closer together than the other buildings I'd seen. Usually, there were twenty yards or so of distance between buildings, but not here. The grouping reminded me more of the silver wolf neighborhood, as if they had been positioned to keep unwanted creatures from getting into the garden.

Between two houses, a large wooden gate stood open, offering entry into the fence line, with two evergreens positioned on either side.

Strange magical energy coursed around me, and it led

past the gate toward another section of forest. Part of me wanted to follow it, while the other part wanted to run, the two instincts conflicting with each other.

"Come on, let's get to work." Midnight hurried to the gate and opened it, gesturing for us to enter.

Echo leaned against an evergreen and yawned. "I'll stay here while you all work. If anything funny happens, all five of you will answer for it. Do you understand?"

"Yes." Minx hurried inside the gate to get away from him. That was her family, and the amount of fear in her eyes made me wonder if both brothers abused her.

Even though I hadn't expected him to do anything useful, I was surprised that he didn't go inside with us. Granted, he wasn't worried about me escaping, and even if I tried, the women were so fearful of their mates they would rat me out. I couldn't blame them. They were doing everything they could to survive, similar to what Cyrus had gone through. Maybe his experiences would help us connect with these women and save them from this horrible pack.

Inside the fence, I saw segregated sections containing various crops of okra, squash, tomatoes, potatoes, cucumbers, and lima beans. The crops were bountiful and in good health.

"Annabel and I will harvest the tomatoes today," Midnight informed the others, and we headed off. She moved to a pile of large brown sacks and grabbed four off the stack. She handed three to me and motioned for me to follow her.

"Okay." Uma didn't look at us as she rushed to grab her own bags, the other two women following.

The tomatoes were in the back of the gardens, farthest away from Echo. When we reached the edge of the fence, the sun was rising and warm on my back. The smell of the sweet tomatoes filled my nose, and I was thankful I'd forced myself to eat breakfast. Otherwise, I'd be starving.

"Make sure you pick the red tomatoes. Leave the green ones there to ripen," Midnight instructed me as I moved down one side of the first aisle.

She followed me, starting at the same spot and working the plants across from me.

I began picking tomatoes, hoping I hadn't misread the situation. I wanted her to start the conversation of her own accord, but if she didn't soon, I'd speak up.

Using the moment of quiet, I linked with Sterlyn and Cyrus and filled them in on what I'd learned.

They're descended from demons? Disbelief coursed through the bond with Cyrus.

That had shocked me as well. *They said that it's a balance thing. When a demon wolf was created and tied to the new moon, the silver wolves had to be created and linked with the full moon. That's why when the silver wolf was born, so was a demon wolf. Sterlyn, did you know?*

No, and no one here did, either, Sterlyn replied, feeling uneasy as well. *Rosemary is calling her parents to see if they have any insight.*

Their darker coat makes sense now. Demons were shadow-like creatures, and these wolves' fur, and mine, reminded me of that. *Also, these women are all being abused, and I think they were forced to join the pack against their will.* I told them the women's vague stories.

Rage flowed from both Sterlyn and Cyrus as she linked, *That is horrible, and I think you're right. Those poor women. All the shifters who aren't from that pack could've been forced the same way.*

That was my fear, too.

Cyrus's disgust was clear. *Those women were probably stolen from loving families and packs like I was.*

Maybe we're meant to lead them together. If you represent angels, and I represent demons, it can't be a coincidence that we're fated. Maybe our union will balance everything.

Midnight cleared her throat, and I looked up from the plant.

"Listen, you have to be careful what you do and say," Midnight whispered. "A lot goes on in this pack that isn't right, but people here don't question it because they either fear for their lives or were raised that way."

I opened my link with Sterlyn and Cyrus so they could hear. "Were you brought here against your will, too?"

"I came here willingly." She pressed her lips into a line as sadness took hold. "Your father didn't become hard and cold until after we'd mated. You see, he was my fated mate."

"Wait, 'was'?" I hadn't thought a fated mate bond could be undone.

She exhaled and averted her eyes to the tomatoes as

she worked. "I don't know how to explain how our relationship changed. He always battled an evil inside him, but there was more good in him than bad. He didn't treat me like the other women, and he protected me, but that changed when I got pregnant with you."

My heart sank. "Me?"

"When we found out we were having a girl, his father became so angry." Midnight seemed lost in her memories and moved robotically. "It was like he was extremely jealous. The two of them went to visit that demon together, and when Tate came back, he was unrecognizable, even to my wolf."

I've never heard of fated mates becoming unbonded before, but the maliciousness I read off Tate felt very similar to what I sensed from Ronnie's father, Sterlyn linked. *I wonder if a demon did something to him that changed their connection.*

"What happened to Tate's father?" I couldn't bring myself to call him my grandfather.

She paused, her face turning pale. "Steve didn't come back with Tate, and his link with us went cold. He died while they were away, and Tate took control of the pack." She shivered. "I thought Steve was bad, but Tate was worse. All the good in him had vanished, and it petrified me."

Things don't make sense. Cyrus's frustration bled through. *Ask her where Tate and his father went.*

"Did Tate not bring his father back to bury?" I asked instead. I didn't want to make her uncomfortable. She might stop talking. I removed a tomato from the plant and put it into the bag.

Midnight shook her head and examined the plant. "No, but the bond was severed, and Tate came back with the alpha power. There was nothing anyone could do."

I watched the thoughtful way Midnight plucked and sorted the tomatoes. Her touch seemed gentle and sure, and I wondered if that was true to her character. Even though the situation was horrible, the one bright spot was meeting my birth mother. She appeared to be a good person who truly cared about me despite her time spent in this pack. "Why did you stay here if you weren't happy?"

"The same reason all the other women are still here." Her focus flicked to me. "If any of us try to leave, they'll kill the people we love. The ones we're desperate to keep safe."

I glanced at the okra section where Uma, who had the most scars on her body, was harvesting the okra with shears. "What did Nyko do to her?"

"She was part of a local pack. She lost her fated mate, and a few weeks later, her ten-year-old son begged her to go on a run with him. They crossed paths with Nyko and Tate." She blinked like she was trying to keep tears at bay. "Let's just say Nyko had his eyes set on her immediately. She was so damn broken."

"Oh, no." My heart broke in two. "Which one of these assholes is her son?" I tried reimagining the cafeteria-style room and all the faces in it. No one stuck out in my mind.

She laughed maniacally, and the edge it held made me uncomfortable. Her voice turned hard and cold. "In a way, his death was a blessing. At least, he left this world as an innocent soul."

No. I must have misunderstood. "They *killed* him?"

"Tate held him down while Nyko ripped his throat out." Midnight wiped a stray tear from her cheek. "They came back drenched in his blood with Uma completely broken. They told her they'd kill her whole pack if she didn't come with them, so she joined our pack immediately, telling her pack not to come looking for her."

Anger burned in my breast, fierce and hot. "Who are they using against you?"

"My parents. I came here of my own free will, but Tate's done such horrible things that even fated love couldn't survive." She moved to another aisle, working efficiently once more.

These women were just like the kids I wanted to protect in the group home.

Her words sank inside me, and my heart ached. "I have grandparents."

She nodded. "They live in northern Tennessee, and maybe, by some miracle, they can meet you one day."

Overwhelming hope spread through me, and my throat dried. I had to change the subject before I broke down. I'd always wanted grandparents and a large family. "I was told a demon is after me. Is that true, or was that something you told the witches to get them to help us?"

"Oh, baby girl." She stopped moving, the blood draining from her face. "I wish that was a lie, and that's one reason we have to get you, your mate, and your other friends out of here before it's too late."

"It still wants me?" My heart pounded as I held my breath, waiting for Midnight to reveal why Tate was determined to keep me here. The look on her face told me I didn't want to know, but we couldn't remain ignorant.

She clutched her neck instead of answering.

My patience slipped. "Tell me, please. I need to know."

CHAPTER SIXTEEN

SHE SHOOK her head and closed her eyes.

I tried not to become frustrated with her. She'd given up so much in her life but shielding me from the truth wasn't helping anyone. "Telling me is the only way my friends, my mate, and I will know what we're up against."

"They'll fight to protect you?" she asked, opening her eyes. Hope sprang inside them. "The silver wolves?"

I had to listen intently since she was speaking so softly. "Yes. I'm part of their pack, and we protect our own. Not only that, but I have other supernaturals that I consider family, and they will fight alongside us, too." She needed to know that, though the silver wolf pack might be small, I had more people on my side. "The witches... one of them left the coven and raised me. That's how I remained hidden for so long. I think she'll help us, too."

Displeasure surged through our bond from Cyrus at my elusive mention of Eliza. *I know she protected you, but I'm still so damn angry over what she might have done to me.*

What are you talking about? Sterlyn asked. She hadn't been linked in when that bomb had dropped the other day.

Cyrus quickly filled her in about the heart-stopping spell the witches had used on us both.

Dear gods. Sterlyn's shock felt like a slap. *I don't understand. Eliza's essence is good.*

"You will need all your friends, and that's one reason I didn't want to tell you. It will be hard to beat your fath— Tate," she corrected herself.

I got that these wolves were descended from demons, but the silver wolves were strong in their own right. "He can't be stronger than descendants of angels."

"But he can." Midnight glanced over her shoulder, keeping an eye on the three mates working diligently over fifty yards away. She ran her hands along a tomato bush as if she was working, but she was making noise to ensure the rustling covered up her whispers. She kept her voice so low. "There is a reason your grandfather was jealous that we were having a daughter." She paused, preparing herself for what came next.

Inhaling deeply, I tried to calm myself. If I pushed her too hard, she might shut down. It was difficult to keep that frustration at bay with Cyrus's and Sterlyn's antici-pation mixing with mine, adding an overwhelming urge to just *know*.

"A daughter is born to a future alpha of the demon wolves every hundred and fifty to two hundred years," she said slowly as if to ensure she didn't have to repeat a word.

Demon wolves. That was what they called themselves. One additional piece of information that I tucked away. "Do they keep track of when a girl is born? I don't understand why Tate's dad would be jealous, given they disrespect women so much. You'd think Tate would have been upset instead."

She leaned closer to me across the top of the plants. Her eyes locked with mine, and fear ran through her gaze. "Demon wolves produce one child, two max, and though women are born in the pack, it's rare for an alpha to have one. And when an alpha does sire a daughter, the demons bestow gifts upon him."

"A gift?" I had a feeling it was anything but.

"More like an exchange." She wiped her hands on her jeans. "If the alpha promises his daughter to a prince of hell, he gets three things in exchange: more power, a longer life, and the guarantee of having another child. Of course, the second child would be a boy who would inherit the alpha role."

"I have a brother?" The thought both excited me and filled me with dread.

Uma glanced at us, so I resumed picking tomatoes. I didn't want one of the women coming over here and interrupting our conversation.

"No." Midnight plucked another tomato, following my lead. "Because you supposedly died, the demon got mad and took away Tate's additional power."

Damn it, where are the princes of hell located? Sterlyn asked.

"He'd already received the power? I figured they'd hand it over to them after the trade." My stomach soured. God, it sounded like a business transaction and not like a father willingly giving up his child to something evil.

She scoffed and whispered, "No. While I was pregnant, Tate was so excited when he heard how fast your heartbeat was—it signified you would be a girl. He and his father ran off to tell the demon, which is apparently standard protocol." She rolled her eyes. "When he came back, I realized why. By granting him power—" She cut off, unable to finish the sentence.

"It corrupted him. All the goodness left him." This whole story made me sick. I wondered how many alpha daughters had been given to a prince of hell. All those women before me sacrificed in the name of power. What had their lives been like? Did they even stay alive?

The demons must want the alpha to alert them so they can give him a taste of that power before he can bond with his daughter, Cyrus linked as hatred filled him.

Sterlyn's words held sadness as she said, *It's purely manipulative.*

Manipulative fit the entire situation.

"Like I said, he'd changed so much that I no longer recognized the person I loved and lived with." Midnight took a moment to collect her thoughts.

I bit my lip, but eventually, I broke down and asked, "Where do demons live? And why wasn't Tate with you when you tried to bury me?"

She laughed, but it was filled with malice. "I don't know where the demons live, but from what I understand, it's another dimension. And as soon as we realized you were dead, Tate left to alert the demon. He was terrified and more worried about what the prince of hell would decide about his fate than grieving the loss of his child."

Though I didn't understand why, that cut deep. I'd hoped that some part of Tate had cared about me. Maybe if a demon hadn't been involved, he would have, but the *what if* didn't matter. I was a means to an end for him; he didn't care about me, only about the power I could bring him.

Do not let him determine your worth, Cyrus linked as he pushed his love toward me. *That asshole alpha never deserved you, and he was a fool for even considering the trade.*

But isn't that how you *feel?* I wasn't trying to be mean, but he was telling me to believe something he didn't believe himself. *That you don't deserve help or love because of the way you were raised? My biological father wanted to trade me for power. How is that any different from you being kidnapped and raised by people who didn't care?*

Shock was his response. He clearly hadn't seen the similarities. The only difference was I'd grown up wondering why I'd been given up and feeling less than adequate. Even though Midnight had done it out of love, if I'd stayed here with my parents, my father would've given me up for selfish reasons anyway. Cyrus had thought no one cared, but he knew now that his family had loved and mourned him every day.

Sterlyn interjected. *Both of you are amazing and deserve love. I'm so glad I found you two and that you found each other.*

I believe you but let me have a chance to feel. I always told the kids in the group home, "Feel what you need to. Grieve and mourn your loss, but don't wallow too long, because the emotions can turn into hatred, and all that does is give more power to the people who abused you."

Becoming full of hate and resembling the man who had made a deal with the devil wasn't an option.

"Thank you," I said simply. I realized this might be my only chance to tell her that.

Her eyes flicked to me. "For what?"

"For loving me and protecting me, even though it caused you pain." That was the love of a true mother— someone willing to live with hurt and pain for the rest of her life to give her child a chance at happiness. That kind of sacrifice wasn't inherent in anyone. "You gave up everything for me."

A smile filled her face as she sniffled. "My child, I'd do it all again in a heartbeat. We *will* get you out of here with your friends and fated mate. I didn't go through all I did, nineteen years ago, for it to be in vain now. You deserve to be happy and to choose your own future."

I already knew what my future would be. All this time, I'd been preparing to be an advocate and fight for people who needed me. For people who didn't have a choice but to do whatever they could to survive. I'd thought it would take the form of protecting children, but I realized I'd been preparing myself for this battle all along. I would fight for this pack and for these women to be treated as individuals worthy of respect. "And so do you."

"Maybe, at one time, I believed that, but not anymore. Tate is my mate. My family is safe, and I can't leave these women behind." Midnight turned to look at the other three. "If I left, their lives would get so much harder, and Tate would hunt me down anyway. I need to stay here to help you remain free after you leave."

There was no point in arguing with her. I already planned to find a way to help every single woman here. *Is there anything else we need to ask?*

How do they get to the other dimension to meet the demons? Cyrus answered.

I repeated the question, and Midnight shrugged. "I have no idea. Only the alpha and the ones he deems trustworthy know."

The air remained full of the fresh scents of the crops. She was telling the truth.

"Now we better pick up our pace before Tate and the others come to check on us." Midnight moved down the section. "Otherwise, it'll raise suspicion."

Yeah, we didn't need that. I bent down and began working faster, trying to make up for the time we'd spent talking.

My body was covered in sweat as I filled my third satchel with tomatoes. I was thankful that my shirt was dark blue and not white; otherwise, people would be getting a show.

The gate opened, and Tate, Ken, and Nyko waltzed through, with Echo following behind.

Tate's icy eyes turned colder as they found me and Midnight far away from the gate and the other women. "What are they doing all the way down there?"

"Working." Echo laughed like he thought it was a joke.

"Did you not notice that they're at the farthest section from you and the other mates?" Tate rasped, the threat in his voice undeniable.

Echo's smile vanished, and he scratched the back of his neck. "Uh…"

Tate crossed his arms, his biceps bulging. "Or were you taking a nap the entire time and not watching over them like I told you to?"

Echo dropped his hand and bounced on his heels. "I mean—"

"That would be a 'yes' to the nap." Ken strolled over to Indra, grabbed her by the hair, and jerked her toward him. He kissed her, despite her eyes watering from pain.

That prick got off on forcing her to kiss him.

"The two of them have three bags full of tomatoes each, so they have been working," Nyko added.

"I was with Annie the whole time." Midnight straightened and cut her eyes to me. She nodded her head toward the women, telling me to head over to them. "We hadn't picked the tomatoes in a few weeks, so I needed an extra set of hands. What do you think could happen with us working in the garden?"

"I'm not worried about you." Tate walked over to us, his gaze staying on me. "I'm concerned with what she might have told you. She wasn't raised the way she should've been, but I see she's pulled her weight. Maybe there's hope for her, after all."

His words sounded insulting, but he nodded like he thought I'd take them as a compliment. He was so out of touch that he had no sense of what was acceptable.

"I've always been a hard worker. I've worked since I was fifteen." I didn't like him insinuating that I wouldn't work hard, but I forced a smirk. "Did you all come here to join us?"

"The mates are responsible for the garden." Nyko headed toward Uma and examined her bags of okra. "We have important discussions, make decisions for the pack, and make sure everyone is pulling their weight." Apparently, the amount she'd harvested was good enough for the man, because he grinned cockily.

"We need to take the food to the kitchen," Minx said as she kept her gaze on the potato plants in front of her. "So, they'll have it for dinner tonight."

"Then let's get a move on." Ken released Indra, who somehow kept her face indifferent. "Lunch will be set out by now."

The men didn't move, and Midnight put her bags over her shoulders. She nodded at me, indicating I should do the same.

186 JEN L. GREY

None of the men had any intention of helping. I care-fully swung all three sizable bags over my shoulders too. Though the bags were bulky, they weren't too heavy to hold. Minx, though, struggled with her four large bags full of potatoes.

If those assholes wouldn't help, I would. She was the smallest of the bunch, coming in around my average height of five and a half feet, but her slender frame caused her to struggle. Now that I was paying attention, I could see that, while Midnight, Uma, and Indra had more muscle, they were skin and bones, as if they were fed just enough to survive.

Yet another way for the men to control them and keep them weak.

I snatched one of Minx's bags and put it over the shoulder that carried only one bag of tomatoes.

"What the fuck do you think you're doing?" Echo snarled, taking on his brother's role as her *protector*.

I stood tall, wanting him to know I wouldn't back down. "I'm helping her since you aren't."

"Let her," Tate said, lifting a hand. "As long as the food gets back, it doesn't matter."

Echo bared his teeth at me, unhappy with his alpha telling him to let me help his mate. It didn't sit well with me either. There had to be a reason Tate was holding back one of his men.

Jaw twitching, Midnight came to the same conclu-sion. It was too late, though, and I refused to give in. The damage was already done.

She hurried to the gate and held it open for me and

the other girls. Now that I didn't have a job to focus on, I felt the air sizzling around me again. With the men following close behind, I didn't have a chance to examine the area for the source.

Minx caught up to me and whispered, "Thank you for helping me. I hope it doesn't cause you any problems."

Her concern warmed me to her more. Despite living in a cold environment, these women hadn't lost their kindness and empathy, at least for one another. "I'll be fine."

"I hope so," she said and stared at the ground again.

The rest of the walk was made in silence, with Tate, Ken, Nyko, and Echo laughing behind us. The four of them sounded carefree, and I gritted my teeth.

Remembering my purpose, I surveyed the area as best I could without being obvious. Nothing struck me as odd or beneficial, other than knowing where Cyrus and the other silver wolf pack members were being kept. The strangest observation I made was the missing sounds of animals in the woods.

The animals could sense the energy surrounding this place and made sure to stay far away.

The large building where we'd eaten breakfast came into view, and I followed the women around to the back. Evergreen trees hid the rear entrance, but there were large bins outside. We dropped the produce into the bins and went to the front.

We entered the building like we had that morning, but this time, there was a table up front with sandwiches. I followed the ladies in line and grabbed a sandwich and a water. My stomach grumbled as the deep ache of hunger took root. My nerves made me feel nauseous, and I hoped I could keep the food down.

When we walked to the other side of the building, away from where we'd sat for breakfast, some of the tension drained from my body, and I sighed. I relaxed further when the men went back to that table.

"They don't like sitting next to us after we've been working in the hot sun," Indra explained, her face more serene than I'd seen it. "We'll have to shower before dinner, but this is the one meal we get to have away from them each day."

As we took a table near the front door, I sat away from the main walkway, next to Midnight and Indra. Once Minx and Uma had sat in front of Midnight and me, we all unwrapped our sandwiches and began to eat. When I took the first bite, my hunger truly settled in. Working in the garden had taken more out of me than I'd realized.

A burly man hurried through the door and slammed into Minx. Her body jerked, and her sandwich dropped from her hands onto the ground.

The guy grabbed her arms, holding them up, his face pinched red with anger. "You stupid bitch!"

"I—I'm sorry." Minx's expression crumpled.

"That's what you get for being in the way," he growled and stepped on her sandwich. "Now you don't get to eat."

I glanced at Troy. He shook his head like he couldn't

believe his mate had done that. He wouldn't stand up for her.

I stood up and slammed my hand on the table, making sure to glare at the prick in the eyes. "I'll get you another sandwich, Minx."

"One sandwich per woman, and that was the one she touched." The guy laughed as he glowered at me. "So, sit your ass down and eat yours before something happens to it as well."

"No way." I lifted my chin, letting him know it was *game on.*

CHAPTER SEVENTEEN

SOMEONE HAD to protect these women, and it looked like that someone was me. My father and his cronies didn't care about the well-being of their mates, and the women had been beaten down too much to even consider standing up for themselves. "If anyone isn't going to eat, it's you. You ran into her. She was sitting in her chair, eating her food."

Ugh, I hate not being with you, Cyrus linked, feeling my angst. *Please tell me you aren't in danger. I feel like every few minutes, I'm asking if you're okay.*

No, I wasn't in danger. This egotistical asshole was. *These douchebags treat the women here like they're property and not people. It's pissing me off.*

"Listen here," the man growled, his beady eyes narrowing. "I get that you're new and the alpha's child, but you need to learn how everything works rather quickly since you're one of us."

Whoa. I was *not* one of them. "I'm not part of this pack."

He laughed so hard his chest heaved. "Uh...no one leaves once they come—"

"That's enough," Tate commanded, walking toward us. His nostrils flared as he scowled at the man. "Do not speak on the pack's behalf. You aren't the alpha."

What the man was trying to say was crystal clear and something I'd already known. Tate had no intention of letting me leave, and the alpha was arrogant enough to think I hadn't figured that out. Normally, I'd find that insulting, but if Tate believed I was that gullible, maybe we'd have a slight advantage over him.

The man averted his eyes, his beige complexion turning a shade paler. "Yes, Alpha. I'm sorry."

His humble reaction must have been enough because Tate turned his cold stare on me. "You may not like how we handle things here, but we have rules in place for a reason."

"A man can run into a woman who's sitting down, and she has to suffer the consequences?" I wouldn't back down like that man—Tate would learn that wouldn't happen. "How is that fair?"

"Life isn't fair," Tate replied, his mask of indifference cracking as the vein between his eyes bulged. "That's something you should be aware of since you were taken from us as an infant. Those damn witches left us behind to deal with the fallout." The hateful man he tried to hide reared his ugly head.

I bit my tongue. I'd caused enough commotion, and

Tate had reached his breaking point. He didn't like anyone questioning him. His word was law, and everyone here knew to abide by it.

Everyone but me, the daughter who'd supposedly died, making him lose the power he coveted so desperately he was willing to give me up again to get it back.

"It's fine," Minx said. "I wasn't hungry anyway."

"See." Tate stared at me as he gestured at her. "You're making a big deal about nothing. Now, sit down and eat."

My wolf surged forward, not liking being told what to do, especially by him. He didn't get to talk to me or anyone I cared about that way.

Whoa. In less than a day, these women had impacted me. All these years, I'd kept people at bay. Then the supernatural world came along and kicked my defenses in the ass.

Midnight touched my hand, distracting me from my hatred. I glanced at her, and her look spoke volumes: *Sit down, and be quiet. Don't make a scene.*

She'd protected me so far, giving my wolf pause. We felt a connection to my biological mother, and it helped that she wasn't commanding but rather advising.

I sucked in a breath to calm my rage. The air sawed at my lungs. *It's infuriating.* At least, I had my mate to talk to frankly.

That's typical of the packs that haven't moved into this century. Cyrus's disgust ran through our link. *And this place seems to be so far behind. I'm sure they're located far away from civilization for this very reason.*

It's like these men equate power with making

everyone feel inferior. I despised people who got hard off the misery of others. That wasn't power but a sick pleasure no real leader would ever want to feel at their people's expense. *They don't want to encourage their pack members to be stronger, even though it would strengthen their pack.*

Cyrus chuckled through our link, but no amusement accompanied it. *They fear someone within the pack will become stronger than them.*

I forced myself to sit back down.

Tate smirked, making me want to jump back to my feet.

"You should eat," Midnight said, pointing at my sandwich. "You worked hard in the garden today."

Yeah, so had Minx, but Tate was still standing close by, so I swallowed the words. A lump formed in my throat.

Tate patted the man on the shoulder. "Go get your sandwiches now that everything is settled."

Sandwich*es.*

I surveyed the cafeteria-like building and noticed that each man had three while each woman had one. Not only that, but the meat on the men's sandwiches was piled twice as thick.

Whatever. I'd be out of here soon enough.

But these women wouldn't be. That thought sat heavy on my shoulders, weighing me down.

When the two men walked off, I tore my sandwich in two and held one half out to Minx.

Her eyes bulged, and she shook her head as she

tucked a piece of hair behind her ear. "No, I'm fine, really."

That was bullshit. Even if she wasn't hungry, she was the smallest one here. I questioned how Troy treated her. I put the other half in the bag and tossed it to her. I wouldn't take no for an answer. "Then it'll go to waste."

"You really should eat that." Midnight tilted her head toward the half sandwich.

Did she expect me not to know what she was referring to? "I'm good. She needs it more than I do."

"Food is sparse around here." Indra bobbed her head. "You'll regret that after a few days."

No, I wouldn't, because I wouldn't be here that long. "Maybe, but I figure we should take care of each other."

Uma took a bite of her sandwich and tapped her dirty fingers on the table. "I like the sound of that."

"Me too." Minx bounced her knee and snatched the half sandwich from in front of her.

Midnight took a sip of water. "Perhaps we should've done better all along."

The rest of the time, we ate in silence.

MY MUSCLES ACHED EVEN after the hot shower. I plopped onto the bed, starving after eating a six-ounce steak and a small potato for dinner. If I hadn't done such hard labor, the food would've been enough.

At least I'd gotten to spend time with my biological mother, Midnight. I couldn't think of her as Mom. Even though I didn't call Eliza Mom, she was that person by all rights. When I'd started to call her that as a little girl, she'd corrected me, saying she wasn't worthy of the title. I'd always assumed it was because she hadn't given birth to me, but now I realized it might have to do with the guilt she carried around over what had happened to Cyrus, leaving her own daughter behind, or, most likely, both.

At least, I thought it was guilt. The way she stared at him. How she seemed uncomfortable around him. It all made sense if she or her coven had been behind his kidnapping.

How are you? I linked with Cyrus, thankful I could connect with him to just talk and not because something horrible was going on.

Miserable, he replied. *I miss you so damn much. We've got to get the hell out of here.*

I agreed with that. *I'll talk to Midnight in the morning. We need to leave by tomorrow night. I'm assuming whatever Tate has planned will happen the day after tomorrow.*

I'm about to go stir-crazy. They didn't bring me lunch or dinner, so I'm starving and stuck inside.

And he was chained. I wondered if Mila and the others were doing any better. I didn't have a way to check on them since we couldn't link to them. I'd asked Midnight about them before we'd left for dinner, and she'd said she hadn't overheard anything. I wasn't sure if that was a good or bad thing.

When we get out of here, I'm never leaving your side

again. Being away from him like this was horrible. I'd volunteer for a root canal if it meant Cyrus would be there. That was how desperate I was to be with him—like he was my drug of choice.

I'll chain us together if that's what it takes, Cyrus vowed.

The crazy thing was I had no doubt he'd do that, and worse, I was okay with it. *The bathroom situation could be problematic.*

I can close my eyes and plug my nose, he teased. *After this, there's no such thing as privacy between us again.*

My laughter surprised me, but Cyrus did that to me. Even in the darkest moments, he was my light and the hope that kept me moving forward. I didn't know how I'd made it so long without him, but damn it, I refused to go through my future without him. *I kinda love you.*

I kinda love you more. He pushed the intensity of his feelings toward me. *I keep thinking about last night. How you looked, tasted, and felt.*

My body warmed. *You better stop talking, or this could get awkward.*

You never need to feel awkward with me.

The thing was I already knew that. *Do you think things will ever calm down and we can just be sorta normal?*

You mean taking you out on dates and watching a movie without my sister and her friends? Cyrus asked.

I don't mind Sterlyn and the others. I chuckled. *But the date part and having time alone without texts or phone calls about impending doom sounds great.*

Unfortunately, I don't think we'll ever get rid of the drama. There's just so much turmoil around Shadow City, but I do think we'll have spurts of that sort of time together. He spoke the truth, even though he could have gotten away with fibbing to make me feel better since we weren't physically together.

Don't ever change. His honesty was one of the things I loved most about him. Well, really our entire group. We all tried to do what we thought was right. The biggest problem we faced was hiding stuff from one another in the name of protection, but I thought we were getting better about that. Withholding the truth caused more drama than it was worth because the truth had a way of coming out—eventually.

A strange mood wafted from him. *Really?*

After a moment, I realized the emotion he was feeling was disbelief. He still didn't think he was worthy of love and acceptance. *Of course. I love you, and it's not solely because of your hot ass. It's also because you're dedicated, hard-working, funny, and take care of the people you love.*

Damn. And here I thought it was my ass. Happiness radiated from him.

I rolled my eyes despite my cheeks hurting from how wide I was smiling. *That does help.* I yawned, glad he wasn't there to see it.

Even though I don't want to stop talking, we need our rest if we're breaking out tomorrow. I'll link with Sterlyn and give her an update. You go ahead and sleep.

He must have sensed I was tired, even though I'd

been trying to hide it. *Okay. Good night. I can't wait until tomorrow night when I can fall asleep in your arms.*

Neither can I.

My eyes closed, but just before I dozed off, I felt his worry.

A SOFT KNOCK startled me awake. I sat up in bed, searching the room. I was alone inside.

The door unlocked, and I bolted to my feet. When it opened, Midnight's musky vanilla scent floated into the room.

Hope blossomed in my chest. Maybe I'd get to see Cyrus tonight.

Her shoulders were tense as she sprinted to me. Her voice was as low as it had been in the garden as she said, "You've got to get out of here."

"What?" My brain was trying to catch up. "I can't leave without Cyrus and the others. We need to get them as well."

"Uma is distracting the two guards." She clutched my arm, dragging me to the door. "We've got to go *now*."

"I thought we had tomorrow too?" As much as I was ready to get away from here, I didn't want to leave her. I wasn't ready. I'd thought I had one more day with her.

Sweat beaded her brow, and she sighed. "Me, too. I was looking forward to it, but your father left after he thought I'd fallen asleep early. Our window was open, and I heard him talking to someone. The person said that the prince of hell wanted to see him immediately, and Tate left. I'm afraid if you don't leave now, you won't have another chance."

"He didn't use the pack link?" Something wasn't adding up. She shouldn't have been able to hear him.

Her hold tightened. "That's what I'm telling you. This person wasn't a wolf, so I'm thinking demon. We've got to move while Ken, Nyko, Troy, Echo, and several other men are on their late-night run. We have to get you out while they're away. After we meet with Uma, we'll break the others free."

That was enough to wake me up completely. I linked with Cyrus and Sterlyn and waited until I knew they were listening. *We're getting out of here tonight. Tate left to meet with a prince of hell. Midnight has a plan to get us out.*

What about Mila and the others? Cyrus asked, completely alert.

He must have been awake already. *We're getting them too.* I headed to the door as an issue popped into my head. "What are we going to do about the guards? They'll alert the pack."

We're on our way to help, Sterlyn replied. *Keep us updated.*

"I have a plan, and it's best if you don't know what it is," she said and yanked me out the door.

With no other choice, I followed her outside. Uma's shaky voice filled my ears. "I...I don't know. The toilet just stopped up, and Nyko is gone."

"Are you serious?" one of the guards asked.

She cleared her throat. "Is that something I'd willingly lie about? Besides, you'd know if I were lying."

I assumed Uma had clogged the toilet on purpose, and I smiled at her deviousness.

"Dude, you can be on shit duty." The guy snorted. "I'll stay here and keep an eye on these two buildings."

"Um...why can't you?" a deeper-voiced guy responded.

The more arrogant one's voice shook with laughter. "Because I'm higher ranked than you. Do I need to prove it again?"

Of course, a male here would love to beat up on someone weaker. Pricks.

"No," the deeper-voiced guy snarled. "I'll be back in a second."

Their footsteps moved away, and Midnight waved for me to follow her. We headed directly to the remaining guard.

As we walked between the two buildings that held Cyrus and the others, Midnight said, a little louder than necessary, "We'll take a quick walk. Then you have to go back inside." She picked up her pace.

We'd just reached the front of Cyrus's building when the guard said, "What the hell do you think you're doing?"

He was leaning against a large tree, scowling as he took us in. He appeared to be in his mid-twenties with the athletic build typical of healthy shifters. His dark roots looked lighter with the slightly more than half moon shining on them, but his eyes held a malicious glint. Without moving, he beckoned us toward him.

Midnight walked over to him and explained, "Annabel hasn't seen the woods around here. I thought I'd let her get to know the area."

Her black shirt inched up, and a dark leather handle stuck out the back of her jeans. It looked like the handle of a knife or dagger.

No, that couldn't be her plan. If she assaulted him, she'd get hurt.

"You know that's not allowed. Take her back to the cabin," the guard commanded.

As her hand inched toward the knife, I knew I had to do something. I couldn't let her take the blame.

I rushed toward her, the guard not paying attention to me. His attention was locked on Midnight.

"You heard him," I said and caught her hand, preventing her from reaching the weapon. "I need to go back."

Her head snapped in my direction, and I had to act fast before she did something rash. I turned and pulled her back toward the cabin so I could grab the knife and make it look like I was the one who'd brought it.

With the hand closest to her body, I grabbed the knife and pivoted toward the guard. His focus landed on the weapon, and his jaw tensed. I pretended to kick him. He grinned cockily as he bent down to block the blow, but I swung the hilt of the knife and hit him in the temple.

He landed on his side with a hard *thud*. I'd knocked his ass out.

"What the hell?" Midnight gasped.

I turned to her, placing a hand on my hip. "I'm saving your ass. If you hurt him, then—"

"We don't have time for this." Midnight bent down and searched the guy's pockets. "He alerted the pack. We've got to move *now*."

CHAPTER EIGHTEEN

JUST MY LUCK. He'd had time to alert the others, but I wasn't surprised. I was sure Tate had given the guards orders to keep me here, no matter the cost. "What are you doing? We need to get them out."

"I don't have keys to those buildings," Midnight said through clenched teeth. "I got the keys to yours because I threw a fit with Tate. I thought he wouldn't budge, but surprisingly, he gave me the keys to your room, likely because he knew I would have only a few days with you before he handed you over to the demon you're promised to."

He didn't care to spend any time with me. I shouldn't be surprised, but a part of me had at least hoped he wanted to get to know me a little.

She pulled two key rings, each with two keys on them, out of his pocket. She handed one to me. "Here are the keys to your mate. One is for the door the other for the handcuffs."

As much as I wanted to get him, I needed to free Mila's group. "No, I'll get the others since they don't know you and I can't link with them. I'll let Cyrus know you're coming."

Her mouth opened, but she closed it and nodded. "Fine. We don't have time to argue."

Midnight is coming to let Cyrus out while I get Mila and the others, I linked with Cyrus and Sterlyn. *The guard alerted the pack.*

You did the right thing, Cyrus responded. *Go get them, and I'll be there as soon as I can.*

Shouts came from the pack neighborhood, and I sprang into action. As I hurried to Mila's building, I heard the creaking of Cyrus's door.

There was no way we could get enough of a head start, but we couldn't stay here and wait for the wolves to return or the demon to arrive.

I reached the small front porch of the house, and my hands shook as I tried putting the key inside the lock. Every time I tried fitting it in, my hands would move, and I'd miss the mark.

My wolf surged forward, lending me patience. Even though we were getting more in sync, I wasn't used to being in threatening situations. I was handling them better than I used to, and I didn't know whether to feel proud or sad about it.

Finally, my hands steadied enough to insert the key into the lock and unlock the door. As I turned the knob, I heard frantic murmurs from the other side.

"It's me, Annie," I said as I stepped in. I paused and took in the room.

Mila was on the floor by the left far wall. Her cinnamon-brown hair was greasy, and there was a black ring around her right cognac-colored eye. Her normally dark olive skin was unusually pale. She sat with her legs folded underneath her and her back against the wall. "Annie?" she whispered.

"Why are you here?" Theo asked from the bed, where he held his mate against his bare chest. His shaggy dark brown hair stuck to his forehead, and the corners of his eyes had fresh lines as if he'd aged ten years in the past few days. He was in his mid-twenties, but he appeared to be in his thirties now, which wasn't normal for supernaturals.

Rudie lifted her head from her mate's chest, her dark sapphire eyes focusing on me. Her long chocolate bangs hung in her face, and she brushed her hair aside to look at me. Her warm ivory skin gleamed with sweat.

"We've got to go." They were in about the same state as Cyrus—not grossly mistreated, but they'd taken a few punches and been underfed to keep them weak.

I hurried to Chad, who was chained to the wall opposite Mila, and let him out first. Of the four of them, if a wolf came, he was in the best shape to fight them off while I freed the others. Mila was bruised, and Theo wouldn't leave Rudie's side.

His wheat-gold hair lacked its usual luster, but his light smokey-topaz eyes gleamed as they scanned me. "Are you okay?"

208 JEN L. GREY

"No, but I will be." I used the second key to unlock the chain then scurried to Mila.

These four had caused a ton of problems for Cyrus, but they were pack members, and Mila was Sterlyn and Cyrus's family—one of the last few members left, though they weren't related by blood. She was the fated mate of Bart, their uncle, who, while protecting Sterlyn, had died at the hands of men Cyrus had trained. To say Mila blamed Cyrus for Bart's death and resented him would be an understatement. She'd encouraged both Theo and Chad to challenge Cyrus for the pack alpha position, but Cyrus was stronger than anyone realized.

"I...I don't know why you're helping us," Mila rasped. "We're the reason Cyrus got captured."

"People make mistakes and do what they have to do to survive." Within seconds, I'd freed her, and even though we didn't have time for a conversation, I needed her to realize this was sincere. I didn't want her to think I planned on using them as a distraction while Cyrus and I got away. "I understand why you're angry with Cyrus, even though it's unwarranted, but we're a pack, and we leave no one behind."

A howl filled the air, and I sprinted to the bed to unlock Theo and Rudie. Footsteps hurried toward us, and Chad jumped to his feet and rolled his shoulders, preparing to fight.

My wolf knew it was my mate. "It's Cyrus and Midnight."

The chains clanked to the floor as I released both Theo and Rudie.

Cyrus stepped through the door, his granite irises on me. "They'll be here in seconds."

In other words, *move*. Mila hesitated, but we didn't have time for that. She was twice Cyrus's age, for crying out loud. "If you want a chance to get out of here, move your asses," I growled, letting my wolf bleed through. "Or be stubborn and risk getting caught."

"She's right," Chad said as he took Mila's arm and tugged her to the doorway.

Mila nodded, and Cyrus and I ran outside. I glanced up to see three wolves fifty yards away. Midnight stood by the door, her face set in a scowl.

When we ran past her, she didn't move. I paused and looked back at her. "Come on. We've got to go."

Midnight bit her bottom lip. "I have to stay here."

"You helped us escape." I had taken the knife from her so the guard wouldn't alert the others that Midnight was helping, but she couldn't stay behind. I was hoping Tate would assume we had forced her to come with us. "You can't stay here."

"If I go with you, Tate will have an easier time finding you even if the witches hide you. The fated-mate connection trumps everything, including magic. I have to stay here to protect you." Her irises darkened as she touched my arm. "Hurry. I'll hold them off the best I can. I love you."

"No, I can't...I won't leave you." Tears filled my eyes as the weight of her sacrifices settled on my chest.

Jaw set, she glanced at Cyrus. "I need you to continue protecting my baby girl."

Cyrus's brows furrowed as he glanced at me and then at her. "Until my last breath."

"That's enough for me. The silver wolves aren't the only ones who can use the power of the moon. Remember, the demon wolves balance the silvers." She dropped her hand and commanded me, "Go, before they catch us all."

Her message was clear—she didn't have to say that everything she'd given up would be in vain if Tate captured us, but that didn't mean I would let her be a martyr. "I love you, Mom, and I'm sorry."

Her eyes turned more honey than brown as she touched her chest. "I love you too, but what are you sorry—"

With all my strength, I punched her in the head. My stomach roiled, but I needed to protect her.

She crashed to the ground, unconscious. I laughed despite the tears streaming down my cheeks and said loudly, "No wonder Tate calls you a stupid bitch."

"Uh...Annie?" Chad said in shock as he and the others waited on Cyrus and me.

You saved her, Cyrus linked, *She might still be punished for trusting you, but not killed. Now we really have to move.*

I needed the others to think she wasn't involved in our escape. I glanced over my shoulder. The three men were only twenty yards away, and ten more were forty yards behind them. Shit! We'd spent too much time here.

Mila and the others spun around and raced ahead with Cyrus and me right on their tails.

Where are you guys? Cyrus linked as we sped through the trees.

Sterlyn replied, *We're three miles in, heading your way. Rosemary took to the sky, and Ronnie is in her shadow form. Alex is in the lead since he can run faster. They should reach you sooner than the rest of us, but we're in wolf form and running as hard as we can.*

We'd have to make it work. The only issue was the demon wolves could see Ronnie in her shadow form, which didn't give her the edge she had with vampires and regular wolves.

Bones cracked as the men behind us shifted into their wolf forms. Fuck. Though we'd gain distance while they transitioned, they'd soon make up that distance and more in animal form.

Even though we couldn't hear the pack, I knew they'd be charging toward us, ready to fight, especially Nyko, Troy, Echo, and Ken. They would, no doubt, love to make me pay for all the *disrespect* I'd shown them.

We'll have to fight, Cyrus linked. *There's no way around it. I'll shift, and I think Chad and Theo should as well. You, Mila, and Rudie need to stay in human form so we can communicate, and I don't want someone to think you're a dark wolf and attack you.*

I wanted to throw a fit about why they automatically thought the women should remain human, but that would be a waste of energy and time. Whether I liked to admit it or not, those three were physically stronger than Mila, Rudie, and me. Hell, I wasn't sure if Mila or I was the stronger between the two of us, but that didn't matter. I was the only one who could talk to Sterlyn and Cyrus.

You better be careful, I linked, fighting the urge to stop and kiss him. We'd been apart too long, but now wasn't the time when we were running for our lives.

He winked at me, and my heart pounded harder. *I have a promise that I made to your mother to fulfill.* He stopped and shifted, his beautiful silver wolf coming through smooth and fast.

This whole night was becoming one of the worst I'd ever had, trumping the vampire attack back in Lexington. At least, that had forced Cyrus and me to connect. All tonight was bringing was more heartache. Leaving Midnight like that, and now separating from Cyrus again, made everything almost intolerable. "Theo and Chad, can you two shift and help Cyrus out? I and someone from your group need to stay in human form to communicate."

"I'll shift with them," Mila said, peeling off and rushing toward Cyrus. "You two keep running. We'll do everything we can to slow them down."

Mila shifting wasn't ideal—I still didn't trust her—but none of us had time to argue. The wolves were gaining on us and quickly. I could hear their heavy breathing and their pounding paws. We were lucky the demon pack had spread out to remain hidden and that a sizable group had been on a run, or we never would've made it out.

How's it going? Sterlyn asked as Rudie and I ran as hard as we could.

Rudie's face was full of fear, but that made her move even faster.

They're gaining on us, but Theo, Chad, and Mila are with me in wolf form. Rudie and Annie are in human form so the two packs can communicate, Cyrus answered.

Rudie's running faster than me. I was holding up the group.

Tap into your wolf and borrow magic from her, he suggested.

I'd forgotten I could do that. My wolf surged forward, and I latched on to her. My legs grew stronger, and my speed increased. Now I had to slow down, so I wouldn't leave Rudie behind.

A snarl came from behind us, and I glanced over my shoulder, only to watch in horror as a dark wolf lunged onto Mila's back. Mila crashed onto her stomach as the wolf completely overtook her.

The dark wolf went for her neck. Right before his teeth sank in, Cyrus slammed into his side, rolling the wolf off Mila. The cinnamon-brown wolf got back on her feet and took off running again. Mila's eyes were wide with terror as she picked up her pace.

Three more black wolves converged on Cyrus while he was distracted by the wolf who'd attacked Mila.

"No!" I yelled and pivoted, running back toward my mate.

"Annie, stop!" Rudie called. "Chad and Theo will help."

The two silver wolves lunged at the two dark wolves on top of Cyrus. The slightly larger of the two—Theo, I thought—bit into the sturdier demon wolf's shoulder. The demon wolf clawed at Theo's neck, hitting the mark, but Theo released his grip.

Chad leaped onto another wolf's back, digging his claws into the enemy wolf's side. The demon wolf bucked like a bull, trying to fling the silver wolf off him.

That left two demon wolves on Cyrus, bettering his odds, but the sound of a larger group of wolves raced toward us. I feared they were the wolves from the night run.

Sterlyn, where the hell are you? I didn't want to have an attitude, but we were greatly outnumbered and needed reinforcements.

Her frustration rang clear through the bond. *We're getting there as fast as we can. I'm sorry. We're trying.*

My chest grew heavy. *I know. We just have a large group gaining on us.*

Throwing caution to the wind, I called my wolf forward. I had to hope and pray no one confused me with the other demon wolves. "I'm shifting, Rudie. Tell Mila, Chad, and Theo that I'll be the dark wolf not attacking them." My bones cracked as my body changed.

"Annie, wait," Rudie said, but it was too late.

My skin tingled as I dropped the knife and dark fur sprouted over my body. Soon, I stood on all fours. I raced by Mila, who was helping Theo, and charged one of the demon wolves on top of my mate.

Before I could reach them, something barreled into me, and I fell. A sharp, piercing pain tore into my back leg. I rolled toward my attacker and spun around so my front paw sliced its snout. He let go of my leg, but it hurt to put weight on it. I was limping toward him when, yet another dark wolf cut me off. He growled, baring his teeth.

The larger pack ran into the area, and the huge wolf in front with cold white eyes glared at me before he threw his head back and howled. It was Ken, and he wouldn't let me go. His eyes flicked to Cyrus, who was still fighting the other two dark wolves, making his target known.

One thing was certain: I'd go down fighting and protecting my mate, even if it killed me. I lowered my head and charged Ken, letting my rage fuel me.

CHAPTER NINETEEN

KEN SMILED in his wolf form, but the action didn't creep me out like it did when he was in human form.

The two wolves that had ganged up on me chased after me, set on taking me in as well. I had a feeling every damn wolf wanted to be the one to bring me back to Tate. Maybe we had a slight advantage over them. *Their focus is entirely on me.*

I'm well aware, Cyrus growled. He bit into the throat of one of his attackers. The demon wolf lunged forward, trying to catch him off guard.

No! My wolf took over, controlling my body and mind. There was no point in fighting it because this was her natural element.

Cyrus had expected the countermove, and he lifted his back legs, kicking the demon wolf in the chest with his claws extended. The demon wolf jerked in pain and surprise as he fell onto his back, blood pouring from his wounds.

My attention turned to Ken. I wanted to hurt the prick like he'd hurt so many others. Ken bared his teeth, his focus locked on me. The two demon wolves chasing me slowed, probably commanded by Ken to let him handle me.

My wolf sprang into action. As Ken lunged for my already injured leg, I attacked his side, twisting my bottom half out of the way. His snout slammed into the ground, missing its mark as I dug my teeth and nails into him.

He sneezed and whimpered at the same time, then went for my injured leg again.

Damn it, Annie, Cyrus linked, his fear coursing through our bond. He rushed past me, sank his teeth into Ken's neck, and ripped out his throat.

The demon wolf's eyes bulged before his dead body dropped.

Under normal circumstances, I'd have mourned the person's death, but we'd just rid the world of an evil being, and maybe Indra would now have a chance to be free—at least before another pompous prick, like Echo, tried to claim her.

Wings flapped overhead, and I hoped and prayed that meant Rosemary had arrived.

Watch out! Cyrus linked.

Something heavy landed on my back, followed by claws digging in and what had to be a mouth biting the base of my shoulder. Pain exploded through my body, and the additional weight caused my already injured leg to tremble. I ignored the pain and used every ounce of my remaining strength to twist over backward, forcing the wolf to bear the brunt of the fall.

Annie! Cyrus linked as he stood on his back legs and shoved the second demon wolf away. The demon wolf stumbled and landed on his side with a sickening *crack*.

He must have broken a bone.

Chest heaving, the demon wolf underneath me released his hold. I'd knocked the wind out of him. I rolled sideways to get away, trying to push through all-encompassing pain, but my leg couldn't bear any weight, and my back felt like it had been ripped in two.

Blood poured down my side, and my head swam.

Cyrus jumped in front of me as twenty demon wolves came into view. Theo, Chad, and Mila charged at them, but they could hold off only a few. Fifteen headed directly at us. There was no way we were getting away. Each pair of eyes was locked on my mate with more malice than ever before. My stomach rolled. If I'd learned anything about this horrible pack, it was that every action had a punishment, and I suspected they would do something to Cyrus to hurt me.

Only one thing would tear me apart—the deaths of my friends, my family, and Cyrus. Tate probably planned to kill Cyrus, but he needed to gain some sort of cooperation from me first to get things lined up before I tried to escape. I didn't know why it had taken until now to put those pieces together. *Cyrus, you need to run. They're going to kill you.*

I figured that was their plan all along. Cyrus stood in front of me, the silver fur on the back of his neck raised.

We weren't on the same page. *Then why the hell aren't you running?*

Because I won't leave you. Cyrus crouched, ready to fight.

The sound of flapping wings grew louder, and I lifted my head to see a dark shape whizzing toward us with long mahogany hair trailing behind. It took me a second to realize that Rosemary was carrying two people. Aurora's hair snapped in the wind, concern etched on her face. Lux's signature wine-red hair mixed with Rosemary's as she held on to the angel's shoulders. A breeze carried a hint of roses and herbs to my nose.

Thank God. Backup was here. I tried to move, but nausea rolled in my stomach. I was in agony, nearly worthless in this condition.

The angel landed next to me, her piercing, purple-tinted twilight eyes surveying me. "Looks like I arrived just in time." She released Aurora as Lux climbed off her back.

Aurora lifted her hands, her eyes narrowing as she muttered some words.

"Stop, that's Annie." Rosemary snatched her hands and gave her a level look.

The young witch paused, and her brows furrowed. "Are you sure?"

"Yes. Her scent is the overly sweet lilac musk with a hint of Cyrus's hydrangeas, since they're mated." Rosemary tapped her nose. "We'll have to keep note of their scents if we lose track of Annie in her wolf form."

The fact that I was in wolf form was probably for the

best, or I would've said a smartass remark. Instead, all I did was whimper.

"Aurora, we need to help the wolves." Lux's arctic blue eyes flicked to Cyrus. "They're grossly outnumbered."

I linked with Sterlyn, *Rosemary and the two witches are here.*

"Go help them," Rosemary commanded. Her hands glowed as she reached for me. What the flipping hell? I jerked away, but she rolled her eyes. "I'm going to heal you then help your mate."

She could *heal* me? I didn't know angels could do that, but I'd take it.

Two demon wolves attacked Cyrus just as Rosemary's hand touched my back. I grunted in pain, and Cyrus looked behind him, distracted.

No! I linked.

Just as a wolf leaped for Cyrus's throat, Chad lunged in front of him, blocking the lethal blow. The striking demon wolf slammed into Chad, but the silver wolf had braced himself for the collision. When the dark wolf hit, Chad stumbled back.

Aurora and Lux ran toward them, Aurora chanting, "*Ventum in misericordia mea.*" A strong gust of wind churned through the trees, pushing against the attacking demon wolves. The wolves hunkered down as the wind ripped around them.

"Stay still. It'll go faster," Rosemary rasped as her hands heated on my skin.

The discomfort eased as her magic flowed through

my body with a warm presence, not unlike the fated mate bond but not nearly as intense. The magic felt foreign yet familiar inside me, which was a strange combination, reminding me of a warm fudge cake topped with ice cream, the two conflicting temperatures complementing each other.

Maybe that was my demon side and her angel side intermingling.

Her magic faded away, and when it had disappeared completely, I slowly moved my shoulder, bracing for pain. The ache was gone.

I looked at her and nodded—the only way I could say thank you for now—and sprinted toward Cyrus.

More demon wolves had arrived, and they ran around the wind, eyeing the witches.

A dark chocolate wolf ran toward us, and I realized Rudie must have shifted too. That was fine—we needed every available fighter.

Rosemary flew past me as she spun around, crashing into two demon wolves before they could reach Cyrus and Chad. The two dark wolves were flung several feet away from the impact.

More than enough wolves were left to fight us.

Out of the corner of my eye, I saw a dark form surge into view. The figure had a head, two arms, and two legs, but there was nothing defined about it until its bright emerald eyes landed on me.

Ronnie.

Now that I was well, I ran to Cyrus's side. *Ronnie's here in demon form.*

Thank the gods. I see her, he linked. *Annie, run. They want you.*

And they want to kill you. There was no way I was leaving them behind. *We need to get to the cars before Tate comes back.* I didn't miss the irony of my statement, but we needed to get away. This was the demon wolves' home turf, and we were outnumbered. While we all still had our health and energy, we needed to run.

"Get ready to run," Lux said and turned toward the demon wolves. "*Natura reflectit voluntatem meam!*"

Vines sprouted from the ground and tangled around the demon wolves. Aurora dropped her arms and wiped the sweat from her brow now that her friend had taken over the spellwork. "Rosemary, can you carry Lux so she can continue the spell while I let my magic recharge?"

"Yes." Rosemary wrapped her arms around the girl and extended her wings, then lifted off the ground.

Chad growled at the shadow, and Rosemary rasped, "That's Ronnie. She's here to help. Do *not* fight her."

That was the one thing about demons—any angel or demon descendant could see them. The silver wolves saw only a hazy outline, but they could still see them.

That was enough for him because Chad ran to Aurora and crouched below her. Aurora's brows furrowed, and Chad headbutted her legs.

"He wants you to ride him," Rosemary said as she turned her back on us to keep Lux facing the demon wolves.

I watched in amazement as the vines wrapped

around the demon wolves like chains. Lux continued to say the words over and over, but her bottom lip trembled.

"We've got to move!" Aurora shouted and jumped onto Chad's back.

We took off running. Ronnie ran next to me, as Cyrus and I stayed at the rear of the pack with Chad in front of us. Aurora kept looking over her shoulder at Rosemary and Lux, her face turning ashen.

With the amount of magic she was using, I didn't think Lux could hold the spell much longer. She was holding off forty demon wolves.

We couldn't run as fast as we'd have liked, since Mila and Rudie weren't true silver wolves, but we moved quickly enough.

Something blurred several yards ahead. Alex had reached us. He slowed, and his body solidified. His sun - kissed brown hair was windblown, and his normally soft, light blue eyes looked navy. He scanned us, and his attention landed next to me, on Ronnie.

Rosemary flew backward, somehow missing the trees and not flying into anything. "You better get your ass moving, vampire, before you get trampled!" she called.

He grunted, his face strained and his eyes glowing as he moved aside, making room for the front of our line to run past.

He was talking to Ronnie, using their soulmate connection. He didn't look happy, I assumed because she was in danger, yet again. I didn't blame him, but Ronnie had always taken care of me even to her detriment. Our last dangerous adventure had brought her to her soul-mate, but I'd created a whole lot of crap in the process.

Lux cried out, "I can't hold the spell any longer! I'm sorry."

I watched as Rosemary spun around, facing us as Lux crumpled into her chest. Even though we were now farther ahead, the snapping of branches alerted us that the demon wolves were escaping their temporary hold and giving chase.

Our group pushed on, and the sound of running paws could be heard in front of us. *I think we can hear you,* I linked with Sterlyn. God, I hoped it was them and not another group of demon wolves that had gotten around us.

Yes, we hear you, too. Some relief wafted through. *I'm running slightly ahead since you are all close by.*

I'd take the extra help.

Lux and Aurora bought us some time, but the demon wolves are already catching up again, Cyrus informed her. *We can't let Mila and Rudie fall behind.*

We must protect everyone, Sterlyn agreed, show-casing what made this group so different. They always protected those in need, even when it was dangerous.

The demon wolves were so close that I could hear their breathing. Every second, they inched nearer. I glanced at Lux, whose eyes were still closed with exhaus-tion, and Aurora, whose color seemed better. I wasn't sure if it was because she'd had enough time to recover, if she hadn't used as much magic, or if she was stronger than Lux, but I hoped she had enough energy to help us out again.

As we cut between trees, Sterlyn raced into view. She was larger than Cyrus by a good foot, and her silver fur glistened more under the moonlight. She moved to the side and nodded for Mila and Rudie to run past. We needed them in front so they could set the pace.

"They'll be here in a few seconds," Rosemary said before she shot skyward, still carrying Lux.

A growl sounded almost right on top of us, and if we didn't turn and fight, they'd attack us soon. *We have to hold them off.*

I'll do it. You just keep going, Cyrus linked, and his fear took hold. *Go with Mila and Rudie.*

Wait. I understood why he wanted to do that, but maybe I could buy us some time. *Their focus is on capturing me.*

I know. Cyrus cut his steel gray eyes at me. *That's why you need to go.*

What if I confuse them? This was the best plan. *If I run off in a different direction, some of them will follow me. If Griffin, Killian, and Sierra—*

I'll tell them. They're nearly here, Sterlyn interrupted. *I'll tell them to run east. Ronnie, Alex, and Rosemary will understand what the plan is when they see us separate.*

This group was so in sync I didn't doubt they would figure it out.

I had one problem. East. Uh, which direction was that? I needed a landmark to guide me

Cyrus shook his head. *We should stay together.*

We are. Theo, Chad, Rubie, and Mila will continue to the cars. Aurora is on Chad's back, and she knows where to go and has the keys. A few will follow them, but the majority will come after the rest of us. We can run faster without them.

Understanding coursed through the bond. *For a second, I thought you were sacrificing yourself.*

I already told you, we're stuck side by side for the foreseeable future. I couldn't leave him at a time like this anyway, not after everything we'd been through. The last time we'd separated, he'd disappeared, and it had taken over a day to locate him. It would've taken longer if it hadn't been for Eliza suspecting his whereabouts.

Teeth snapped right behind me, and something tugged on my tail. I yanked my tail forward, and fur ripped from it. Luckily, the wolf had missed the meat. *We've gotta go.*

Let's move. Sterlyn veered left, and the three of us took off running as fast as we could.

The demon wolves didn't miss a beat as the majority of them chased after us, right on our heels, exactly as we'd planned.

CHAPTER TWENTY

THE DEMON WOLVES could run faster than a normal wolf, which meant I could as well. I connected with my wolf, nudging her to take control.

The demon wolf that had nipped my tail was now within striking distance.

"Keep running," Ronnie said as she spun around and attacked my pursuer. I heard the slicing of skin and knew she had used her demon dagger on the wolf.

I glanced back, watching Ronnie's shadow wrench the shadow dagger away, and the wolf fell with a whimper, blood pouring from its neck. The demon wolves right behind him tripped over the body, allowing me a slight lead.

"Damn it, Ronnie," Alex growled.

Ronnie didn't miss a beat and caught up to us effortlessly.

My wolf surged forward, taking control. She tugged at something inside me, and a tether appeared that I'd never noticed before. Silver magic filled me, strengthening my wolf. My legs moved faster, and I was able to pass Cyrus unexpectedly.

How'd you do that? Cyrus asked. He caught up to me, and we ran side by side.

Good question. *I don't know. I think I finally accessed some of my demon power, but still, you can run faster than me.* I'd seen him run during an attack and he was still holding back to keep pace with me.

Meaning that a full moon makes us stronger and the demon wolves weaker, Sterlyn linked as she picked up her pace too. *And when it's a new moon, and we're the weakest—*

—the demon wolves are the strongest, I finished. Even though that could prove to be problematic later, now that the moon was waxing, at least, the silver wolves had an advantage. However, the opposite held true when the moon was less than half full. Knowing the differences would give us something to consider when strategizing.

Our group ran hard as the demon wolves tried to catch up.

Killian, Griffin, and Sierra are ahead, Sterlyn said as we pushed ourselves harder. *They can't run as fast, so prepare to fight.*

We couldn't lead them to the vehicles. I had hoped we could put off fighting a little longer, but we'd have to stop them the best way we knew how.

Maybe we shouldn't have had Aurora go with Chad. Stress rolled off Cyrus. *We could use her right now.*

We didn't have much of a choice, Sterlyn replied,

scanning the area ahead. *Chad had her on his back, and Theo couldn't fight them on his own. They needed Aurora to help fight them off.*

Arguing would accomplish nothing. We needed to work on an action plan. *Ronnie bought us some time. Maybe we should split up?*

That won't work because I'm not leaving you, and they're focused mainly on you and me. Cyrus glanced at the sky as if it held answers. *Maybe a couple demon wolves would stay to fight Sterlyn and the others, but you and I can't take on thirty at once.*

Griffin's honey-blonde wolf appeared in front of us. Killian's cappuccino wolf stood on one side of him and Sierra's sandy blond and slightly smaller wolf on the other. I hated that Sierra was in this situation—like me, she hadn't been raised with intense combat training. Yet, here we were, getting thrust into one precarious situation after another.

A demon wolf howled behind us, both in warning and as a call for help. More wolves had to be running to assist them. We didn't need more demon wolves joining the fight. We were already outnumbered.

"Get ready," Alex rasped. He blurred ahead and stopped next to the three wolves staring us down.

I guessed we were drawing the line in the sand. At least, Killian and Griffin were stronger than Mila and Rudie, despite the women's training.

When they catch up, we all fight. Take out the closest and biggest threats first, Sterlyn instructed, but I could feel the concern and worry she was trying to hide.

We were in a bad situation, and I wasn't sure what else we could do.

Cyrus huffed beside me. *They're all threats.*

Then we do the best we can, Sterlyn replied as we reached the others. *Sierra is holding her own, so I don't think they've gone through extensive training like we have.*

All at once, Cyrus, Sterlyn, and I spun to face the demons head on.

The enemy wolves hadn't expected it, and they slowed to a stop, taking us in. We might not have the numbers, but we would each fight for every person here. To their disadvantage, the men of the demon pack cared only for themselves.

Ronnie and Alex surged forward. Though the demon wolves could see her, Ronnie moved quicker than them in her demon form, while Alex blurred with vampire speed.

The impending threat was enough to make the enemy wolves rush into action. Ronnie sliced her dagger into a demon wolf in front, and blood squirted from its body. The demon wolf closest to her lunged, but Ronnie floated high, and the wolf couldn't catch her.

Alex grabbed the offending wolf's head in midair and snapped its neck. It crumpled. In two seconds, they'd eliminated two of the forty demon wolves here. If we kept up that pace, maybe our odds wouldn't be as bad as we'd expected.

Let's go, Sterlyn linked as our entire group moved at the same time. We pushed ourselves to reach the wolves we'd been running from moments ago.

A demon wolf raced past Ronnie and Alex, his ebony eyes locked on me. He paused, and his eyes glowed faintly as ten other demon wolves stepped in behind him.

I'd know those heartless eyes anywhere—Nyko.

He opened his mouth, baring his teeth, and charged at me. The evilness swirling around him almost stole my breath away. I had no doubt he planned to kill me, upset that I'd killed Ken. He would have our entire group focused on fighting so he could attack me.

I pawed at the ground, antagonizing him. I wanted him to bring it and make him so irrational he couldn't think clearly.

Nyko and the ten other demon wolves raced toward us. They split up, making it obvious who would attack whom. Nyko fixed on me, while three others locked their attention on Cyrus, and another three went after Sterlyn. The final four stayed focused on Griffin, Killian, and Sierra behind us. The others attacked Ronnie and Alex, but I couldn't do a damn thing to help them.

When Nyko was within lunging distance, he leaped, his dark eyes locked on my neck, as the others attacked as well.

My wolf snarled, and I ducked, letting his body sail right over me.

He landed behind me, and I spun around and bit into his side. I thrashed my teeth, shredding the skin. His metallic blood filled my mouth, but I ignored it, inflicting as much damage as possible.

An angry snarl resonated from deep within his chest. He moved his legs, forcing me to release my hold. Vomit inched up my throat when my gaze landed on the big chunk of missing skin. That was what the prick deserved for underestimating a girl.

Nyko swiped a paw at me, and I stepped back so he missed the mark. Drool dripped from his mouth, and rage filled his dark eyes. He attempted to pounce on me again, but his legs buckled from the injury I'd inflicted.

Instinct took over, and I sank my teeth into his throat and jerked my head. His skin ripped, and blood spilled down my snout. I pulled back and dropped the fur in my mouth as he died right in front of me.

"Ronnie!" Alex screamed, and I spun around to see three wolves attacking my sister while she was distracted by another wolf.

A wolf jumped on the vampire king's back as he desperately tried to reach his wife. He no longer cared about his own safety.

I ran toward my sister, wishing I could tell Alex to pay attention to himself. The horror on his face had everything to do with my sister being in danger.

Ronnie surged upward, but not in time. A wolf bit into her shadow, and a strangled cry left her.

That was what I got for getting confident. The moment I thought we might make it out of this without injury, our luck ran out.

"Get out of the way!" Rosemary screamed, the thunder of her wings filling the air.

I wasn't sure what she was doing, but I had to help Ronnie and Alex. I watched out of the corner of my eye as Sterlyn ripped out the throat of her third enemy wolf and ran toward Ronnie, linking with me, *Help Alex. I'm stronger than you.*

There was no question there. Sterlyn was the strongest silver wolf, with Cyrus a close second. With the moon over half full, she was stronger than any demon wolf.

Pivoting toward Alex, I glanced at my mate as he killed his last attacker. Thank God both he and Sterlyn had been so well trained.

I'm going to help Sterlyn, he linked and rushed after his sister.

Alex leaned forward and flipped the wolf off his back. His shirt was ripped, and the claw marks were so deep I could see muscle through the blood pouring out of him. I ran to the demon wolf, who was rolling back onto his feet, and slashed at his neck with my claws. His eyes bulged as he drowned in his own blood.

I forced my eyes away and ran to Alex, turning so he could climb onto my back.

"No, Ronnie," he said, staggering toward his mate.

Not being able to communicate with them was super inconvenient. I jerked my head in Ronnie's direction as Sterlyn and Cyrus freed my sister from her captors. She moved a little slower but still faster than I could run as she rushed to her mate.

Alex was not in the best shape. I linked, *We have a problem.*

The remaining demon wolves attacked Sterlyn and Cyrus at once, ganging up on them to end the deaths on their side.

Pain ripped through our mate bond, and fear squeezed my heart. *Cyrus!*

Now that Ronnie and Alex were together, I charged toward Sterlyn and Cyrus, desperate to help. Griffin, Killian, and Sierra, finally done with their fights, ran toward them too.

Stay back! Cyrus linked. *You'll get hurt.*

Like hell I would. *Then we'll get hurt together.* I wasn't being rational, but I had to get to my mate and Sterlyn.

Rosemary landed in front of me, blocking me and the others from the silver wolves. "Stay here," she said.

A now-perky Lux stepped out of her arms. She lifted her hands to the large pile of wolves and repeated the chant that Aurora had said earlier, *"Ventum in misericordia mea!"*

A breeze swirled, growing stronger and stronger. Lux continued to chant and circle her hands. The wind followed her directions, churning into a tornado. She pushed it toward the large group, and the demon wolves were tossed into the air away from the others. Every time the demon wolves tried to get back to us, the wind threw them backward, until Cyrus and Sterlyn were free. Bite marks covered their bodies, but their injuries weren't serious.

Lux fisted her hands, and the magic stopped. She sagged and said, "Rosemary, recharge me."

Rosemary touched Lux's arms, her hands glowing as they had with me earlier.

I'd moved to reach Cyrus when Rosemary

commanded, "Stop. You'll make it harder. Sterlyn and Cyrus, move!"

The demon wolves attacked again, but Sterlyn and Cyrus ran toward us.

Run, Cyrus linked, his desperation bleeding through.

I couldn't. Not until he was next to me. I couldn't leave him behind again. *When you get here.*

Annie, I swear, he growled as he and Sterlyn passed Rosemary and Lux.

Lux raised her hands again, her palms facing the demon wolves, and yelled, "*Somnum nunc!*"

At first, I wasn't sure what the spell did. Then the closest demon wolves shut their eyes and dropped. Their heartbeats slowed to a restful rhythm, and I realized they were asleep.

One by one, the rest of the demon wolves followed suit. Perspiration beaded on Rosemary's forehead. She looked at us and groaned, "Go! Hurry. I'll meet you back where it all began."

Sterlyn nodded, indicating she understood, and spun toward Alex. *Let's go. They'll meet us back at the coven.* She ran in front of Alex and crouched on the ground.

You're injured—maybe Griffin, Killian, or I should carry him, I suggested, hating that she would carry the burden after being hurt.

Sterlyn shook her head. *They already run slower. I can pull strength from the moon.*

I'll do it, Cyrus linked and trotted over to her.

Her lavender eyes glowed. *You took the brunt of the attack protecting me. I'm doing this.*

Now that she'd mentioned it, I noticed that Cyrus had more bite marks than Sterlyn. That made me both proud and infuriated. I loved that he was willing to do anything for the people he loved, but it pissed me off that he'd made himself the main target of the attack. I'd have done the same thing for Ronnie, so I bit my tongue.

"I can—" Alex started, but he stumbled.

Rosemary's chest heaved as she grunted, "I can't do this all day. Get on Sterlyn. You won't make it on your own. You're losing too much blood. You know Ronnie won't leave you."

That was enough to make him crawl onto Sterlyn's back. Griffin stood next to his mate, rubbing his head against hers as the vampire king climbed aboard.

Alex settled in and grunted, "Go."

Our entire pack took off, running as fast as possible toward our vehicles.

The trees were back to being cypresses and redbuds, indicating we were getting closer to the motel. We made decent time, and I hoped Rosemary and Lux could hold them off long enough for us to get away.

The trees grew thicker, and when I heard the rustle of raccoons and flying squirrels, my body relaxed marginally. We were far enough away from the demon wolves that the animals felt safe to come out.

How much farther? Cyrus asked, limping.

He was hurt worse than he'd let on, but there wasn't anything we could do about it now.

Sterlyn replied, *About half a mile.*

Two engines purred in the distance, and I prayed it

was Theo, Mila, Rudie, Chad, and Aurora. Not long after, the motel came into view.

Theo and Chad stood in human form outside the cars. When they saw us, they ran to the vehicles and opened the doors. I hadn't considered that we wouldn't have time to shift back into human form.

Luckily, it was past one in the morning, so no humans were awake to see a pack of wolves jumping into cars.

Cyrus and Annie, Sterlyn linked to us, *I'll take Alex to his car and let Ronnie drive if she can. I'll get Killian to tell Sierra to ride with you because it'll be a tight squeeze in the Navigator.*

That sounded like a good plan to me.

Okay, Cyrus replied.

We ran, and he jumped into the back of the SUV first and slid to the far side. I slid into the middle, and Sierra jumped in after me. Theo ran over and shut the door as Ronnie materialized outside the passenger door and helped Alex off Sterlyn's back and into the car.

Alex's face was pale, which was saying something. He dropped into the seat, and his head leaned back against the headrest, as if he couldn't hold it up on his own. The others ran to the Navigator and got situated, and Ronnie climbed into the driver's side of the Mercedes SUV.

Alex's heart slowed, and Ronnie sobbed, "You better not die, Alex!" She peeled out of the parking spot. "Annie, please help."

He didn't even respond.

CHAPTER TWENTY-ONE

I WANTED TO HELP, but I was in wolf form. If I didn't do something, though, Ronnie's soulmate could die. I glanced behind us and noticed the ice chest and duffel bags. *I'm shifting.*

"The others can stay in wolf form in case they catch us, but please help me," Ronnie begged.

Cyrus growled, *Everyone will see you naked.*

I'm not asking for permission. Alex is passed out and near death, and only Ronnie and Sierra will see me anyway. His wolf didn't like the idea of others seeing me naked, but this was a dire situation. *I can't do nothing.*

You're right. Regret wafted from him.

Hopefully, since Ronnie was driving so fast, that wouldn't happen, but we needed to be prepared.

I focused internally, pushing my wolf back inside. She resisted, still sensing danger, but after a few minutes, she finally retreated.

My bones cracked as they repositioned themselves

into human form. It didn't hurt, but the sound was painful. My skin tingled as the fur pulled back, and smooth skin reappeared. Within seconds, I was back in human form.

"What can I do to help?" I asked.

Even though the car interior was dark, it didn't truly help my situation, not with everyone's supernatural sight. It might as well have been a sunny day, but I pushed my discomfort away.

"Oh, thank God." Ronnie's voice broke with a sob. "He needs blood. There's an ice chest—"

"I see it." I spun around, climbed over the back seats, and reached into the hatchback. My bare ass stuck up in the air, fuller than the moon in the night sky. I solely focused on the task of saving Alex.

Cyrus lay across the bottom of my legs, keeping me from falling into the back as I desperately reached for the ice chest. It was just an inch out of my grasp.

A hard swerve had me falling to the side, the headrest digging into my ribs. I grunted but ignored the throbbing pain. I would probably have a bruise, but Alex was hurting a whole hell of a lot more than me.

"Annie, hurry," Ronnie sobbed. "Our connection is fading."

I've got you, Cyrus vowed.

Can you give a little on my legs? I need to reach a little farther. I didn't want to be tossed around like a ball, but I had to reach the damn ice chest.

He lifted off my legs, and I pulled myself deeper into the hatchback. The car had jostled the damn ice chest right against the door. I stretched, ignoring my screaming muscles. The vehicle swerved again, and the chest slid toward me. I grabbed the handle in the nick of time. *I've got it.*

I pulled the chest into the back seat and set it on the floorboard. Hands shaking, I opened the lid and saw ten blood bags sitting on ice. "How many does he need?"

"All of them." Ronnie glanced in the rearview mirror at me. The area around her emerald eyes was pink from tears. "He needs every bit of blood we have."

That I could do. I grabbed a pouch and ripped the top corner off. "Uh, it's cold. Do I need to warm it?"

"No, but he won't be able to drink. I'd give him my blood, but vampire blood doesn't heal other vampires." Ronnie's hold on the steering wheel was so strong her knuckles had turned white. "You'll have to drip it into his mouth."

Yeah, I was going to drip cold blood into the mouth of a dying vampire while completely naked. As if my life hadn't been strange enough.

Focusing on the task at hand, I used my right arm to cradle Alex's neck while bringing the bag of blood to his lips.

His breathing was shallow, and his heart was murmuring. Shit, I needed to move fast.

I lifted the bag and rubbed my fingers along the cold liquid, hoping to warm it so it would drip better. Blood trickled into his mouth, but nothing else happened. I expected him to suck or gulp, but he didn't react.

"He's not drinking," I said, not quite hiding my hysteria. Something clawed at my chest, and my breathing quickened. I didn't want to be the reason he died, but I wasn't sure what else to do.

"It's fine," Ronnie said reassuringly. "Just keep doing it. The liquid will slide down his throat. If his mouth gets too full, rub his throat hard to force him to swallow."

Desperate, I squeezed the bag harder, filling his mouth with more liquid. I repositioned him on my arm so I could hold his head in place while rubbing his throat as instructed. No matter how hard I rubbed, I couldn't get him to swallow. The only thing keeping my sanity from breaking, and probably Ronnie's too, was that his breathing and heartbeat weren't growing fainter, but they still weren't good.

Blood trickled from the corner of his mouth, and I realized his mouth was full. I dug my fingers into his throat. Then I felt something magical.

He gulped.

I lifted the bag again, pouring more into his mouth. When I was getting ready to make him swallow again, he did it on his own.

"He's drinking!" I exclaimed.

With each squeeze, he drank more and more. Soon, he lifted a hand, snatching the bag from me. He slurped and squeezed the entire bag within seconds.

"More," he rasped.

That was easier said than done. "Okay." I loosened my grip on his head and reached down for another bag.

When I lifted it, he snatched it from me, biting the top off and draining the liquid.

Not needing him to tell me he'd need more soon, I snatched another bag out of the ice pack and held it out to him. Within seconds, he'd finished the one he had and grabbed the other.

"You scared the shit out of me," Ronnie rasped, her breathing leveling out. "I thought I'd lost you."

He glanced at her, responding through their connection.

After he'd finished the bag, he sat up a little and glanced at me. His eyes widened before he shut them and groaned, "You're naked."

Oh, shit. I'd forgotten. How was that possible?

Cyrus growled, not amused, *If you don't get dressed, I may wind up killing Alex after all.*

Yeah, there was no graceful way of getting out of this situation. "I had to shift to get your blood since you were near death, and Ronnie couldn't pull over because the demon wolves might attack again." Great, now I was rambling. Clearly, I wanted to see just how awkward I could make this situation.

"Hand me the chest. I can take it from here," Alex said, his eyes still closed and his arms extended.

Despite him talking and sitting up, he was still pale and sweaty, hinting he could take a turn for the worse. I handed him the ice chest and practically leaped into the back of the car, snagging the duffel bag that smelled like me.

Cyrus stood on the floorboard to his full height, covering my ass from Alex's view. *Be careful,* he warned.

"Can you slow down? I'd like to get dressed before

they catch up in the Navigator." We were at least five miles down the main road and hopefully out of danger enough for Ronnie to drive at a more reasonable speed. "I'd like to get dressed without flashing anyone else."

"Yeah, we should be good." Ronnie inhaled deeply and reached over the center console to take Alex's hand. "And yes, please put your clothes on. Now that Alex isn't near death, my crazy possessive side is kicking in."

Cyrus growled low in agreement.

Sierra made a loud choking sound. It worried me at first until I realized she was laughing in animal form. Great, I'd almost forgotten who was in the vehicle with us. She would never let us live this down.

I unzipped the bag and pulled out shorts and a shirt. I wouldn't worry about a bra and panties right now. I needed to cover myself. I quickly turned back around and found Cyrus, so tense he could have passed as a statue, covering me to keep me from being seen from every angle but Sierra's.

I dressed as quickly as possible with Cyrus practically on top of me, and when I was finally covered, his body sagged.

Let's never have that happen again, Cyrus linked, his relief flowing into me.

I chuckled. *Deal.* I looked at the front to find Alex almost back to normal. His color was returning, and he drained the last bag of blood from the ice chest.

"Are you still in a lot of pain?" I glanced over my shoulder into the back seat like I expected another ice chest to magically appear.

He kept his attention forward and cleared his throat uncomfortably. "I'm much better. The rest of me will heal on its own slowly, after all the blood I consumed."

Ronnie giggled, almost sounding carefree. "She's dressed."

"Thank the gods." He grunted and turned to face me. "And thank you."

I hadn't expected that. "What for?"

"If you hadn't done"—he waved his hand up and down—"what you did, I might not be alive." His cheeks turned pink, and he scratched the back of his neck.

Cyrus huffed. *Tell him not to mention it again.*

His meaning dawned on me. "You're my brother. I'd do anything to protect you, and Cyrus said to never mention that again."

"Gladly." He straightened, looking forward again. "I feel the same way about you, and I'm very proud to call you family."

That was the nicest thing Alex had ever said to me. I knew he cared about me because of Ronnie, but maybe our relationship was developing beyond that. "And if it weren't for me, you wouldn't have almost died."

"That isn't your fault." Alex leaned over the center console and kissed Ronnie's cheek. "Just like Ronnie being a demon isn't her fault. In all my three hundred years, I've learned that destiny always makes sure your fate is followed."

Sierra whined and pawed at her nose.

A second later, Sterlyn linked to Cyrus and me. *Sierra is harassing Killian to get me to tell you two that old men get off on saying shit that doesn't make any sense, and to just nod and pretend you understand.*

Sierra hated that she couldn't smart off to us in the car. At least she hadn't told Killian about what had happened.

And she wanted you to know you have tan lines from some skimpy two-piece bathing suit you like to wear. Even though Sterlyn wasn't in the vehicle with us, I could feel her laughter through the link.

I groaned and cut my eyes to the dirty-blond wolf. "You couldn't wait until we got to the coven?"

Her gray eyes lightened with amusement, and she gave me a wolf smile with her tongue hanging out.

"I'm assuming she pestered Killian until Sterlyn linked with you?" Ronnie asked.

Alex groaned. "Of course, she did. Her mouth is always running. And here I thought we'd have some peace before she transitioned back to human."

Don't encourage her, Cyrus replied. *The only reason I'm not losing my mind is because Alex was saved.*

I'm glad about that. Sterlyn's sincerity floated into us. *He's part of the pack.*

Her words made sense. I hadn't pieced it together until she'd said that. Our group was a pack, despite not all of us being wolves.

As we turned onto the road that led back to the coven, my leg bounced. We were out of danger, but we were about to face another issue—Eliza. Had this coven taken Cyrus away?

Are you okay with going to the coven?

Yes. I need answers, Cyrus linked, knowing what I meant. *If this coven took me from my parents, sister, and pack, I need to find out why.*

I understood that. I'd always wanted to know why Midnight had given me up, but the truth hadn't made things better. In some ways, it had made them worse, but I couldn't discourage him. Sometimes, only answers could give us closure.

Cyrus laid his head on my lap, and I ran my fingers through his fur. I was careful not to touch the bite marks, not wanting to hurt him. He calmed at my touch.

My eyes landed on his leg. *How bad are you hurt?*

It's already healing. He brushed off my concern. *I'm fine.*

I didn't push. We were safe. He'd have time to heal before we were in danger again.

Hopefully.

The closer we got to the coven, the more restless he became.

Even though Eliza and the coven had saved me, if they'd kidnapped Cyrus, I wasn't sure which side they were on. All this time, I would've trusted Eliza to do what was right and keep everyone safe, but now that foundation could fracture.

The vehicles stopped, and Aurora jumped out of the car and ran past the Mercedes. Just like last time, as the witch stepped over the cloaking spell boundary, the neighborhood flickered into view with the moon shining behind it. She waved us into the neighborhood. Ronnie slowed as we reached her and rolled down the window. "Do you want to jump in?"

"I need to stay here and put the spell back up. I don't want to chance the wolves finding us." Aurora motioned for us to go. "I can't do it until you're inside."

Ronnie pressed the gas, coasting through the barrier with Theo following close behind. As we drew closer to the houses, Circe, Eliza, Herne, Selene, Sybil, Kamila, Cordelia, Aspen, and Eliphas rushed from the community building.

They looked behind us, as if they expected to see the demon wolves after us. Despite helping us, they didn't trust us to keep their location hidden.

Ronnie pulled into the gravel spot next to the building, and I climbed over Cyrus to open the back door. When I got out of the car, Cyrus and Sierra bounded after me, heading toward the back. Ronnie opened the hatchback, pulled out duffel bags, and handed one to each of them. They took off into the nearby woods as Sterlyn and the others followed suit beside us.

Slowly, Alex walked around the vehicle, still not back to normal, with Theo, Mila, Rudie, and Chad following behind.

"Where are Aurora and Lux?" Circe asked, her jaw tense. "And are these your friends?"

"They're the ones we went to save, and Aurora is resetting the boundary." Circe was tense, expecting something horrible.

"And Lux?" Herne asked, her onyx eyes turning darker.

"She's—" I started, but the sound of flapping wings interrupted me. The sound wasn't strong and sturdy like normal.

We all looked up as a dark form dropped from the sky. Rosemary groaned and wrapped her wings around Lux before slamming into the ground between the community house and the woods.

Dirt and grass exploded as Rosemary's collision formed a crater in the earth.

A petrifying silence followed. For a second, we stood there in shock.

Sterlyn ran from the woods, dressed and in human form, yelling, "Rosemary! Lux!"

The rest of us sprang into action. The others ran from the woods as we charged toward our friends.

I reached them first. Rosemary's dark wings blocked her and Lux from view.

I touched one of Rosemary's wings, and something warm charged through me like it had when she'd healed me. That had to mean something. She had to be alive. "Rosemary," I murmured.

She groaned faintly, and her wings fluttered.

Sterlyn reached us and fell to her knees on the other side.

"I'm fine," Rosemary grunted. "Just tired."

"What about Lux?" Herne asked breathlessly as she reached my side.

Unwrapping her wings from her body, Rosemary revealed Lux lying against her chest. The young witch's

252 JEN L. GREY

breathing was steady, and her eyes were closed. "She used a lot of magic just like me."

Strong arms wrapped around my body and pulled me against a hard chest. I closed my eyes, enjoying the warmth of his skin. The buzzing of our connection sprang to life. Cyrus was here, supporting me in my time of need.

Killian and Griffin flanked Sterlyn, and Killian bent down to take Lux from Rosemary's arms. "Let me have her."

"Okay." Rosemary handed Lux off to him and slowly sat up.

"Are you hurt?" Griffin asked, concern etched across his face.

She stood slowly, and the moonlight hit her face, revealing dark circles under her eyes. "Once I get some rest, I'll be fine."

Killian looked at Herne. "Where do I need to take her?"

"You take care of your friend," Aspen said and held his arms out for Lux. "I'll take Lux to her room."

They didn't want us going into any of their houses.

"Okay." Killian handed Lux to him and wrapped an arm around Rosemary. "Are we staying here another night?"

"We need to get back to Shadow City, but if Rosemary needs time—" Sterlyn started.

Rosemary waved her hand. "I can sleep in the car. It's fine. We need to get out of here. Those wolves will be looking for us."

"Yes, I think it's best you all leave." Sybil crossed her arms, her face tense. "Every time the barrier comes down, we risk discovery."

"They all need rest," Circe said, looking at our party. We were all beaten and tired with Cyrus, Rosemary, and Alex having taken the brunt. "They will stay the night, and we can plan in the morning. Those wolves won't find them if we're cloaked. Eliphas, go help Aurora reset the perimeter, and your group can stay in the same house as last night."

We should stay, I linked with Cyrus and Sterlyn. *And rest for a few hours.*

You're right. Sterlyn yawned. *Just a few hours, though. Then we need to get back. Luckily, we hurt their numbers, so they won't be in a hurry to attack, but we don't need to wait for them to make their move.*

"We'll take you up on your offer," Sterlyn said and smiled. "But we will head out by nine in the morning. We don't want to put you at risk, and the wolves will be hunting you down after Lux and Aurora helped us."

"Go get some rest. We'll meet you at the community house in the morning," Circe said and moved back toward the houses.

Killian stalked off toward the house where we'd stayed, and I realized a few of us might be sleeping on the floor, but at least, we were safe.

Our group followed Killian, but Cyrus took my hand, halting me. His eyes glowed, and angst filled him. *I'll be a minute. I need to talk to Eliza and Circe. The longer I'm around her, knowing they could have been involved, the more obsessed I become. I...I can't sleep until I get answers, now they're so close.*

I'll stay with you. I didn't want him to do this alone.

He smiled tenderly at me. *I don't want to make you uncomfortable. She raised you.*

I'm here for you. You mean the world to me, and I want to hear what she has to say, too. I wanted to make sure I knew the woman who had raised me.

"Eliza. Circe," I called out. "Can we talk to you?"

The women stopped in their tracks, their bodies tensing.

They knew what this was about.

CHAPTER TWENTY-TWO

MY HEART POUNDED in my ears, and I had to remind myself that even if they knew who had orchestrated Cyrus's kidnaping, it didn't mean they were responsible. But the tightness in my chest wouldn't let up.

What's going on? Sterlyn linked, pausing several steps away.

Cyrus cleared his throat. *We're going to ask Eliza and Circe about the spell that made it look like I'd died as an infant. Since they know the same spell, maybe they can shed some light on who's at fault.*

I loved him so much for giving Eliza the benefit of the doubt. He could have accused her out of anger, but he was keeping a level head.

After a second, Sterlyn responded, *I'll stay with you. If they know something, I want to hear it, too. You weren't the only one affected.*

Because of the same person or coven, Sterlyn and

Cyrus didn't get to grow up together, and their parents never learned the truth before they were brutally slaughtered. They'd both been robbed of time they could never recover, and Cyrus had gotten the worst end of the deal.

He'd been kidnapped and given to someone who'd thought he was the rightful silver wolf alpha. Sterlyn had been born first, though, and the alpha power had been gifted to her. That was what sexist assholes got for assuming a female couldn't lead.

You're right, Cyrus sighed. *Sometimes, I forget you're a victim, too.*

"Do you two have a moment to speak to us?" Sterlyn asked with an edge. "We have a few questions we hope you can answer."

"Well, it's late—" Eliza began.

"This is important," I cut in.

The others in our group paused.

Cradling Rosemary against his chest, Killian said, "Let's go. They can fill us in later."

Ronnie tilted her head, squinting at me.

She wanted to know what was going on.

I mouthed, *I'll tell you later. Just give us a minute,* knowing Cyrus wouldn't want an audience. These questions were personal and asking them would make him relive a dark past that had left him scarred and broken.

"But—" Sierra pouted, glancing at us.

When Ronnie set her jaw, my stomach dropped. She was going to argue about leaving.

"Come on," Ronnie said, looping her arm through Sierra's. "I need your help getting the old man settled."

"Really?" Alex rolled his eyes, though the corners of his mouth tipped upward at his mate. "She already gives me a hard enough time about my age without you egging her on."

"Hey, you look good for your age." Sierra's eyes sparkled, her attention diverted to ragging on Alex. They had a strange relationship. She purposely liked to give him hell, and he tolerated it for Ronnie. And Sierra took full advantage of his tolerance. "You're three centuries old. You could be her great, great, great"—every time she said *great*, she held up another finger—"great grandfather's age. Wait, was that enough greats?"

Rudie snorted, her face smooth instead of lined with terror or worry. I hadn't seen her look like that ever, even back at the silver wolf pack, likely because Theo and Mila were constantly upset over something Cyrus had done.

"Not funny." Alex glared and moved slowly toward the house where we'd stayed a few nights ago.

"He moves like an old man now." Sierra chuckled and bumped into Ronnie's shoulder. "Have fun with that tonight. Don't take his hip out with your young, bendable ways."

Aurora laughed, and Circe and Eliza turned their heads in the young girl's direction. She mashed her lips together as Circe gestured to the houses. "All of you can go, too. Mom and I can talk to the wolves alone."

"Are you sure that's wise?" Herne crossed her arms and arched a brow.

Circe lifted her chin. "You need to check on Lux."

The witches obeyed, though Sybil stayed back, even after the other witches had obeyed their priestess.

"Go," Eliza bit out. "You heard what Circe said."

Sybil tensed, but she spun around and followed the others.

Sterlyn came and stood beside Cyrus with Griffin at the other end of our small line. We were standing tall next to one another, ready to face their answers as one.

With the two witches standing side by side, it was easy to see the family resemblance. They had the same high cheekbones and sharp nose.

"Do we want to go into the community building?" Circe asked, pulling her shoulders back.

Cyrus did one sharp headshake. "Out here is fine." *I don't want to chance anyone interrupting us or feel trapped. I need you and the moon.*

Always. Those were two things he'd never have to risk giving up.

"What is it, then?" Eliza said gruffly and rubbed her hands together. She liked getting straight to the point, no matter the discussion.

I waited for Cyrus to say something, but he remained quiet as fear penetrated our bond.

My heart broke for him. Sometimes, getting answers was scarier than never knowing them. "Midnight—my birth mother—told me something that sounded oddly familiar."

Eliza's brows furrowed. "How so?"

Circe's breath caught, and her face paled. "Maybe we should talk about this tomorrow before you leave."

My blood ran cold. She was nervous.

"I want to hear this." Eliza dropped her hands and stepped toward us. "What did she say? If they're on to the coven, we need to know now."

"They are on to the coven, but they couldn't find you. Whatever cloaking spells you have in place work. It's about how I was taken." I couldn't force myself to come right out with the words. A chill ran down my spine, and I inched closer to Cyrus, needing his touch.

Eliza's shoulders dropped, and she inhaled deeply. "Thank goddess. I'd hate for the coven to be at risk again after everything we gave up. What is it?"

Hope surged through me, lifting the weight on my chest. Eliza was clueless. "The way Cyrus and I were taken from our parents was very similar. We were afraid—"

"What?" Eliza exclaimed and spun around to face her daughter. "You performed that spell *again*? After all we went through?"

Circe dropped her head and closed her eyes. "I didn't have a choice."

Acid churned in my stomach, and the shock blazing into me from Cyrus made my eyes water. It would soon turn to rage.

Justified.

"Like *hell*, you didn't have a choice," Eliza rasped, her irises darkening to hunter green. "I gave up *everything*—"

"You stole my brother?" Sterlyn gasped and clutched Griffin's hand. "You're the witch who attended our birth?"

All the anger left Eliza as she pressed a hand to her stomach. "Yes, I am."

Cyrus's shock swirled into pain and fury. "Why?" He held his voice steady, but it wouldn't take much for him to explode.

"The reason doesn't matter." Her chin quivered. "It doesn't change anything."

"It does *too*," Circe cried. "Don't stand there and pretend you were a willing participant! You weren't. You did what you had to do to save our family."

"What do you mean?" Griffin asked, his eyes duller than the warm hazel I was used to. His face was stern, the veins in his neck visible. He was feeling Sterlyn's emotions just like I felt Cyrus's. When someone hurts your mate, they hurt you equally.

"Wolf shifters snuck into our coven one night and stole Aurora from her crib." Circe clutched her chest as she relived that horrible night. "We had the cloaking spell up, but somehow, it came down. They left a note with a number to call."

Griffin's jaw twitched. "What were their names?"

"They didn't give us any." Eliza lifted her head and stared at the sky. "But they said if we wanted Aurora back alive, there was something we had to do."

Sterlyn ran her fingers through her hair, her skin glistening under the moon with her movement. Her bite marks were already healed, proving how strong the silver wolf's magic was. "But how would they know Mom was pregnant?"

"Because our coven always attends the alpha heir's

birth." Eliza pushed her fisted hands against her thighs. "When the Nightshadow Sisters used the death of Ophaniel and the birth of the silver wolves to take our place in Shadow City, we were cast out and told to never come back again. Little did we know, the silver wolves would soon follow us outside. The silver wolf alpha found our descendants because our magic stems from the same power—the moon."

"Nightshadow Sisters? What the hell is that?" Every time I thought I was up to speed on the supernatural front, something like this was thrown my way. I hated feeling like an outsider.

"The coven that lives inside the Shadow City walls," Eliza said venomously. "Their magic stems from the shadows."

Everything came back to shadows and the moon. That couldn't be a damn coincidence.

Griffin tugged at an ear. "I never knew Erin had a name for their coven, and I've lived in Shadow City all my life."

"That's because a coven's name is sacred, and anyone who knows it is a threat." Eliza waved a hand dismissively. "The point is these wolf shifters found out about us and had a witch help them take down the spell."

Circe's head jerked upward, and she gasped, "What? You never told me that."

Eliza sneered, "I investigated after I split from the coven to figure out where the boy had been taken. I found out some things, but wanted to keep you out of it for your own protection. I called off my investigation when you called me about Annie."

Eliza was dropping so much information that I couldn't breathe. "You helped them kidnap Cyrus to get Aurora back?"

"I gave up another innocent child to save my granddaughter." Eliza's voice cracked, and her shoulders shook. "It wasn't right, but I couldn't let Aurora die. I did the unforgivable."

Cyrus's emotions swirled between us. They were conflicted; he didn't know how to feel. Only one sentiment was constant.

Unworthy.

Replaceable.

Undeserving.

I refused to let him see himself this way. He had to see that her actions had been wrong. "You didn't consider asking for the silver wolves' help? To share your burden so neither one of you had to lose someone you loved?"

"They had Aurora, Annie." Eliza's breath hitched. "I didn't want to risk her life."

"You risked his instead?" I couldn't get over it. The person I'd thought was moral and always did the right thing had been a coward. "He was just an infant, too!"

"Do you think I haven't lived with that regret?" Eliza snapped, her chest heaving. "That I don't think about that poor baby boy and those parents who thought they lost a child every day? I couldn't even stand to be with my coven after that, because I realized I should've made a different decision."

Circe barked a laugh and backed away from her mother with a shudder. "You *would* have risked Aurora?"

"Of course not." Eliza threw her hands up in surrender. "But like Annie said, I should've talked to the silver wolf alpha, Arian, and told him what was going on. Instead, I not only violated his trust, but I also broke my oath to always do what was best for mankind. I harmed a family and pack. I can't come back from that."

I don't know how to feel, Cyrus linked with me and leaned into my side.

Blinking rapidly, Sterlyn tugged at the roots of her hair. "You should've known better. I understand you were scared, but you were their priestess. Their leader. You let emotion overrule everything."

"Why do you think I stepped down?" Eliza averted her gaze. "I couldn't lead any longer, and I made Circe promise to never use that spell again."

"Don't you *dare*." Circe pointed at her mother. "You don't get to step down and then criticize me. This was about balance, and I don't regret my decision."

Now we were all pointing fingers and making the situation worse.

"You're right." Eliza stared at her feet. "All I can say is I'm sorry. I've regretted my decision and thought about your family every day. I tried to find you to check on you, Cyrus, but you'd disappeared. When you and Sterlyn became involved in Annie's and Ronnie's lives, I couldn't believe it, couldn't even look at you without feeling my soul being ripped to shreds."

"You think guilt makes things better for me?" Cyrus

said measuredly, but his voice shook. "That your regret erases the years of abuse I received?"

"Not at all," Eliza murmured.

Rage was taking hold of Cyrus, controlling him. "I didn't grow up with my twin sister. I never met my parents. Because of you, I trained the very men who slaughtered my pack. Damn it, I've only been able to connect to my wolf and shift for the past five months, and I struggled until Annie and I mated."

Eliza said nothing, taking his wrath.

"This coven blocked Annie's magic, concealing my fated mate." Cyrus's face turned red. "Did you want to take *everything* away from me?"

"That's enough." Circe moved in front of her mother, shielding her. "She left us—our entire coven—because she couldn't move past what she'd done to you. She abandoned us, and yeah, you're right. It doesn't change the fact you had a shit life. I get it. But tell me you've never made a mistake, one you wish you could undo."

"Every mistake I've made was a result of the shitshow she handed me." Cyrus's body shook. "So, please, tell me how I'm not supposed to blame *her*—no, wait—all of *you* for everything?"

This was a no-win situation, and I wasn't sure how I felt. On one hand, my heart hurt for Cyrus. He never should've been made to endure such a horrible upbringing, one where the basic joys any child should have the right to had been stripped from him. It was the same for the women in the demon wolf pack and for the kids in the group home where I'd worked. On the other, Eliza had made a terrible decision to protect her family—something we could all be guilty of—but she'd also saved me.

"We should separate and sort through how we feel before we say things we'll regret," Griffin said, his gaze on Sterlyn's face. "There are a lot of emotions coming out. We're all tied together, and we can't undo the past."

Sterlyn's eyes glowed faintly. "You're right." She glanced at her brother. "Are you okay with—"

"I need a walk." Cyrus pulled away from me and turned toward the trees.

"Don't go more than a mile out," Circe called out to him. "Otherwise, you'll break the spell."

Without responding, he marched toward the trees.

My eyes burned with unshed tears. "I'm going with him," I told the others.

Sterlyn nodded. "Keep him safe."

She thought he might do something stupid, too. I was jogging to catch up to him when he linked, *Stay with the others.*

My blood boiled.

He didn't get to push me away. I picked up my pace, ready to fight if that was what he needed.

CHAPTER TWENTY-THREE

THERE'S no way in hell I'm leaving you alone out here, I linked and let him feel my determination.

He walked faster to the trees as a sadness filtered through our bond. Then it faded like he was attempting to hide it from me.

Who the hell did he think he was? We were mated—that meant we had no secrets. At least, not secrets like this. If he was hurting, I was the person he should rely on.

I heard the footsteps of the others head back to the house. They didn't speak. Hell, we'd said everything there was to say. Like Griffin had said, the best thing we could do was go back, lick our wounds, and process everything we'd learned.

Just as Cyrus hit the tree line, I caught up to him. Luckily, he wasn't trying to outrun me because he could if he wanted to. The magic from the growing moon would make him faster than me.

Talk to me, I linked and touched his arm. I didn't like

having distance between us. It felt as if I were standing on the shore, watching him float down the river on a branch, trying to tread water. Every time I reached out to help him, he went under.

Squirrels scurried around us, oblivious to our presence, like we were part of nature and posed no threat to them. When I'd been human—er, spelled—animals would never get close to me. Another change that had happened since I'd embraced my true self.

I walked behind him, waiting—no—hoping he would turn around and open up to me like I'd asked, but he never did. The only sound was our breathing and the forest animals we passed.

After a quarter mile, I couldn't take the silence any longer. I grabbed his arm, and borrowing power from my wolf, I jerked him toward me. He stumbled as he turned, surprised.

When I saw his face, the world crumbled around me.

His eyes were red, and a tear trickled down his cheek. A prominent line formed between his eyebrows as his face twisted.

My heart broke, and I moved to hug him.

Don't, please. Cyrus rubbed his eyes.

His words stung, but I pushed away my own emotions. This needed to be about him, not me. *Why?* Such a simple question, but the answer could destroy me.

I'll break down. Cyrus inhaled shakily. *I'm trying to keep it together and see things for how they are.*

You don't have to keep anything together for me. I cupped his face and lifted his head, so he had to look me in the eye. *I'm your partner. Your mate. I want you all the time, even through the hard stuff.*

Even if I'm broken? His irises lightened to pale silver, and his bottom lip quivered.

Don't you realize we're broken together? I stepped into him, our chests touching. Well, my chest to his belly if we were being technical. *Within the first few days of our births, we had the same spell placed on us. We grew up not knowing our parents and with a feeling of not belonging in the world. Doesn't that prove we're each other's perfect other half?*

You aren't broken, he linked, placing his forehead against mine. *You're beautiful, strong, caring, and want to help any struggling person you come across.*

Then you aren't broken either. I kissed his lips softly. *You're loyal, sexy as hell, care more than anyone I know, and hold yourself accountable to a fault.*

I'm none of those things. Another tear slipped out of the corner of his eye and trailed down his nose. *I'm the man who was raised alone and trained the very people who murdered my parents and the pack I should've grown up in. And now I learned that if I hadn't been taken, Aurora would've been raised like that, if not killed. So I feel guilty about wishing my future hadn't been taken away.*

I brushed his tears away as my throat dried. *See what I mean about caring too much? You have every right to be upset about the childhood you lost. Neither you nor Aurora should've been put in that position. Besides, you can't blame yourself for what happened to your parents and pack. You didn't know what your captors had planned, and you were doing everything you could to survive.*

Even though that's true, I still helped them. They tried to capture Sterlyn. Hell, we still don't know the identity of the alpha willing to breed with her. He's still out there, and I haven't done a damn thing to find him. He stepped back, his body sagging. *Everyone I love gets hurt, and I can't protect them. If something ever happened to you—*

Oh, hell no. You don't get to pull away. You don't get to back out now. I gestured to my neck and fisted his shirt, pulling him back toward me. *You claimed me, and I claimed your irritating ass. We are* forever. *And who did I just have to save because my biological father captured him? Huh? If one of us puts the other more at risk, it's me.*

The corners of his lips tipped upward. *You did save me.*

My heart squeezed, and I focused on my anger instead of his sexy, stupid lips. *I did. So stop being stupid.*

I'm not trying to hurt you. He ran his fingers through my hair and wrapped an arm around me. *It's just...when I feel happy, things seem to fall apart again.*

You're not happy now? I arched a brow and placed a hand on his chest. The warmth of his skin and his thrumming heart had my body relaxing. Whenever I was near him, he kept the nightmares away.

He sniffed. *I wasn't until a minute ago when my stubborn ass mate put me in my place.*

You can thank the group home. Working there taught me the wise ways of telling it how it is. Those kids don't appreciate sugarcoating or bullying. They realize quickly that the people who are honest with you care about you the most. I stared into his eyes as my heart grew so large that it hurt with everything I felt for him. *And I most definitely care about you.* I winked. *Just a little.*

He chuckled and pulled me into his chest. *I don't know what I'd do without you.*

You won't be finding out anytime soon. I closed my eyes, focusing on his breathing and the rise and fall of his chest. *And seriously, be upset with Eliza. I am. What she did wasn't right, even if she didn't have bad intentions.*

Placing his chin on my head, he exhaled. *I don't want to come between Eliza and you. She kept you safe and raised you.*

So? That doesn't erase what happened to you. I will always be grateful for her, but most importantly, I will always be on your side. I opened our bond so he could feel the sincerity of my declaration. Yes, I needed Eliza, Ronnie, and the others, but I couldn't live without *him*. He was the most important person in my life, and I'd fight heaven and hell to be with him, which, scarily enough, might just happen. But I'd face whatever came as long as I remained next to him. *I love you, yet that doesn't convey exactly what I feel for you.*

He tilted my head up and kissed me. His lips were soft and warm, and when he slipped his tongue inside my mouth, his signature cinnamon taste exploded across mine. *I don't deserve you.*

Yes, you do. He had to stop thinking of himself as unworthy and that he had to prove his value to me, Sterlyn, and the rest of the world. He wasn't perfect—none of us were—but he was my *perfect. You complete me.*

And you make me feel alive after feeling dead inside for so long, he replied and deepened our kiss.

The scent of his arousal filled my nose, increasing the warmth charging through me.

We'd gone days without each other, and my chest tightened at the thought of not connecting with him. My hand slipped between his legs, and I found him hard. He groaned as my hand brushed against him, and his hand slid down my side.

We should go back, he linked, but his fingers were already digging into my hip.

I pushed him against a redbud tree, and a few branches rattled, raining leaves down around us. *I need you, and we'd have to be quiet in the house.* My fingers brushed his arms, and I felt the scab of one of the many bites he'd endured. *Unless you don't feel like it. You were hurt.*

Oh, I most definitely feel like it. His hand slid under my shirt and cupped my bare breast. I hadn't put on a bra or underwear in the car. *Besides, they're just scabs and no longer hurt.* His finger kneaded my nipple, and my body flamed with need.

He moved his mouth to my neck and sucked. The pressure and suction while he massaged my nipples had me ready for him.

My hands urgently unfastened his jeans, and I pushed them and his underwear down. *Thank God you're back in your normal clothes.*

Yeah, I didn't like wearing someone else's things. With steady hands, he removed my shorts.

I kicked them from my feet as he slid both hands between my legs. My head fell back, and he rubbed in a circle, teasing me. Refusing to be outmaneuvered, I stroked him as he kissed his way down my chest and captured a nipple in his mouth.

His hands worked magic on my body as he sucked, nipped, and rubbed. The tension in my body escalated, and I quickened my pace on him. He groaned, and with my free hand, I pulled his hair gently, and his noises became more guttural.

I stepped away from him, and he ogled me like I was his favorite dessert. He rasped, "Get back here."

If my need for him hadn't been overpowering, I'd have teased him some more, but my wolf howled, needing the fated-mate connection. I climbed him and straddled his body. He slid inside me easily as he leaned his back against the tree.

You're going to get splinters. I panted, slightly concerned, but my body wouldn't stop riding him.

He thrust inside me, his silver eyes glowing. *I don't give a fuck.*

As he filled me over and over, I wrapped my arms around him and kissed him. I couldn't get enough of him inside me, his taste, his smell. He was all around me, and I wanted to get lost in the moment.

We opened ourselves to each other, and my pleasure intensified. I could feel his desire and need building. The growing friction between us strengthened as time stopped. For one small moment, things were perfect.

The way they were meant to be.

Just him and me.

An orgasm ripped through me with his following right after. The combined sensations made my head grow dizzy as our bodies convulsed together.

After the high had left, we stood there, silent and unmoving, enjoying the last few moments of our time alone together.

With perfect timing, Sterlyn linked with us, *Are you two okay? It's been thirty minutes, and we're getting worried.*

We're fine, Cyrus replied and pushed a strand of hair behind my ear. *We're on our way back.*

Okay, good. Sterlyn's tiredness trickled through. *We saved you the bed Annie slept in.*

Thank you. I didn't want this moment between Cyrus and me to end, but we needed our rest. We had to get back to the other silver wolves tomorrow and form a plan. Tate and the others would attack again, and we couldn't leave our pack unprotected.

I moved to step back, and Cyrus anchored me in place. He grunted. *Let's just stay here.*

We can't. But, God, I wanted to. Everything inside me screamed to stay here with him, in this moment. For a second, we felt separate from the rest of the world. Though Sterlyn had forced reality to trickle back in. *They're already worried.*

Fine. He booped my nose and winked. *But only because I kinda love you.*

I kinda love you, too. My chest felt full to bursting. I climbed off him, begrudgingly, and we got dressed.

He intertwined his fingers with mine as we walked leisurely back to the houses.

Cyrus glanced at me. *Do you think Mila and the others will ever forgive me?*

That was a hard question to answer, and I didn't want to say something I wasn't completely certain of. *After all this, if she still doesn't wake up, then it's better if that group doesn't hang around.*

She has a right to hate me. Cyrus huffed and cast his eyes downward. *I did train those men.*

Had you known what would happen, you never would've trained them. He had to stop with all the guilt. It was tearing him up inside. *The real person you need to seek forgiveness from is yourself.*

He paused, and his forehead creased. *What do you mean?*

You beat yourself up more than anybody over what happened. The past can't change, and you made what you thought was the best decision at the time. You must believe that and hold on to that knowledge. I kept trying to break through to him and smacking into a brick wall. *How can you expect others to forgive you when you can't forgive yourself?*

I hadn't thought of it like that. Pursing his lips, he tugged me forward again. *But you're right.*

You can only do the best you can each day and be kind

to yourself. I moved closer to him, hoping he would finally listen. *Besides, you're my mate, which means you have to be a badass.*

A huge grin spread across his face, and he stared into my eyes. *You may have a point there.*

We walked through the clearing and, within minutes, entered the house. Mila, Theo, Rudie, and Chad had taken the floor while Killian snored next to the couch Rosemary slept on. He was worried about the angel, but I had a feeling she would be just fine.

We crept up the stairway and into our room. Once Cyrus and I had gotten settled, a faint tapping sounded on our door.

Cyrus tensed, but the smell of sugar cookies informed me who it was. *It's Ronnie.* I had a feeling I knew what she was coming to see us about. "Come in."

The door opened to reveal my sister's hunter green irises. "Hey. I'm sorry to bother you, but I wanted to check on you. Sterlyn told us ..." She trailed off, her gaze settling on Cyrus. "I can't believe it. I'm sorry."

"We're fine." I didn't want to talk about it, but my heart tugged that she'd made a point to check on us, despite her mate still recovering. "Thanks for asking. Can we talk about it tomorrow?"

"Yeah, sure." She turned to leave but paused and looked at Cyrus. "There's no one better for my sister. I want you to know that."

He jerked his head back and scratched the top of his head. "I'm the lucky one."

"We both are," I murmured.

"Well, good night." Ronnie smiled sadly and shut the door behind her.

Cyrus radiated happiness. Ronnie had no clue how much her words had impacted him. He'd needed to hear that affirmation from someone other than me tonight.

The two of us cuddled until we fell into a peaceful slumber.

A KNOCK at the door startled me. I opened my eyes and found Cyrus already wide awake.

Sierra asked, "Hey, are you two up? I doubt it, since it doesn't reek of sex outside your door like Sterlyn and Griffin's room did."

"Shut up!" Griffin shouted from their room. "We were up and packing when you came down here."

"Obviously, not for long. The stench of sex was still thick!" Sierra hollered back, over the moon that she had an audience. "You should be like these two and Alex and Ronnie when around others. Celibate."

If she only knew what we did last night in the woods, Cyrus linked and nuzzled my neck.

My body warmed, and I gasped in need.

"Okay, I'm coming in," Sierra warned as the door opened. "I can smell what's brewing in here, and we need to leave."

I glared at Cyrus. "You didn't lock the door?"

He shrugged. "There's no lock on it."

Figured. Damn witches.

"Get your asses up." Sierra stepped to my side and yanked me out of the bed. I tumbled onto the floor in a heap. "I want to go home. I want my own bed. Well, I want the bed in Griffin and Sterlyn's guest room."

That was enough to get me moving. We needed to go back and figure out what to do about the silver wolf pack. The demon wolves knew where we lived, and Cyrus had called Darrell last night to give him a heads-up about what had happened. "All right, we're getting up. We're already packed, so we can walk right out the door."

Cyrus stood and scowled. "If you pull her onto the floor again and she gets hurt, I will take revenge."

"Is that a dare?" She let me go and propped her hands on her hips.

I wouldn't be part of this standoff. I got to my feet and chuckled. "I'm out of bed, so there is no risk."

"Where there's a will, there's a way." Sierra waggled her brows at me.

"I fully understand why Alex looks at you the way he does sometimes." Cyrus rolled his eyes.

"Thank you," Alex called from down the hall. "She's not as endearing as she likes to believe."

"I'm loveable, damn it." Sierra pointed at me. "Tell them."

If I hadn't known any better, I wouldn't have thought there was a psycho demon wolf pack after us. "I'll save my energy to load the car."

Sierra's jaw dropped. "Traitorous hussy."

A low growl emanated from Cyrus's chest. "Watch it."

Before these two could break out in a battle of wills, I moved past Sierra and reached for the bag.

"I got it." Cyrus caught my hand and pecked my cheek. "I'll let you stay here with the little she-devil." He placed the strap over his shoulder and headed toward the stairs.

"Oh, you won't get too long of a reprieve. We have a two-hour car ride to enjoy ourselves!" Sierra beamed, then snapped, "You get to sit in the middle because he's your mate, and he won't risk slapping me and getting you caught in the crossfire."

"You're incorrigible." Even though I secretly loved it, I'd never admit it to her. I gave her a small hug and headed down the stairs.

Downstairs, the wolves who had broken away from the silver pack were standing awkwardly in the middle of the room. They all looked rested and must have bathed before going to bed last night.

Rosemary stood at the window, staring outside, her body tense.

I exhaled, and something inside me loosened. Rosemary was standing on her own. Her skin was back to its healthy fair complexion, and anyone who hadn't been there last night would guess she'd been exhausted a few hours ago.

She glanced over her shoulder and frowned. "Sterlyn told us about the conversation last night. Killian's outside, but you need to be there."

I followed her gaze, and my stomach tightened. Eliza was standing in front of Cyrus with her hands raised.

CHAPTER TWENTY-FOUR

WHY DIDN'T you tell me she was out there with you? I linked and charged out the front door, heading to stand beside my mate at the trunk of the Mercedes SUV. My body ran cold as I feared what Eliza might be saying to him.

Killian stood next to Cyrus, his hands in his pockets, looking off to the side.

I didn't need to be able to link with him to know he felt awkward as hell.

Everything is okay, Cyrus assured me, and when I reached his side, he took my hand. *She just got here.*

I glared at Eliza, angry she hadn't given him the space and time he still desperately wanted. I understood she felt bad and that the guilt had been eating at her, but that didn't mean she had to rush Cyrus.

He had a right to be angry and grieve.

"What's going on?" I inhaled deeply to ease the tightness in my chest, but frustration bled into my tone.

Circe came out of the house next door and stood on the porch. Her lips mashed into a line as she watched the confrontation.

"Annie," Eliza groaned. Dark circles were prominent under her eyes, and her cotton shirt was wrinkled like she'd slept in it and tossed and turned all night. Even her messy bun was...well, messier. The tangles she hadn't brushed out put her look over the top. She tugged on the waistband of her khaki slacks and grimaced. "I didn't come here to talk about"—she lifted her head skyward, searching for answers—"what you all asked about last night. Don't get me wrong, I want to, but I came out here to discuss how to help you get everyone back to the silver wolf neighborhood."

My entire body sagged. I hadn't considered that. We had thirteen people in two vehicles that ideally fit twelve.

The front door to the house we were staying in opened, and Rosemary, Sterlyn, and Ronnie headed outside. They must have overheard the conversation because Rosemary waved a hand and said, "I can fly."

"Are you sure?" Killian asked, his irises turning dark chocolate. "You were exhausted last night."

"I'm fully recharged." Rosemary's wings exploded from her back. "And flying is like walking. It doesn't require magic."

Ronnie crossed her arms, scowling at Eliza, saying more than words ever could. Sterlyn placed a hand on my sister's arm, knowing what she was feeling, since she'd told Ronnie about everything last night.

Out of the two of us, Ronnie hated to upset Eliza the

most, like she had a crazy need to please her. She'd been raised in a group home until her fourteenth birthday, when she'd thought a shadow was trying to attack her. It had been her demon side trying to manifest, but she hadn't known that. Eliza had taken her in the next day. I hadn't known anything about the shadow—Ronnie had never said anything when she'd come to live with us—but I'd slowly wiggled my way into her heart. Soon after that, we'd become family. For the first time, the shadows had stopped haunting Ronnie, and she'd felt safe with us. We'd learned that was because Eliza had spelled her to suppress her demon side.

"Are you serious?" Circe huffed, her face twisted in pain. "You're leaving us again when those demon wolves are hunting us, too?" She stomped off her porch and stepped into the midmorning sun.

Her appearance wasn't much better than Eliza's. Though she didn't have dark circles, her eyes were red and swollen as if she'd been crying. There was no telling what they'd said to each other after we'd left them last night, but Eliza had been clear: She shouldn't have given up Cyrus for Aurora, and that hadn't sat well with Circe.

"Don't you realize that all I do is cause pain?" Eliza's face hardened. "I'm better off on my own, like I tried to be nineteen years ago."

My chest felt like it had been ripped wide open. "But I messed that up?" Even when I'd been angry at her before, I'd never felt hurt. This was different. She was blaming me for things getting worse again. "Why'd you take me in the first place, then?"

"That's not what I meant." Eliza rubbed her temples. "You didn't mess anything up but look at you. I couldn't keep you safe, like I couldn't keep my granddaughter safe or the silver wolf I sacrificed to get her back."

Sympathy surged inside me, but it wasn't from me. The blood-boiling anger was mine, rising to levels that would make me implode. This was from Cyrus. *You feel bad for her?* I asked. The conflicting emotions distracted me from the rage coursing inside.

I know what that feels like. Cyrus tightened his hold on me. *If something happened to you or Sterlyn, I would sacrifice someone to save you without a second thought. You two are the most important people in my entire world, and I know what it feels like to know that everything bad that has happened is because of a decision I made.*

This was insane. I was more upset with Eliza about her decision than he was. I didn't have a shitty life because of her, but I resented what she'd done to him. *You were a child trying to survive. You didn't know any better. You had no other choices. It's not the same thing.*

Do you think she felt like she had a choice? Cyrus pulled me against him. *Because, in that moment, she didn't.*

Damn him and his maturity. That was fine. I could be angry for the both of us.

"I can't believe you're choosing to leave us again." Circe fisted her hands. "We need you. You know magic better than me, and you're the strongest witch among us."

"You should stay," Sterlyn said sternly. "Rosemary

says she's fine flying home. We can manage two full vehicles for a two-hour drive."

Eliza scoffed and shook her head. "I can't do that. I need to go back and help cloak where you live."

"You'll go to Shadow City with *them* to help, but you won't stay with your own family and coven?" Circe's eyes glistened. "Why? We need you too."

"Because me staying here isn't good for anyone. I'm not a leader that can be respected. I broke my oath." Eliza took her daughter's hand. "I don't want to leave, but it's the right thing to do."

She was punishing herself, but she didn't realize she was hurting her coven too and, most importantly, her family.

Alex and Griffin joined us outside, their faces tense as they glanced at everyone.

"Unless you're staying indefinitely, we can't cloak the pack homes," Cyrus said. "We still have to run and get supplies weekly for necessities. Even if we didn't leave, someone would have to bring them to us. Either way, the barrier would come down. Maybe you should stay here and help your daughter and coven."

Sterlyn leaned against the side of the trunk. "The best thing we can do is move the silver wolf pack to Shadow Ridge, into the pack neighborhood where we live."

"But we'll be exposed." Cyrus's forehead lined. "I thought we wanted to stay hidden."

I snorted, letting the irony of his words take hold.

"That didn't do much good. I brought a new enemy straight to your door."

"You didn't know what you were," Cyrus said roughly. "You don't get to blame yourself for that. It doesn't matter. Fate determined we would be together."

"Which proves Sterlyn's point." Killian steepled his fingers. "What's the point in hiding when you're going to be found anyway? We have several vacant homes in the back section of the neighborhood. A few people may need to share a house, but it's not like there are a ton of you."

Ronnie nibbled her lip. "What about the council? They didn't want Annie there, and they still aren't happy about Sterlyn."

"She's right, though," Griffin said, agreeing with his mate, "about how things are going. The time will never be perfect. Maybe having more silver wolves in the community will ease the tension among the races, since their ancestors trusted you to be the council representatives for our race."

Alex frowned. "Are you thinking they'll want to replace you as council representative?"

"No. The city doesn't like change, and my family has been on the council since it was formed. All the representatives are from the founding members, but I think if the silver wolves protect the city again, it will create goodwill among the shifter race."

"Like they came back to protect and not just to lead." Sterlyn nodded. "It could work. A silver wolf is on the council, and having the pack come might strengthen my standing."

"Or tear it apart." Rosemary sighed. "Azbogah and Erin will use the situation to turn the council members against you."

"Maybe, but that's a risk we'll have to take. The entire silver wolf pack can't be cloaked, and the demon wolves know where to find them." Sterlyn lifted a hand. "We have to do what's in everyone's best interest."

I hated that we were in this situation because of me. Acid swirled uncomfortably in my stomach, and though it gurgled, the thought of food made me want to vomit. "I'm sorry."

"If the demon wolves attack Shadow Ridge, you'll essentially be signing over the council to new leaders," Alex interjected. "Of course, I'll back you, but that would give Azbogah the leverage to move against you successfully."

"Then what do you propose?" Killian shrugged. "What's the right answer?"

"Taking Annie there will only cause more problems." Eliza straightened her shoulders. "What if she came back to Lexington with me?"

"Not a chance in hell that's happening, unless you're willing to let the rest of the silver pack live with you, too," Cyrus said sternly. "I can't abandon them when things are difficult." His eyes flicked to the building where Mila and the others waited. They were at the windows, watching everything.

"And what if we're attacked?" We had to make the

best decision possible. "We wouldn't have the coven, Sterlyn, Ronnie, or any backup close by."

"I wish I could offer you refuge, but we can't support that many extra people for long." Circe rubbed her hands along her arms. "It's hard enough to make do with the people we have living here permanently, and that's one reason I wish Mom would stay."

Eliza tilted her head as she examined her daughter.

"Our best bet is to integrate back into Shadow Ridge society, but instead of descending on the town, what if we move back to the old pack land?" Cyrus turned to Sterlyn. "You own the land, and it's not being used. The silver wolf pack could live there and guard the city like you suggest, but we wouldn't be living *in* the city. If the demon wolves track us, it would be to that location, and everyone would be close enough to help."

Griffin rocked in place. "There are plenty of houses they could live in without having to double up. They'll need to be cleaned, and Sterlyn and the other men who lived there before splitting off already know the area."

Sterlyn exhaled, and her eyes glowed faintly. She was talking to someone using the pack or mate link.

Are you okay living at Sterlyn's and my parents' house? Cyrus linked with me. *Sterlyn wants to make sure I'm okay with the plan. Maybe we can find something there about the demon wolves.* Warmth spread through our bond—hope.

He wanted to stay there, probably to get a sense of his parents. *Of course. That's probably the best solution.* It was off the grid too, so maybe the demon wolves wouldn't find it.

Sierra marched outside, two bags on her shoulders, and took in our various expressions. "What the hell, people? Why are you all standing out here like this? If we had a truck with the bed open and the grill going, it'd look like a tailgate. But you're standing behind a bougie hatch-back Mercedes, so this just looks sad."

I snorted. "How do you even know what a tailgate is?"

"I've seen movies, and a few of the university kids talk about them." Sierra rolled her eyes. "Not that any of these guys would know that since they never show up for their classes anymore."

"We've been busy, and we're working on a new curriculum for the vampires." Ronnie stuck her tongue out. "And technically, I'm not an official student yet, so I'm not one of the skippers."

For a moment, things felt normal. Well, other than the part about being around a coven of witches and all that jazz.

"I'm taking off," Rosemary said and walked away from the group. "I need to get back to the city. We all need to."

That was enough to sober up the mood.

Circe crossed her arms. "When she flies out, it'll take down the barrier, so can you all leave together?"

"Yeah, we do need to get back." Alex hurried back to the house and grabbed two bags. "Last night, Gwen told me Azbogah tried to call a council meeting, but she thwarted it with the help of Yelahiah and Pahaliah."

"I'm assuming Ezra didn't vote in favor of waiting until we'd returned," Griffin growled, his jaw tense. "I don't know what's up with him. I thought he was a friend, but ever since he got the shifters to attack and take Ronnie—" He cut off, his face turning red.

I'll help the others load up the car, and you say goodbye to Eliza. Cyrus kissed my cheek.

I wasn't sure I wanted to talk to her. I was so damn angry I could very likely punch her. *Do I have to?*

She saved you, and that's the main reason I can't hate her. He cupped my cheek, his eyes turning light. *If it weren't for her and this coven, you would've grown up there, and I can't bear to consider how that would've shaped you.*

He had a point. She'd sacrificed for me, even when she'd wanted to be alone to wallow in her guilt. *Fine. Be all mature-like.*

I'm learning from the best. He kissed my cheek and patted Killian's shoulder. "Want to help me get the rest of the bags?"

Killian nodded, and as the two of them headed off, Alex cleared his throat. "Maybe a few of us should help them."

They wanted to give Ronnie, Eliza, and me some time alone.

As the others shuffled off, Circe stayed and fidgeted. She was having a harder time with her mom's presence than I'd realized.

"Annie, I'm sorry—" Eliza started.

"You don't need to apologize. I get why you did what you did, but it still hurts." I needed her to understand that I didn't hate her; I still loved her. "Nothing has changed between us. It's just hard knowing you're the reason Cyrus suffered the way he did. But you were doing what you thought was best and have beaten yourself up about it ever since. I just wish you had told me." I glanced at Ronnie. "Both of you have kept so many secrets from me, making me feel like I wasn't part of your world. That you two had a bond you didn't find me worthy of. It's just... I'm done with secrets. And if we mess up, I need to know we're in it together."

"I only found out about all this a few months before you," Ronnie tried teasing, but it fell flat. She grimaced and nodded. "But I understand what you mean. I hate secrets, and it wasn't that we didn't think you were strong enough—we just wanted to protect you."

"I'm sorry too, and I'll do whatever I can to make it up to you, Cyrus, and Sterlyn." Eliza hugged me, her herbal scent filling my nose.

We hadn't embraced each other like this in so long. "Then you can stay and help your family. They need you."

She glanced at her daughter and frowned. "But—"

"Don't be a martyr. Help them." Ronnie patted Eliza's shoulder. "And if we need you, we'll call. Besides, you'll need to head back to Lexington at some point."

Eliza blew a raspberry. "Fine, but you have to promise me you'll call if things get even slightly weird."

"Promise." I didn't have to hesitate on that. We might need all the help we could get.

"Fine." She hugged Ronnie and turned to her daughter. "I'll help so they can leave."

Within a few minutes, the cars were loaded, and we all climbed in. Sierra demanded to ride with Alex, Ronnie, Cyrus, and me as Rosemary took off. We rode out of the neighborhood on edge, scanning the area for demon wolves.

When we finally made it to the interstate, we each took a deep breath, and Sierra started singing Katy Perry at the top of her lungs.

Two and a half hours later, we pulled into the silver wolf pack settlement. I'd been dreading coming back here, unsure what kind of shit Mila planned to pull.

Cyrus had linked with Darrell when we'd gotten within range, so the entire pack was waiting for us outside. Darrell stood in front, his blood-orange eyes stern. He had his hands clenched at his sides, and his honey complexion seemed paler than normal. His dark brown hair was drenched in sweat, and he held his feet shoulder width apart, like he was ready for a fight.

What's going on? I linked to Cyrus.

He told the pack the plan, and a few of them aren't happy about us moving again, Cyrus linked. *He's been arguing with them for the past ten minutes, and they want to talk.*

We got out of the vehicle with Ronnie and Alex right behind us. When the other car emptied, Martha ran over to Mila and pulled the woman into her arms. Her short, dark auburn hair contrasted against Mila's brown, and she closed her aqua eyes. Martha whispered, "Thank the gods you're okay."

"No thanks to *him*," Mila answered, pointing at Cyrus.

I moved, not even registering my actions. That bitch's first words were to throw my mate under the bus, and I was done humoring her.

CHAPTER TWENTY-FIVE

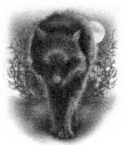

"HE JUST *SAVED* YOUR ASS!" I pivoted and jabbed a finger at her. I was done with her irrational anger, done with her animosity, and done with her complete disrespect. I'd recognized the signs of trauma in her from losing a loved one. I'd tried to understand and connect with her. I thought I'd made headway when she'd promised to give us time before blackmailing Cyrus. She'd found us making out next to a stream before we realized we were mates. But at the first opportunity, she'd used that information to undercut Cyrus. During the demon wolves' first attack, she'd dropped it like a bomb, resulting in her, Theo, Rudie, and Chad leaving our pack.

Mila lifted her chin and pulled away from her friend. "That's what a real alpha does for his pack."

"You're not his pack," Martha murmured loud enough for everyone to hear. "How can you be so self-righteous?"

"We've been best friends for years. Even our girls

are best friends." Mila narrowed her eyes at Martha. "Gods know why your mate supports Cyrus, but I'm your best friend, and you want to speak out against me like that?"

If compassion hadn't gotten through to her, maybe bluntness would. Maybe she needed hard love. "You aren't the only victim here, Mila. Everyone here has been through some kind of hell. Stop being so narcissistic and stop causing problems!"

Annie, Cyrus linked, but the warmth of his love spread into my chest. *I love that you're standing up for me, but—*

But *my ass.* If I'd been in my right mind, I might have snickered at that horrible retort, but my blood was boiling, colliding with the coolness of the demon influence in my veins.

Ronnie, Sterlyn, Alex, Griffin, Killian, and Sierra walked up behind me, but none of them interjected.

That was fine. I didn't need anyone's help. I could take her ass down on my own.

"*I'm* the one causing problems?" Mila's jaw dropped. She glared at me and gestured at my mate. "He's the one—"

"—who trained the people who killed your fated mate." I spread my arms out. "We *all* know, and we all *hate* the loss you're experiencing. But you're spewing so much anger, and you need to move on from that stage and get to grief and acceptance. Or you can leave again... because that went *so* well last time."

Mila flinched, and her nostrils flared. "Who the *hell*

do you think you are? You're a dark wolf, and no one should be okay with you being part of this pack."

"I'm Cyrus's mate, and *I* didn't abandon this pack because things got too hard." I wouldn't let her get to me. On the TV law dramas I enjoyed watching, lawyers often tried to anger witnesses on the stand to make them appear irrational or suspicious. Even though it was fiction, it was a tactic many lawyers used to discredit people. She was trying to do the same to me. We were on trial with the silver wolves as our witnesses. "Cyrus struggles every day with his role in Bart's death, but he shouldn't have to. He was stolen from his family and pack as a baby, and he did what he thought he had to do to survive. If he'd known what would happen, he would've risked *everything* to protect the ones he loved. For you to spew hate and throw that in his face every chance you get makes you cruel, heartless, and unworthy of this pack. You're threatening pack dynamics and causing conflict. You do it because it's the only damn thing you can control, but then you get angry with yourself and shit even more on Cyrus!"

Her chest heaved as her hands fisted at her sides. "You don't know *anything* about me."

"Maybe not, but I know if you hadn't split off from the pack, you and the others wouldn't have been captured." I stepped toward her, wanting her to realize I wasn't backing down. "Cyrus was captured because we were desperate to *save* you. That's what a pack—a family —does. They forgive, even when they shouldn't." I turned to Chad, Theo, and Rudie, her followers. "And despite it all, Cyrus and I made sure to save you from the demon wolf pack. We fought and protected you and took you to safety. And the first thing you do is *blame* him for your capture?" I laughed bitterly. "No, you don't get to twist the story, and if you're going to blame anyone, it should be me."

Martha's brows furrowed. "Why would anyone blame you?"

"No one should," Cyrus growled, his silver eyes glowing. *Stop. This is ridiculous. She won't change her mind.*

They need to know everything. The secrets and half-truths have to stop. Mila had been using them as ammunition, and they were why the others had struggled to follow Cyrus. He wanted to prove himself by carrying the burdens alone. That was what he'd done his whole life, and it ended now. "Because the demon wolf alpha is my biological father. As you all know, that was why they came here—for me."

"*See,*" Mila cooed, her cognac eyes shining with victory in the midday sun. "Neither of them is fit to lead."

"Stop it," Chad growled. He grimaced and inhaled as he stood straight to face down the woman who'd been a huge influence in his life. "Annie's right. This has to stop. Yeah, I didn't like Cyrus at first. He wasn't one of us, and he had a different way of thinking, but like Annie pointed out, he risked his life for us, even after we turned our backs on him and made his life hell."

Mila scoffed and blinked repeatedly. "You can't be serious. After all I've done for you."

"That's why I followed you for so long, even when I

disagreed with you." He shrugged, and his face twisted. "I didn't want to leave the pack, yet I did it out of loyalty to you. But I can't do this anymore." He shook his head and walked over to Cyrus, Sterlyn, and me.

Holding his breath, Cyrus tensed, ready to spring into action, and pulled me against his side.

Calm down, Sterlyn linked as she stepped up beside me. *He's making a point.*

I know, but what point is he making? Cyrus replied, his uneasy emotions filling me. *He's challenged me and taken every opportunity to talk to Annie, so I'm not super fond of the asshole.*

He was always a friend. I wanted to calm the raging animal inside him. *My heart was yours the moment we met.*

Chad stood before us and glanced at Sterlyn, casting his eyes downward. The fuzzy sensation that was his spot in the pack link refilled with warmth.

Chad then looked at Cyrus and linked, connecting to the three of us, *I'm sorry I was such a pain in the ass. I view all three of you as my leaders and will follow you anywhere from here on out. My loyalty is to this pack, and no one else.*

Something changed inside Cyrus. The uneasy feeling switched to one of surprise.

"That doesn't change anything," Mila huffed. "Theo—"

"Chad's right." Theo stepped beside Chad with Rudie next to him. He clapped his best friend on the shoulder and submitted to Sterlyn as his friend had.

"This entire group, including the angel and the vampire king and queen, saved us. They refused to leave us behind, despite how poorly we'd treated them. That is a group I want to follow." Theo's eyes darkened. "And I'm sorry I challenged you."

The warm spots for him and Rudie reformed in my chest. The only straggler was Mila.

"I...I can't believe this." Mila shook her head and clutched her chest. "You're going to force me to rejoin this pack?"

Sterlyn arched her brow. "We would never do that. We aren't dictators. That would make us no better than the demon wolves or anyone who seeks power. You will always have a place here in our pack if you want it and when you're ready to come home."

This was exactly what Mila had needed to hear from her ultimate alpha: she wouldn't be forced to do anything, but we all wanted her with us. This would eventually lead to her defining moment—she would either wake up and grieve, or she'd remain angry and tear away from us.

"That's fine," she said a little too loudly and licked her lips. "I'm better off on my own."

"You have our number if you ever change your mind," Cyrus said and wrapped an arm around my shoulders. There was an edge to him but also calmness—like he was finally finding peace.

Mila marched off toward her house, instead of the woods, and disappeared.

Darrell rubbed his chin. "Most of the pack isn't happy about moving again."

Cyrus exhaled and glanced around the neighborhood. "We can't stay here. The demon wolves will retaliate, and they know this location. If we stay, they'll attack us hard. Tate is desperate to get Annie back."

We quickly updated him on everything we knew.

I said, "Even though some of them were killed in the last attack, they still have over a hundred wolves in their pack, greatly outnumbering us. If they attack on a new moon, which I'm assuming they will, they'll be twice as strong as you are. We can't stay here. We have to move, so we can control when the battle begins."

"It's been hard enough not having all the houses completed." Theo frowned. "How much worse will it be in the new location?"

"Every house there is complete, and some of you will feel as if you've come home," Sterlyn said, emotion thick in her voice. "We eliminated the enemy that attacked us in the older silver wolf neighborhood. There's no reason the pack can't move back there."

The corner of Darrell's lips tipped upward. "I hadn't thought about that, but you're right. Many of us already know that area, too."

A few whispers of affirmation followed suit, and the pack links in my chest warmed. They liked the idea.

Since everyone is on board, are you two okay with handling the move? Sterlyn linked, turning her lavender eyes on us. *Griffin, Ronnie, Alex, and I really need to get back to Shadow City. We'll gauge what's happened since we've been gone and meet up with Yelahiah to see if she has any answers about the demon wolves.*

I hated to see them go, but we had a lot to do.

Cyrus squeezed his sister's shoulder. *Go ahead. Annie and I can take it from here.*

She winked. *I know you can. Otherwise, I wouldn't be leaving.*

I turned around and hugged Ronnie. "Come visit me soon?"

"Of course." She kissed my cheek, and her cool skin sent a chill down my spine. "If you need *anything* before then, let me know."

"Stay safe," Alex said. He took his wife's hand and tugged her to the Mercedes. He pointed at Sierra. "You can terrorize Killian, Griffin, and Sterlyn since they have room in their car."

We said our goodbyes, and Cyrus got our luggage from the trunk. When we turned back to the pack, they were brimming with excitement. I'd expected more push-back, but eagerness surrounded us.

Only pack what you want and need, Cyrus linked with the pack now that Griffin, Killian, Sierra, Alex, and Ronnie were gone. *Even though I don't think they'll attack this fast, we need to move quickly. The other neigh-borhood is only fifteen miles from here. Let's get there by tonight if possible. Don't worry about furniture—the houses should have all we need.*

I hadn't realized the other place was that close, but it made sense, since Sterlyn had fled from there and found

Killian and Griffin shortly after her pack had been slaughtered.

Everyone moved, and soon, we were all hard at work.

THE SUN WAS SETTING, and the pack was in their loaded vehicles, following Cyrus. Darrell was coordinating where everyone would stay once we got there, which would give Cyrus and me time to acclimate to the house we'd be living in—Cyrus's parents' house. His emotions had been all over the place since we'd decided to move.

We took a turn around a section of oak, ash, and maple trees.

We're almost there, Cyrus linked.

The sky was full of pinks, purples, and oranges, the sun setting behind a neighborhood that appeared ahead of us. Much like the settlement we'd left behind, each brick house was modest and of similar design. Everything looked untouched. The grass was high, indicating no one had lived here for quite some time. A gigantic, circular grassy clearing looked nearly identical to the one they'd used for training.

The neighborhood is one huge circle, Cyrus explained as we drove through the streets. We passed fifty houses before he turned down a street and into the driveway of a home with dead hibiscus and hydrangeas lining the entrance. *I've only been here a handful of times, but Sterlyn said she and our mom planted those flowers each year.*

My heart ached for him and all the conflicting emotions coursing through him—longing, jealousy, and pain.

Maybe we can do that next summer. I had no clue how long we would be here, but hopefully, we could stay here indefinitely. *Something we can do to honor her together.*

He stopped the SUV and glanced at me, his eyes darker than granite. *I'd really like that.*

We climbed out of his vehicle, and I waited by the car while Cyrus made his way to the side of the house where the air conditioning unit sat. Darrell pulled up to the house on our right, while Theo and Rudie parked at the one on our left. At one time, Theo living next to us would have panicked me, but now that he'd submitted to Sterlyn and Cyrus, I had a feeling things would be all right.

I watched as Cyrus picked up something from under the rocks surrounding the unit. I met him at the sturdy, red chestnut door. He inserted the key into the lock and paused.

Hey, we don't have to stay here. I touched his arm and leaned my head on his shoulder. *We can stay in any of these houses.*

No, I want to. He inhaled sharply and opened the door, then stepped into the living room.

A beige cloth couch sat against the tan wall, with a brown leather recliner in the corner. The dark walnut floor gleamed, and the faint scent of lavender swirled around me.

Beyond the living room, on the right side of the

house, was a large eat-in kitchen with maple cabinets and an empty pot on the black stove. A round table with four chairs sat to one side, and I caught a glimpse of the back door beyond it.

Cyrus stopped and shook his head as pain coursed through him.

I wrapped my arms around him. *I'm here.*

I just wish things were different and they could've met you. Cyrus's chest shook. *I wish—*

I know. How I wished I could make his parents appear, but I was at a loss as much as he was. I wanted to say or do something to take his pain away, but I couldn't do anything to make this easier or better.

Come on, he sighed and led me through the living room and down the hallway on the left side of the house.

I held on to him tightly as if that would reduce some of his pain, and when we passed a door on the left, I glanced inside. A collage of Sterlyn with people I didn't know hung on the wall. Even though it was clearly her, she looked nothing like the strong and confident woman I knew today. Crumpled teal sheets covered the bed, and the stale stench of dust hung in the air.

Pictures lined the hallway, including photos of Sterlyn through various stages of childhood. I spotted two family pictures of his mom, dad, and Sterlyn. Cyrus looked so much like his father. I took a deep breath, trying not to linger and cause him any more discomfort.

We passed an office on the right where papers were scattered across the top of a huge mahogany desk. *This would've been my room. You know, if I would've—* He cut off, his pain stealing my breath. A tear trailed down his cheek as he headed to the last door in the hallway.

As we stepped inside a sky-blue master bedroom, I noted the king-size bed with its wrinkle-free navy comforter, which contrasted with the white bed frame. The walls made the room feel too bright for the staggering hole his parents' deaths had left behind. A white chest of drawers occupied one corner of the room, but other than that, everything else seemed barren.

Let me wash the sheets while you unload the car, I linked, but he lifted a hand.

His eyes twinkled, losing the edge of pain. *I want to show you something first.*

What? I asked, but he only smiled as he walked to the dresser and reached inside the space where the bottom drawer was missing. Something clicked, and he grabbed the right side of the heavy furniture piece and pulled it toward us. A large gaping hole appeared with steps leading down to a hidden room.

My stomach churned. What secrets was I about to learn?

CHAPTER TWENTY-SIX

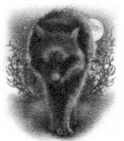

FOLLOW ME, Cyrus linked and extended his hand to me.

This is how horror movies begin, I teased, but my heart raced, revealing my discomfort.

He chuckled and arched his brow. *Do you think I would put you in harm's way?*

We both knew the answer—no.

I trusted him completely, so I tried to calm my nerves. *If we die down there, this is on you.* I scrunched my face at him.

And here I thought you weren't one for dramatics. He took my hand and kissed me. *Come on.* He tugged me toward the dim stairwell.

Tapping into my wolf, I sharpened my vision and followed him down the stairs. Despite being significantly shorter than him, I had to hunch my shoulders. With each step, the wood creaked underneath us but remained secure.

Dust floated in the air. *Is it normally this dirty, or is it neglected because the pack hasn't lived here?*

No one outside of Sterlyn, Griffin, Killian, me—and now you—knows about this. My father didn't even tell my mother about it. He turned right, ducking as he entered a room. *This stays between us.*

It meant the world that he was sharing this with me. *Are you sure Sterlyn is okay with me knowing?* She was the only family he had, and I didn't want to cause a problem between them.

I told her what I was going to do, and she didn't object. She and I think similarly—we're strongest when our fated mates are a partner in everything.

Those words were beautiful, and I believed them as well. I'd never imagined having a permanent relationship, but not only had I found my fated mate, but I'd also found another amazing sister.

Cyrus ran his hand along the wall, and light flooded the opening as I turned toward the room. The rectangular space was around three hundred square feet with beige stone walls. An air vent was in the ceiling, so the area was temperature controlled. A large, white marble statue of a male angel with strong, chiseled features stood in the center of the room. Wings fanned out behind him, and a moon sat in the palm of his hand.

Is that the father of the silver wolves? I couldn't remember his name, but I knew he was Rosemary's uncle. *Or are you guys just creepy with some random angel in your hidden basement?*

God, I love you. He wrapped his arms around me.

Though we may be weird, yes, this is Rosemary's uncle, Ophaniel.

My chest expanded at his words and touch, but the statue intrigued me. I freed myself and walked over to the statue, running a hand down the marble. It wasn't as cool to my touch as I'd expected. The angel was gorgeous, and even though he was stone, I could picture his hair and eyes matching Sterlyn's.

Cyrus strolled to a desk in the corner of the room where a leather journal lay. He rubbed his hand over the front reverently and opened the book.

I walked over and looked at the yellowed pages. They were blank. *I expected entries or something.* Why would they keep a blank leather journal down here?

They're there. We just can't see them. He stared at the pages, and his forehead lined. *I've tried to get a glimpse of the letters but never had any luck. Only the true silver wolf alpha can read the pages.*

Ugh. Badass for Sterlyn, but another thing he couldn't experience.

It's fine. He glanced at me with a tender smile. *At first, I was upset, but it's not my sister's fault. It took me a while to figure that out, but I don't know what I would've done if I'd lost her, too. The first entry is dated 1125.*

Do you think it has information on the demon wolves? I scanned the pages as if the words would suddenly form, revealing all the secrets I wanted to know.

He shook his head. *It's all about the silver wolves' history. It's about how Ophaniel impregnated a wolf shifter, creating the first silver wolf. He had a child born only a decade earlier, and for angels, that timing was supposed to be impossible, making it clear that the silver wolves were destined to exist.*

Which meant the demon wolves had been destined, too. *I wonder what my heritage is like. If the demon wolves were created at the same time, did a demon impregnate a wolf shifter first, forcing the silver wolf to be born, or vice versa?*

Cyrus lifted his head and stared at the angel statue. *I never considered that the silver wolves were created because of the demon ones. Obviously, they came together near the same time to balance each other, like the demons and angels, but... That scenario could have merit, not that it changes anything now.*

That was true. It didn't matter whether Ophaniel or the demon had begun the craziness; we were still in the same situation with the demon wolves hunting me and my fated mate being silver. Maybe our mate bond could finally balance everything so we weren't constantly under threat. One could hope.

Cyrus had brought me down here to share a piece of his history—of his family. He wanted me as involved in his world as I wanted him in mine. *Thank you.*

His silver eyes locked on me. *For what?*

For bringing me down here. I kissed his cheek and pushed the warmth in my chest toward him. I needed him to know how much this meant to me. *I kinda love you.*

He beamed. *And I kinda love you.*

He set the journal back on the table and pointed to

the stairs. *I wanted you to know everything I did and see the great lengths my father and his ancestors took to hide us. Unfortunately, I think the silver wolves have made things worse by staying in hiding.*

Maybe, but either way, you, me, our family, and our allies will make things right. I looped my arm through his and tugged him upstairs. *And our first step is getting this place cleaned and set up. You bring our things in, and I'll tidy up the house, so we don't sneeze to death.*

Sounds like a plan, he linked, and followed me back up the narrow staircase.

The two of us got to work.

THE NEXT FEW days passed in a blur. Mila contacted Darrell and stayed at a house farthest away from us, afraid to be on her own. She didn't cause trouble and kept to herself.

The rest of the pack settled into the houses, working the gardens, and getting the lawns maintained, while keeping up a light training regimen. It was nice to be busy, and things felt normal.

Are you awake? Cyrus asked as he turned to me in bed.

I pretended to be asleep to determine what he was up to.

"Annie," he murmured and began kissing my neck. "I know you're pretending."

His kisses made my skin buzz, and my body yearned

for him. I'd thought after we'd completed our mate bond that things would become less intense, but I'd been so wrong. Every day, our attraction grew stronger. Sometimes, I felt like I couldn't breathe unless he was touching me.

I remained still, not wanting him to stop. A strong hand slipped under my shirt and caressed my breast. My eyes fluttered, and my body turned hot.

He moaned in my ear. *God, I love your scent mixed with arousal.*

I bumped my ass against him, his hardness defined already.

He nipped my neck and gently pinched my nipple, shooting flames through my body. No longer able to pretend, I turned to face him. His shaggy dark silver hair was disheveled, and his eyes were dark with desire.

He was damn sexy and *all* mine. I yanked his boxers down to his knees and rolled on top of him. I straddled him, admiring his six-pack.

His eyes widened. *You aren't wearing any panties.*

The past few mornings, he'd woken me up like this. It was incredible to have time to explore our connection, safely hidden away, and feeling like life was normal. Cyrus still had moments of sadness, but we were figuring out how to make this our home. We had to—even with the ghosts that hovered nearby.

Reaching underneath the brown satin covers, I guided him inside me. He kicked off his boxers and grabbed my hips.

He lifted himself up and kissed me, then removed my shirt. *You're so beautiful.*

Without words, I opened myself up to him and began riding him.

He threw his head back and guided me into the rhythm he wanted with his hands on my waist. We moved slowly, not at our normal quick pace.

Every time he filled me, the friction between us grew stronger. Sweat covered our bodies as we moved steadily in sync with each other. He released my hips and cupped my breasts, and the building pressure intensified.

I leaned down, kissing him. I wanted to taste him. Feel him. Enjoy him.

He sucked on my tongue as his fingers worked magic on my breasts. I lost sense of time, place, and location, completely wrapped up in everything Cyrus. I never wanted this moment to end. If I could, I'd stay locked in the bedroom with him forever.

All too soon, my body was ready for release. I moaned as he thrust faster inside me.

His pleasure mixed with mine, and I stopped kissing him, sitting straight up and increasing the pace.

Our eyes locked as we peaked. His mouth dropped open, and his body shuddered, causing the orgasm to rip through me even stronger. My body quivered as the intensity crashed between us, riding out longer than normal.

When it was over, we sat there for a second, completely caught up in each other.

Are you two up? Sterlyn linked.

That was the equivalent of a cold shower. Thank God we'd climaxed, or Sterlyn would've ruined the moment. I begrudgingly lay back in my spot. *Yeah, what's going on?*

Cyrus spooned my body, and I covered us up with the thin sheet, feeling a little weird talking to Sterlyn while naked. He chuckled and nuzzled my neck.

Yelahiah doesn't know anything about the demon wolves. She tried to find the information discreetly and couldn't, so she's on her way to ask Azbogah if he knows anything.

He tensed and pulled away, completely alert. *Is that a good idea? If she doesn't know anything, why would he?*

He's the likeliest person to know things about them, since he told Matthew where to find Ronnie's father. Sterlyn's frustration bled through the connection. She wasn't happy about it, either. *If he knows something, we could learn why Annie was promised to a demon. What would a demon want with a demon wolf? We're missing something, and unfortunately, that prick might be the only one who can help us.*

We didn't have a better option. If we could find out why a demon wanted me, while we figured out how to take down the demon wolf pack and save the women, we'd be in a better position. *I know you or Yelahiah wouldn't talk to him unless it was the only option.* Yelahiah had left Shadow City for the first time in centuries to help Ronnie fight her demon father, so between that and Sterlyn's trust in her, I knew she wouldn't purposely lead us astray. *You'll let us know if you hear anything?*

She's talking to him now. I'll be in touch, Sterlyn replied. *How's the pack doing? Is Mila behaving?*

Yes, but who knows for how long. Cyrus exhaled as reality smacked us in the face. *She's keeping to herself.*

At least she's here. She wasn't causing trouble and wasn't in danger. Those two things were more than we could have hoped for.

We'll get over there soon. We're dealing with some issues Ezra created while we were gone. Sterlyn's displeasure was strong. *In our absence, he got even closer to Azbogah.*

Is his intent dark like the angel's? Cyrus asked.

He and Sterlyn could read people's intentions, and I was slowly learning I could, too. What I'd always thought were red flags about people was actually my demon side recognizing a person's essence. I'd really noticed it while with the demon pack.

No, but he probably thinks he's doing what's best. Azbogah isn't pure evil either, which makes him hard to read. Sterlyn paused for a second. *Hey, Rosemary is calling me. I'll keep you updated.*

She disconnected, and I climbed out of bed. It was time to get going and focus on training. We needed to attack the demon wolves as soon as possible while they were still licking their wounds.

LATER THAT EVENING, Cyrus and I sat in the backyard on a blanket, eating a frozen meat pizza I'd heated up. We'd had a good day of training, and we were finally making the house feel more like our own.

The gibbous moon was high, and my blood ran at a normal temperature and not the enhanced coolness I'd felt when I first shifted into my wolf. Since demon wolves were the opposite of the silver wolves, I'd be at my weakest during a full moon, whereas the silver wolves were weakest during a new moon.

The scent of honeysuckle tickled my nose as I took a bite of food and leaned back to look at the stars in the cloudless sky.

I still can't believe Azbogah said he couldn't help. With everything I'd heard about the dark angel, I should've known better than to get my hopes up. At some point, we had to catch a freaking break.

At least, we tried to get answers. Cyrus sipped an Amber Bock. *Killian is working with his pack to determine who can help us when we attack during the full moon. He can't take everyone, but hopefully, with his pack, we'll be evenly matched.*

The demon wolves were stronger than regular wolves, except during a full moon, but that meant I would also be at my weakest. I had to keep reminding myself that it was better to be weak if that meant the demon wolves would be too. That was why I'd been training so hard. I wanted to kick Tate's ass.

Unease filtered through the pack link, and when I realized it was coming from Darrell, my stomach rolled.

He was one of the wolves standing watch.

Even though we expected to be safe here, we'd developed a schedule of four wolves keeping guard when everyone went home for the night.

He linked with the entire pack, *Five black Suburbans are heading our way.*

Cyrus jumped to his feet, knocking over his beer. *Do they have tinted windows, including the windshield?*

Yes. How'd you know? Darrell asked.

My mate tensed. *I think it's the men I trained—the ones who slaughtered this pack earlier this year.*

Sterlyn responded, her fear bleeding through, *We're on our way. Run! Do whatever you have to do to survive.*

I stood, ready to protect our home and our pack. *What do we need to do?*

Before he could answer, gunfire filled the air.

CHAPTER TWENTY-SEVEN

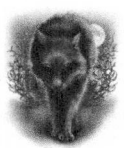

SCREAMS ECHOED IN MY EARS, and the cold tendrils of fear permeated the pack links. My breath caught, and my lungs couldn't expand.

We were being attacked with firearms.

Everyone get to the woods, Darrell linked as his warm spot in my chest filled with urgency.

No! Cyrus spun around, examining the tree line. *They'll take over our homes and displace us. We've been training with guns. We need to fight them with our own firearms. Get into your houses and aim out the windows. We need to hold them off and protect our home until Sterlyn and the others arrive.*

Protect our home.

He was right. If we ran, that would give them more power over us. We had enough enemies—we needed to handle this, instead of dragging it out.

Tires squealed as the Suburbans headed toward the back of the neighborhood where we were staying. Our pack had chosen homes deeper in the neighborhood and away from the entrance, in case we were attacked, and to prevent ourselves from being as easily seen. The only time we were near the front was during training.

Cyrus snatched my hand, and we ran to the front of the house. The vehicles hadn't made it here yet, and we wanted to check on everyone. The sun had disappeared, and I assumed the attack had been timed down to the second. The living room window of Darrell's house was open, and moonlight reflected on metal. Martha was prepared, but alone.

The sound of an engine grew louder, and more gunfire sounded.

Come on. Cyrus ran to our door and threw it open. *They're almost here.*

No one was outside, and my wolf surged forward, allowing me to see better. In the surrounding homes, our pack members had their guns aimed through slits in the windows, prepped and ready.

I bet the silver wolves were relieved they'd learned how to fight with firearms.

I continued to the front door just as a vehicle swerved toward us. Two men with black helmets hung out the back door, pistols lifted and ready to shoot. My heart pounded in my ears. Running to the door, I tapped into my wolf.

Cyrus held it open, and as I reached him, shots were fired.

A bullet grazed my arm as I ran inside the house. Another hit the doorframe as I passed through.

I leaned against the wall beside the door, breathing raggedly. That had been way too damn close.

Cyrus sniffed, and his face turned a shade paler. *I smell blood.*

It's nothing, I assured him. *The bullet grazed me.* I gestured to my upper arm where I'd been hit.

His nostrils flared. *Still unacceptable.*

More shots went off as another engine drew closer—so close it had to be on this road, too. Half the pack lived down here, since not all of us could fit on this one road.

Cyrus rushed to the couch. He knelt and removed two pistols and several clips of bullets he'd stashed there.

Glass shattered as someone in the Suburban shot out the living room window. The jagged pieces flew everywhere. Cyrus lunged on top of me, protecting me from the onslaught, but digging the shards that had already struck me deeper into my body.

Cyrus! I linked and tried pushing him off me, but he kept me pinned down.

I bucked underneath him. *Get off. You've got to be hurt.*

He gritted his teeth. *I have the moon. It'll help heal me.*

Remember that when it's a new moon. If he was going to throw that in my face, I'd return the favor during the new moon.

Doors slammed outside.

Damn it, they'll have bulletproof vests on, so aim for the head, Cyrus linked with the pack as he stood and hurried to the window with both guns. *They wouldn't be getting out of the car without protection.*

They have helmets, too, I added. I wasn't sure if Cyrus had seen that.

So their kill spots will be harder to hit, Theo replied. *We need to aim for the legs and arms to disable them.*

Injure them as much as possible, Cyrus agreed and fired.

I bit the inside of my cheek as a ball formed in my chest. Overprotective Cyrus hadn't given me a gun, but that was fine. There was a rifle in our bedroom. Fighting with him about it would only give the enemy a bigger advantage.

I scurried into our bedroom and slid on my knees across the hardwood floor to the bed. I snatched the rifle and headed into Sterlyn's room. Maybe they wouldn't expect someone to fire from there.

I kept the lights off, so they couldn't see inside the room easily, and lifted the blinds. Four men ran toward our house and Darrell's next door, while four more stayed in the two vehicles, firing. The ones running to the houses held shields in front of them, and our bullets ricocheted off without harming anyone.

This had been planned better than I'd imagined.

One guy heading toward our house had a greasy, scruffy beard that hit his chest. A huge smirk filled his face as he lifted a hand. The enemy gunfire stopped, and the bearded guy said, "Julius, we know you're here."

Julius? The name tingled in the back of my mind.

Cyrus wasn't amused. *That was the name I went by growing up.*

"And you're shooting, Diego." Cyrus laughed without humor. "I thought we were friends—well, until I pieced together that you were the asshole who coordinated the attack that killed my parents." *Go into the hidden room, Annie.*

My heart tugged toward my mate. He'd been manipulated and used his entire life, up until he'd found the silver wolves.

Wait. Did he just tell me to hide? *I'm in Sterlyn's room.* Technically, it was still her room. We hadn't touched this room or their father's office, focusing on the living areas instead.

"We *were* friends." The man's voice deepened as the wind changed directions and blew a grassy scent toward us. "Until you left to play house with the enemy. Did you think we wouldn't figure it out?"

Please go to the hidden room. Cyrus's fear swirled around me, adding to the iciness prickling my body. *If Diego is here, they brought their top men. When we trained together, I was the only one who could beat him, and only when the moon was to my advantage.*

I understood he was worried about me, but our whole pack was at stake. We needed every person to help against men Cyrus had trained. *No,* I answered simply.

His frustration wafted into me as he replied to Diego, "Nah, I figured you wouldn't care. It's not like any of us cared about Dick, but what I can't fathom is why the hell you're here now. He and Saga are dead."

"And I don't answer to you, anymore." Diego snickered. "I want you to know that I wasn't aware they were your pack—not that it would've made a difference. I'll extend you the same courtesy offered to them, since we have history. Come out now and give yourself up or...die. The choice is yours."

Cyrus growled, his rage building so everyone connected to him could feel it. "We know that even if we gave up, you'd kill us eventually. Don't pretend I don't know how you operate." He linked with the entire pack, *Shoot them. Do whatever you can to slow them down. He's toying with us.*

That moment was the calm before the storm. The energy and testosterone swirling between the two groups were palpable.

"But not right away. You'd have more time to live." Diego shrugged. "Maybe you'd escape."

I was done with bullies threatening us as if we were in the wrong. I aimed the gun between his eyes, not even three inches below his helmet, and pulled the trigger.

The bullet lodged between his eyes, and he dropped dead instantly.

"What the hell!" exclaimed a man a few feet away. "I thought this pack wasn't trained with weapons!"

Fire! Cyrus commanded, and our entire pack shot at the enemy.

The three men standing outside the vehicle turned and ran for cover.

The driver yelled, "Hold our ground. You know the plan."

My stomach dropped. *This is a diversion.*

A crash from the kitchen confirmed my suspicion. Someone had entered our house.

I charged out of the bedroom and into the hall as three men came into view. They were dressed all in black to blend in with the night. Diego had been a distraction to buy his people time to approach from the woods.

The whole attack had been planned meticulously.

Be prepared for them to come in the back, I linked, lifting my gun.

The man chuckled darkly as he charged at me, and the other two headed for Cyrus.

Cyrus, behind you. I had to help him. Bouncing on my feet, I lifted the gun as blood pumped through my body. I felt the rush inside me as my wolf surged and brushed my mind.

The man coming at me shot at my hand, and I dropped the gun as he continued toward me. The gun slid toward him, and he holstered his gun.

Everything inside me screamed *defense*, but if he expected me to be a weakling, I'd do better to wait and surprise him. *Are you okay?*

I'm fine. Just hold on. I'll be there in a second, Cyrus vowed.

Yeah, I'd take care of this guy before Cyrus reached me just to prove a point.

The man drew closer, and the hint of grass overwhelmed me again. *Why do they all smell like grass?*

They're bear shifters, Sterlyn answered, her tension

high. *We're ten minutes out and driving as fast as possible.*

Surely, we could last that long.

The bear shifter stood in front of me and removed a cloth from his pocket. He moved quickly, placing one hand around my head as he attempted to put the cloth over my nose.

A sweet smell hit my face, confirming my suspicions. The cloth was drenched in chloroform.

I grew lightheaded and had to fight back before it could impact me more.

I ducked, and the man caught air and stumbled.

When I punched him in the gut, his eyes bulged, surprised by the onslaught, and he crumpled. I rolled out of the way and kicked him in the same spot. He landed with a *thud* on the floor.

As I rushed past him, the man grunted and caught my leg. I fell to my knees, and they throbbed with pain. I placed my hands on the ground and twisted, kicking the guy in the face with my free foot.

His head jerked back, but the asshole kept a strong hold.

The sounds of fighting from the living room were the only things keeping me sane. I could hear Cyrus grunting as he whaled on his two attackers. The bear shifters were thick like freakin' Ford trucks and almost seven feet tall, but it sounded like Cyrus still had the advantage.

Five more people ran into the back of the house, and I glanced into the kitchen. They ran into the hallway, and when their gazes landed on me, two ran to me and grabbed my arms. The other three ran to help their friends fight Cyrus.

What the hell was going on? Why were *these* guys focused on me? *Cyrus!* I linked, needing his help. *Five more men are here, and three are heading your way.*

The guy on the ground released me as the other two men dragged me toward the kitchen. I used all my strength to swing my legs upward, kicking each one of them in the face. Their heads snapped back, and the one on my left growled.

"Get off her, Blake!" Cyrus ran toward us, but the tallest bear shifter punched him in the back of the neck, and he fell to his knees. "Joey, I swear I'll kill you both." *Can anyone help Annie?* Cyrus linked as a crazed sensation filled the bond. He was desperate and petrified, and it was all because of me. Again.

The taller guy on the right snorted, and the one on the left said, "Oh, I'm so scared."

I'll find a way there, Chad replied, determination coursing through his words. *We're all under attack. They aren't trying to hurt us, just holding us off from getting out.*

"You should be." I dragged my feet, but the floor was slippery. I might as well have been wearing socks. They manhandled me through the kitchen, and I heard Cyrus lose control. Gunshots were fired in rapid succession.

"We've got to move," the one on the right grunted.

I wasn't sure which one was Blake or Joey, but it didn't matter. I stomped on their boots, but they were steel-toed. I twisted to kick one of the guys in the nuts, but he anticipated it and stuck out his leg, blocking the blow.

The kitchen table was right next to me, meaning the door was less than five feet away. I had a feeling if they got me outside, it would be harder for the others to help me.

When the guy on the left reached for the knob, I kicked him in the jaw. His head smashed against the broken door, and the door slammed back into its frame.

"Damn it, Joey," Blake grunted and grabbed my jaw, holding me still. "Open the fucking door."

"He's coming," a guy in the living room yelled as Cyrus growled. His feet pounded on the ground as he charged toward us.

Thank God. Even if they got me outside, Cyrus would be there in seconds. At least, they didn't seem inclined to kill him, probably from training together. They wanted to detain him more than anything.

Joey opened the door, and a man stood there dressed in a cotton shirt and jeans. His mossy green eyes scanned me. Then tawny brown wings exploded from his back. I went slack, shock freezing my limbs. The angel rasped, "It's about damn time," and pulled me into his arms as his wings flapped, blowing back his ginger-blonde hair. We lifted off the ground as he took flight.

I tried to wriggle out of his grasp, but I couldn't budge. My chest grew tight, and I sucked in his mossy scent.

"Hold on tight. It might get a little bumpy," he warned as he lifted me.

Cyrus ran into the kitchen, his granite eyes locked on me. *Annie, hold on. I won't let him take you. I'll bite his legs.* He began to shift into his wolf.

No matter what I did, I couldn't get any traction, and we reached the roof's overhang. Silver fur sprouted across his body, and I lost sight of him. My heart ached as Cyrus's howl of pain filled the air and his despair mixed with mine.

"Let's take you back where you belong." The angel chuckled darkly, like he'd told a joke and I was missing the punchline.

No, we couldn't be separated. Not like this. *Not again.*

ABOUT THE AUTHOR

Jen L. Grey is a *USA Today* Bestselling Author who writes Paranormal Romance, Urban Fantasy, and Fantasy genres.

Jen lives in Tennessee with her husband, two daughters, and two miniature Australian Shepherd. Before she began writing, she was an avid reader and enjoyed being involved in the indie community. Her love for books eventually led her to writing. For more information, please visit her website and sign up for her newsletter.

Check out my future projects and book signing events at my website.

www.jenlgrey.com

ALSO BY JEN L. GREY

Shadow City: Silver Wolf Trilogy

Broken Mate

Rising Darkness

Silver Moon

Shadow City: Royal Vampire Trilogy

Cursed Mate

Shadow Bitten

Demon Blood

Shadow City: Demon Wolf Trilogy

Ruined Mate

Shattered Curse

Fated Souls

The Wolf Born Trilogy

Hidden Mate

Blood Secrets

Awakened Magic

The Hidden King Trilogy

Dragon Mate

Dragon Heir

Dragon Queen

The Marked Wolf Trilogy

Moon Kissed

Chosen Wolf

Broken Curse

Wolf Moon Academy Trilogy

Shadow Mate

Blood Legacy

Rising Fate

The Royal Heir Trilogy

Wolves' Queen

Wolf Unleashed

Wolf's Claim

Bloodshed Academy Trilogy

Year One

Year Two

Year Three

The Half-Breed Prison Duology (Same World As Bloodshed Academy)

Hunted

Cursed

The Artifact Reaper Series

Reaper: The Beginning

Reaper of Earth

Reaper of Wings

Reaper of Flames

Reaper of Water

Stones of Amaria (Shared World)

Kingdom of Storms

Kingdom of Shadows

Kingdom of Ruins

Kingdom of Fire

The Pearson Prophecy

Dawning Ascent

Enlightened Ascent

Reigning Ascent

Stand Alones

Death's Angel

Rising Alpha

Made in the USA
Las Vegas, NV
31 July 2022

52428961R00198